AMERICAN TOTEMS

Terence S. McNamara

Publisher: Inspiring Publishers,
P.O. Box 159, Calwell, ACT Australia 2905
Email: publishaspg@gmail.com
http://www.inspiringpublishers.com

 A catalogue record for this book is available from the National Library of Australia

National Library of Australia The Prepublication Data Service

Author: Terence S. McNamara
Title: American Totems
Genre: Fiction

Paperback ISBN: 978-1-923087-40-8
Hardcover ISBN: 978-1-923087-39-2
eBook ISBN: 978-1-923087-38-5

Dedication:

A thank you to Grant Wood's wonderful painting, *American Gothic*,
in part an inspiration for this novel, and to AP.

CHAPTER ONE

I understand why nature puts us on a clock. There is an aggregation of mistakes in all our lives with their indelible memories, unremovable from our psyche except by dementia. Paths not taken, relationships abandoned or mishandled, opportunities lost, and, worst of all, strengths abused and weaknesses conceded. It all weighs on a person until the inevitable welcome reset. Life was never meant to be self-evident and sadly, surviving life isn't the same thing as living it. Existence for many of us is illusory. We carry so many self-inflicted limitations with us, so many constraints and encumbrances and, of course, those annoying social constraints and legalities that sometimes stand in the way of living life to its fullest. *Do what thou wilt shall be the whole of the Law* according to Crowley, not meaning it hedonistically but as a philosophy for living. Certainly it is difficult to find a survivable mix of saint and devil that allows our inner rat to find its way through life's maze.

For a large part of my life I was sure that I was moving forward; married but no kids, a business owner making mortgage payments and assiduously accumulating debt and friends. Little did I know that I was sliding toward a catharsis brought on by the fact that I had married too young, my debts were too large, and my friends were actually acquaintances. I was ignorant of the consequences of all the choices I had made up to my forty-second birthday. Forty-two years is a long time to be on the planet before you actually get it. It struck me like the birthday gift from hell, that suspension of self-esteem that appears mid-sentence asserting something that you once fully believed but suddenly realise isn't true. I'm paraphrasing Mark Twain, but it isn't the things you don't know that bring you undone, it's the things that you are one hundred percent sure of that turn out to be wrong.

At forty-two, my marriage was in the crapper. I'd had a brief affair five years before my recent divorce; I thought we were on a break, thank you, Ross Geller. Nonetheless, apparently, that makes me a bastard, an unworthy, less-than-human husband, not acceptable in the eyes of social media, all of them co-offenders or enablers. It magically meant that all of my efforts, my expended funds and time and wasted emotional resources up to that point in the relationship, were made worthless. Before the affair, our marriage had deteriorated into routine role play. I met someone who wanted to have sex with me because of what her body said rather than what her sense of duty dictated. My apologies to those who think that is either crude or meaningless but that, in fact, sums up the twenty-first-century man's dilemma: is the sex in your life socially scripted or raw physical need? Men's inability to distinguish between the two, a special thank you to Meg Ryan in *When Harry Met Sally*, brings an anxiety that all men dread. Is a six-pack more arousing than a six-figure income? I was ambushed by someone who actually wanted me physically. She just wanted to screw me and, with all respect to Meg, it is unmistakable when you see what that looks like up close. My misconduct, in the confines of our modern world, made me less than a man. All my previous accomplishments and contributions over a twenty-year marriage were nullified and I turned to dirt in the eyes of my wife and more importantly in the eyes of her friends and her mother. The problem was I didn't think I was dirt, even though she began walking all over me. Nonetheless, I compliantly dug a hole in it to submerge myself below it. I had no frame of moral reference other than that provided by my father, who was silent on most matters of importance to a young man except for sport. I discovered there're two things you can't waste time doing: going out of your way to do something because you want to stick it to someone (this is particularly relevant when it comes to ex-girlfriends), and going out of your way to please someone (this is particularly relevant when it comes to your wife). The former is futile and the latter is, in the long term, totally unproductive. Both lead nowhere, except to an empty feeling of disenchantment with the Totems we erect to our misapprehensions about ourselves, our community, and our universe.

After those realisations, the voices began to admonish me for wasting my precious emotional resources. It's no good putting your hands over your ears, because the voices you're hearing come from inside your head. You can, of course, dismiss them and instead look to the future. We all look to the future. We use the future to pay today's expenses and we mortgage our emotional resources to deal with today's issues, all without realising our resources are finite and the consequences of our avarice are inevitable. Postponing a reckoning only makes the shortfalls bigger and their reconstitution more difficult.

We have no idea what value we represent to the planet and what we risk by embracing that ignorance. Sentient beings carry a burden that other life forms do not and that is the need to figure it all out rather than just take it as it comes. We want to be right, not wrong; we need to be better than others, not worse; and we have a desire to live, not just survive. It's a burden that is not mitigated by religious mythology. We look through confused eyes at a world that is moving too fast for us to catch up, a world sufficiently dissembled for us to be unable to understand it, even if we did momentarily manage to pull alongside as it speeds away.

It is difficult to look back and realise that twenty years had passed in my adult life without evaluation or measurement and that, in the end, I was beneath that pile of dirt before I saw it being dumped on me. Those twenty years went by fast. My choices were mired in misinformation and cherished misapprehensions, mostly given to me by my parents and childhood friends, and that confusion was untempered by self-awareness. I know that there is nothing noble about blaming your friends or your mother or your ex-wife for the things that happen to you, that it is better to look to your own self-improvement rather than risk losing yourself in sophistry. Hemingway might recognise that sentiment, but I had that moment of lucidity all on my own. I began seeking those things that we all seek: freedom from the hole I had put myself in, the right to live life without harassment from my wife, and the right to be the best version of myself. It turns out that we are all alone in constructing that state of being, contending, as we must, with the self-inflicted wounds of perceived inadequacy. Booze only delays the reckoning, inaction all the while consuming us, stalking us like a wolf who understands the inevitability of its bleeding prey's submission. Society can't help us with the requisite transformation, our social environment is often the main impediment to our personal growth. You have to find your own way forward...

"Good morning, Mr Jamisen," the receptionist said.

I keep telling her to call me Jim, but she won't. I was greeted as I walked into the office carrying a throbbing head, the effect of a whiskey picnic the night before in my new, salubrious, post-divorce digs. I am a lawyer, but please don't hold that against me. I work casually in a friend's practice since my own practice went bust amid all my personal chaos. It was hard for me to adjust after twelve years in my own business. I don't mean adjust to not being the boss, that's a terrible job, I just mean losing the sense that I was the master of my own destiny. I satisfy myself these days with the realisation that I was kidding myself to think that I was any kind of master, let alone being master of something so difficult as controlling my own destiny. My father was master of his household, as all the men in the sixties and before that time had been. That role was assigned to them by God and State and he had no choice. Men back then were just as stuck as women were in their assigned roles. I remember my mother telling me a story about how my father was acting strangely toward her a couple of days into their honeymoon. It turned out that when she had sat them down for lunch at the long dining table in the cottage they had rented near the beach on the first day of the honeymoon, just the two of them, she had put them both at one corner of the table but unwittingly put herself at the end of the table. In Irish parlance, that means the *head of the table.* The honeymoon didn't amount to much after that innocent but mortal sin. Those clearly defined roles prevented most from looking past their designated function to the humanity beneath or the opportunities beyond. But a larger social problem was created when those roles were abandoned without a clear structure being put in their place. Enter the seventies. Acid and weed helped obscure the pain of the transition for some, but not in my family. That change set my parents' marriage and many other relationships like theirs adrift. Just like the central character in *Mad Men* who began as the Master of Madison Avenue and head of his family and ended up being a weed-smoking hippy. I'm sorry I ever watched that show. I hate it when they make the hero fail or, worse still, die. Shows or movies like that should come with a warning at the beginning: *before you get emotionally invested in the hero, please know that we intend to make a fool of him or her and/or kill him or her off. Watch, knowing that you will inevitably be let down.* The writers of such shows or movies are trying to be realistic, you see, and your viewing pleasure takes second place to their desire to be *artistic*. So, screw the viewer and their simplistic objective to be entertained. The fact is that we have all too much *realism* in our own lives to pay to see a film or stream a TV show whose producers lecture us about how hard life can be or, more broadly, how we should live it. We already know life's misery all too well and we definitely are not looking for a lecture.

As you can tell, I sometimes allow myself to contrast events in my life with those depicted in movies or television or, better still, literature. It comforts me and sometimes provides me with a better understanding of my predicament, and almost always brings a belief in more palatable outcomes. Most of all, I love the unspoken understanding that sadly only exists in fiction. There's a scene in *The Rifleman*, a sixties Western TV show, always the preferred moral reference for a young man growing up. In this scene, Connors, the Rifleman is standing with his love interest, Miss Lou, who is, as it happens, the owner of the Mallory Saloon. Who wouldn't want a girlfriend who owned a saloon? Some bad guy comes into the bar and makes an inappropriate suggestion to Miss Lou. The bad guy disparagingly flicks a dollar piece at her face for the booze she had just served in retaliation for her disinterest in his advances. Connors catches it in his gloved Rifleman hand, without looking at it or at Miss Lou, without ever shifting his unblinking gaze from the bad guy. Miss Lou doesn't blink either or flinch. They both know with absolute certainty that Connors would intercept the dollar piece mid-air. I just love that shit. She knew he'd protect her, and he knew she knew. A man can sometimes, but rarely, see that belief in his close friends' eyes, particularly war veterans. It's primeval. It comes after 300,000 years of the male of the species hunting together. Male or female, you can always smell the stench of its absence. Even the undeserving man can be enlarged by the presence of the belief of another, and the greatest man can be defeated by its absence. It was mortifying and debilitating for me to witness the metamorphosis in my wife from supporter to saboteur as my business failed. Don't get me wrong; I don't see myself as a victim, just numb from my recent troubles. I had drifted into the *blah-zone,* which can be quite comforting, really. I always assumed my psyche was healing quietly in the background.

Jim, my boss, collars me before I have a chance to get settled.

"I have a new client for you. She's waiting at reception. She asked for you." I peered over his shoulder to see who he was talking about. "She's got some gripe with her husband, and it seemed to me to be the type of case you would like."

"What, inconsequential with no hope of any decent fees?"

"Yeah, that's the one."

I waved at her to come in. It's not that large an office, but I couldn't be bothered being polite enough to go over and get her. She was a tall, good-looking woman, blonde, late-thirties, with large breasts. I was a little perturbed that I had noticed her breasts; part of me wasn't numb it seemed.

"Hi."

"Jim Jamisen. Come in, take a seat."

"Pamela Fredericks, nice to meet you."

"I thought you were going to say Anderson there for a minute." She didn't get it. It was a clumsy compliment. You could tell where my head was at. "What can I do for you?"

"I hear you can fix things."

"Who on earth would be silly enough to say that?"

"A friend of mine, actually. The wife of an old employee of yours, Bob Bow."

"I'm not sure I recall the guy." He used to work for me and stole from my business. I remembered him, alright.

"He's dead. My friend was there when he got shot on her front porch as he left for work and she had a terrible time cleaning the stain off her favourite cotton dress."

"Oh, that Bob Bow, I remember reading about it. So why would Mrs Bow be sending you to me?"

"Well, I own a cotton dress that I am particularly fond of, as well."

"I'm not following you."

"Apparently, she met you when you went to confront her husband shortly after he started up his new business with your clients. It must have been quite a scene because the bullet hadn't hit the wall of the house before she figured you for the shooter or someone you sent. She's been keeping an eye on you ever since. Through the press, I mean."

"I haven't been in the press."

"There have been other long-range shootings in the last couple of years since her husband died. Same M.O. for all of them. She thinks it's you."

"Really! I think I'm… flabbergasted." I was going to say flattered.

"I am not without means and am potentially very wealthy."

"Good for you."

"Look, no one is accusing you of anything."

"Why would they?"

"My take on this is you have declared open season on some arseholes in your life and have decided to do the world a favour by removing them."

"If only."

"Well, I know an arsehole and I want you to put him on your list."

"I don't have a list."

"Do you know someone who does?"

"No lists. I can help you find a good divorce lawyer."

"More legal bullshit?"

"You know who's office you're in, right?"

"Pass." She stood. "Been there, done that, copped the repercussions. Here are my details, if you decide to be helpful."

I muttered something about wanting to be of assistance but she left frustrated, without engaging my legal services. I was afraid my extended sexual dry spell would end up with me making a decision about this case that would be bad for my health. There is a lovely old Spanish saying that *blaming a man for following his dick is like blaming a compass for pointing north.* I'm guessing it was a man who said it, I don't know who, but I'll bet that adhering to it didn't always guarantee his wellbeing. North can be dangerous territory.

As I headed home that day, I began to grasp what had happened to me in that meeting with Pamela. She had caused me to take a look at the man I had drifted into becoming in recent years. For me, it had become the worst of times without wisdom or belief, just Dickensian disenchantment. At forty-two, the vision I had as a child, of what I would become as a man, had not been realised. I had compromised and I had done it without knowing that the bargains I had made along the way were permanent. I am an honest person who has done dishonest things, necessitated, I wanted to believe, by the day-to-day practicalities that afflict us all, those forces that require us to re-interpret the rules and relinquish our adopted purpose that, once conceded, make us lesser beings for having acquiesced. I am not religious, nor am I amoral. The echoes in my head from Martin Luther testified to my predicament, not my beliefs. *Out of the depths, I cry to thee* repeats as evidence that I was terminally diminished by my belief in the inconsequence of my life. I found myself deep in that hole I had dug that now reached part way to hell and all the way to the end of my rope, a rope to which I had clung long past my desire to hold on to it had been extinguished. But like any religious allegory, my tale was to become one of fundamental redemption. The journey to my deliverance, however, took a winding path that may disquiet the righteous soul. To them, I would say this: God rescued Lot for *He knows how to rescue the godly from temptation and to keep the unrighteous under punishment for the Day of Judgment [Peter 2:8]*. I was, I had realised long ago, more interested in what punishment I could personally impose upon those that had trespassed against me than concerned about what God might have in store for me on Judgement Day. It was Wilde rather than the Bible that I now embraced: *things are what they are and will be what they will be*. The inevitability of that proposition permitted me to shed my fears of what the next morning might bring and instead wallow in unexplored resignation. That escape was my bulwark against the tragedies that were piling up in my life like so many empty whiskey bottles in the kitchenette at the shithole hotel where I lived. Perversely, my acceptance of the availability of an alcohol-induced death was the only thing that had kept me alive to this point. *I don't care* was my mantra but I would not add the word *anymore* because that would imply I had aspirations to care again.

"Hello there, big boy." I had accepted Pamela's invitation for a drink. She was persistent. I was weak. What can I say? The Spanish guy was right.

"Knock it off, that's not going to work on me." It was working. She had showered and changed. I could smell the soap or whatever it was that she used on her body and I could see a lot more of those breasts that I was telling you about. I knew what she was trying to do and *she had me at hello*, thank you, Cameron Crowe. We had settled in on a pair of bar stools at the cosy end of a local bar.

"I'm immune to flattery," I reiterated.

"All evidence to the contrary."

I found myself glancing down at the front of my pants but she was talking about the emotional transparency that came with the numbness I carried around with me now like a cloak of invisibility and the fact that she caught me looking at her breasts.

"Look, I don't know what you were talking about in my office. I'm just a lowly lawyer. I have trouble getting up enough motivation to shave in the morning, let alone doing the sorts of things you think I do."

"Yeah, but you are a lawyer and I figure you might know someone who knows someone who could do something. I didn't believe Jill when she told me, Mrs Bow that is, but I thought there was no harm in meeting with you. You've been fucked over by some bad people so I figured you might at least understand."

"Understand what?"

"My husband is cheating on me."

"I thought that was compulsory. If husbands got shot for cheating there would be no more husbands, Pamela."

"Or no more cheating." She paused for effect; here comes the sob story. "He beats me and my son. Has done for years."

"Go to the police."

"I have. He just beats me for going to the police. They do nothing. He is a wealthy man, very well connected all the way to the mayor's office."

"Then leave him."

"Not an easy thing to do."

"Why don't I believe you?"

"You don't have to. Here is the whole sordid story, the photos, the medical records, the police reports." She handed me a thumb drive. "The boy is only twelve, for God's sake. It's not as if he can defend himself."

She had hit a nerve. "Your husband wasn't Christian clergy at some point, was he?" I said, thinking about my own unhappy school days. I got up to leave. "I'll have a look and see what I can recommend."

"Don't bother coming back with any of that legal bullshit. I've gone down that road before and he tried to have me committed to a mental hospital."

Another nerve gangling. I didn't want to hear anything more about mentally unstable women. Because of previous encounters with such creatures, the thought of it made my backbone shiver and increased my desire to leave. I hate myself when I jump to conclusions, this one being that he was right about her being crazy.

"I'll have a look at the material and get back to you," was the best I could muster. In the meantime, consider divorcing him."

"Thanks for nothing."

"No problem. It's what I do for a living."

I left, she stayed.

CHAPTER TWO

So, I was at Pamela's place the following Friday. Yeah, that's right, Pamela's place. Sniffing around like a dog. It was a big house, the staff had been sent off with chores, the hubby was off on a business trip, and the kid was upstairs studying, she said, so the coast was clear. It was good for me that the house was almost empty because if she succeeded in getting someone to bump off her husband, I didn't want any association with her. Yet, there I sat. So far, my relationship with her was turning out to be just another wonderful experience with an unstable woman.

"Have you changed your mind about helping me?" she said as she sat in the lounge opposite me. Did I mention the legs?

"No, I haven't changed my mind."

"Why are you here?"

"Not sure. To bring your file back." Feeble.

"Thanks. Just leave it on the coffee table. None of that moved you?"

"It all did."

"So, why won't you help me?"

"I keep telling you, you've got the wrong guy."

"So, why are you here?"

"Didn't we just...no, I guess we didn't." I thought about the question more seriously the second time around. I knew why. "I can't stay away. I'm following my baser instincts."

"How base?"

"Home base."

"If my husband heard you say that, you would have another reason to shoot him."

"Being?"

"He'd be looking to shoot you."

"I told…"

"Yeah, you don't know anything about that. I'm not sure that I believe you. I am not that unhappy with the baser instincts thing, though. We've all got them." She smiled a baser kind of smile and it looked to me like it might have been a while for her, too. "Can I get you a drink?"

"Scotch, neat, thanks."

It was about three in the afternoon, but what the hell? After five was my rule but three was an odd number too. She got up and walked over to an antique drinks trolley buried in partially filled bottles; someone was a drinker. It was a slow, deliberate walk and I watched her all the way across the room. She didn't need to look back to know I was watching. I'm sure she could feel my stare burning on her back. Dear me, it had been far too long. I think a four-year dry spell qualifies you for virginity again because mine had definitely grown back. She needed to be very gentle with me. I was fragile.

"You look a bit fragile."

"What?"

"Like a guy who hasn't had one in a long time," she said, as she gave me the glass and went back to pour herself one.

"Do you mean a drink?"

"No."

"Are you clairvoyant?"

"Just horny, but I have an excuse. My husband likes to dominate me. In his head that doesn't include sex, just hitting and emotional abuse. He gets his sex somewhere else."

"I knew someone who liked to hit people, once, mainly young boys. No one that could hit back effectively, God knows I tried."

"Is he dead?"

"Yes. He met with a terrible accident not so long ago."

"It didn't involve a cotton dress, did it?"

"No, a brick wall." I'd said enough.

"Are you married, Jim? You don't mind if I call you Jim?" She sat again.

"No, divorced."

"How does that make you feel?"

"Numb."

"Which bit is numb?"

"My soul. Not the important bits… apparently."

"What's made your soul numb?"

"Arseholes. The lying, cheating, stealing kind. Whiskey helps. Cheers."

"Is that why you started shooting people?"

"I told you…"

"Yeah, yeah. The woman-beater is not back until Sunday, he is in Frisco on business, or that's what he says. Are you a risk taker, Jim?"

"What have you got in mind?"

She thought pretty hard about it.

"A swim?"

I was going to say that I didn't have a costume but I wasn't that virginal.

I remember seeing Jake for the first time through the water as I came up for air. He was standing beside the pool. Jeans, tee-shirt, and a stern look.

"So, you're the lawyer?" he said. His mother was sitting on the steps of the pool in her one-piece with her feet in the water.

"A lawyer," I said as I wiped the water out of my eyes, "sure."

"You don't look like much."

"I'm not."

"Mum says you can fix this for us, that you are some kind of big shot."

"Did she say big shot or good shot?" I pulled myself up out of the pool clumsily, it was hard. I didn't think he would get the play on words.

"If you're here when he comes home, you'll be shot. You know that, right?"

I said *right* in return, incredulously trying to focus with the water in my eyes. He was angry with me and I didn't know why. Maybe he was just angry. I sat in my boxers on the pool's edge looking up at him. He was not a happy twelve-year-old. He turned and went back inside. I looked over to Pamela who had the look of a mother whose child was terminally ill and she couldn't do anything to save him. I swam over to her and gave her a kiss. We both responded immediately to the intimacy in a way neither of has had foreseen despite our sexual bravado over the drinks cart. The *what if?* was left behind and replaced with *what now?* It had been a long time for us both and consequences ensued. I think she was glad to have the opportunity to express her sexuality or she was trying to sweeten the deal. Either way, I was happy to oblige.

I was walking in Bali, Andy Warhol said *and I saw people in a clearing having a ball because somebody they really liked had died and I realised then that everything was just how you decided to think about it. Some let problems make them miserable for years when they should just say, "So what?"* Many such things in life depend on your vantage point, like a sniper attempting to judge what is a threat and what is innocuous. All of which led me to consider my propensity to hate people who had fucked me over. It's a word laden with foreboding, *propensity*, pregnant with potential danger. In the opening scene of *American Sniper*, a mother and her son lie shot dead, predetermined to be culpable because of their *propensity* to harm, rather than them being guilty of a deadly act. I know a lot of people that display that same trait, just not as openly as that mother and her son. The sniper believed the boy was going to throw a grenade at the approaching American military column. In today's terrorised social environment, we accept the child's *propensity* to harm. Some even accept that he needed to be shot, both the boy of six and then his mother. But it is a huge leap to believe that they would have fared well had they engaged a column of armed soldiers secured within armed vehicles, the two assailants together had just one grenade between them. So, a respected SEAL became judge, jury, and executioner and, yes, I know the complexity of that argument. I will give Mr Eastwood the courtesy of assuming that he knew it wasn't going to be a fair fight. He, too, was making the social comment I just illuminated.

I think it is hard to identify the point when my marriage ended. Twenty years of talking, then no talking but still *living* together, un-divorced and un-killed. Whatever our differences, it was difficult to walk away from a twenty-year investment, half of my life, all of my adult life. Time is the only investment that really matters and turning your back on an outlay of that size is unwelcome. It was a mistake to marry her, I was very young, and she was the wrong person. I remember her legs when she got out of bed. I would look at them sticking out from that short nightie as she put on her makeup. I was twenty. The legs, as it turned out, were not enough to base a lifetime investment on and I now realise that a penis is as much of a curse as a disapproving father when it comes to such matters. Her sister hated me and my parents hated her. Their disapproval only spurred me on because I was so young and so moralistic. Unbeknownst to me, she had another agenda and an eternal fear of rejection. I saw pictures of her with her previous boyfriend dancing and the look in her eyes before he rejected her. I wish I could send her back to him for them to suffer the disappointments that arrogant arsehole would bring to her. But, unfortunately, she didn't give up her virginity to him, she gave it to me, and my goose was cooked. All in all, it was a set-up. I capitulated happily then but eventually not so much. There is no greater betrayal than to be with someone for twenty years and then have them reject you. The so-called sin of *cheating* can't compare to such brutality. Cheating in a marriage is just a venial sin. Rejection after such an investment of time deserves the needle. *Lies are a necessity, they are the source of meaning and hope,* thank you, Titus Abrasax. But with great respect, sir, there is no hope, you idiot.

For some time, I couldn't afford to live somewhere other than the marital home and in accepting that *contre ton gré*, I joined many non-living un-dead around the globe who had accepted that same contract. My brethren in silence, stuck in their downstairs study or backyard shed smoking their choice of drug and abusing the *misses* unheard and unseen because it was more palatable than not smoking and abusing her out loud and in person. In consenting to my marital farce, you have clear evidence of my obfuscation as to both its cause and the options available to me. *Life moves pretty fast,* Ferris Bueller entreated, asking us to slow down and smell the roses: *if you don't stop and look around once and a while, you could miss it.* The problem for me was that I had already missed it and it had been surprisingly easy to do. Clearly, Ferris was describing a life lived better than my own, but the movie filled the void left in my brain by my absent self-esteem. *The facility for quotation covers the absence of original thought*, thank you, Sherlock. An accusation to which I plead guilty. Life engulfed Ferris like a warm blanket; he was immune to all the things that afflicted me.

At that time at home, I lived on the line between reality and dreaming and my next step wasn't clear. We all feel it just after we wake up in the morning. Coffee is supposed to fix it and fix the paranoia that goes with it but, for some of us, it doesn't go away. The hypnagogia persists all day, yeah, that's right, there's even a word for it. You find yourself accepting people and things around you only because you are dreaming. You hope that they are the right people and you are in the right place, but neither is true. I think I have spent much of my adult life in that state, like a cork bobbing in a river, washed from side to side and not possessed of the clarity needed to set my own direction. I couldn't come up with the right choice at any given decision point and even my strongest inclinations were swayed by the next interrupting phone call. It was John Lennon who proposed that *life is easy with eyes closed, misunderstanding all you see.* He was right to suggest that many of us live in that blind state but it doesn't make life any easier. In that dream, the real world closes in on you and squeezes out all understanding and opportunity.

I have never gotten my head around the denial of cause and effect in a marriage. I don't mean excuses for infidelity, I mean that infidelity is this huge and, apparently, only crime of any substance in a marriage, aside perhaps from violence. Violence carries so much weight in some cultures but not as much as infidelity does in ours. You could be subjected to endless emotional hardship or continued physical rejection and it all equates to a breakdown in the relationship for which perhaps no one is to blame. All that counts for naught. If you go out and find some physical relief without your unloving partner's consent, then you are the devil incarnate. I remember a line in an Al Pacino movie where the estranged wife of Pacino's character told him that she had to go out and demean herself by having sex with his best friend to get closure from him. I never understood what she meant at the time; in fact, I found it offensive. But I understand it now. Infidelity is the bullet in the heart of any relationship, regardless of how much that relationship has going for it and what other emotional crimes have been committed. Infidelity is the only thing that carries sufficient weight to send everyone packing. What about demonstrating by your actions that you don't love or respect your spouse anymore, or telling them there will never again be physical affection? None of that works, but sleep with someone else and it's: *you arsehole, fuck off.*

In my case, the relationship needed a bullet in the ear, but sadly, infidelity also ends otherwise great marriages. We are, after all, human. I could have taken Pamela to dinner and walked along a beach sharing intimate thoughts with her and we could become nothing more than dear friends and confidants, sharers of intimate emails and texts. In our soap opera world, that would have been OK. She would just be a *friend* to me. But if the genitals meet, then boom, light the fuse and retire, because your life is about to explode. Is it such a crime when compared with all other possible crimes? Are we all that puerile and shallow? Clara, my ex-wife, was wrong for me from the beginning and we had both known that for some time. I wonder about how much of the relationship I invented and how much of her was real. She is one of those people who paint their life by the numbers; numbers printed on her brain by her mother and her friend Catherine. When I was young, my personality was overwhelming, driven and confident, and I think Clara was overcome when we first met. What I saw reflected in her was my enthusiasm for the relationship rather than her affection returned in kind. The result was that I ended up making a hell of an investment of life resources and ending up with nothing to show for it.

Moving out of the marital home when the time came was easy. My laptop, one bag of clothes, a pillow, a doona and a mattress that had none of the crabs or bugs that I was sure the room I was about to rent contained. A couple of clean sheets and I was done. The sum total of who I now was and what I now had all fitted in my campervan. I didn't want to take anything else from that house. Most of my clothes were too big for me since I had started drinking and not eating, and Clara loved that furniture more than she loved me. No pet, it wasn't allowed, even though I think you can build up karma points by looking after any living being. One of the by-products of going numb is that everything around you turns a uniform shade of grey and becomes meaningless to the unenthused mind. None of my accumulated junk from school or college was of any interest to me. Boxes full of reminders of me falling short of ancient and now meaningless objectives, mementos of long since excused non-performance, the substance of a life half-lived. I told Clara to throw out anything she didn't want.

The decision to move out surgically removed the last vestige of my childhood. I had gone from my mother's house to living with Clara and it was not until I left that house that I realised I hadn't fully let go of the little boy that resided within both homes. Santa was finally dead, as was the residue of my childhood belief system. I wondered whether that meant I could finally grow up, but I realised it was both too much to hope for and too late to implement. Instead, I said my final farewell to Clara and drove to a fleabag hotel close to work. At the hotel that first night, I settled in with a fresh bottle of Scotch to welcome myself to the real world. That hotel room summed it up perfectly for me; it had nothing I owned or cared for except the bottle of Scotch and the *unmistakable whiff of existential despair.*

It was lucky for me that the sprawling house owned by Pamela's husband was in something of a gully. It was about a week after my swim in his pool and the day after I read in the papers that Pamela had *died from injuries sustained from a fall at home.* She had tripped and fallen down the stairs, the police asserted. Fredericks was the very well-connected bereaved husband and the death was ruled an accident. I don't mind admitting that I cried for her but despair was quickly replaced by guilt about my inaction and from there the jump to anger was easy.

It would usually take me a month to set up a shoot but, in this instance, it was hard to wait even twenty-four hours. I was emotional and I was probably about to make a mistake because of that emotion, but I didn't care. I had seen the bruises on her back that night in the pool and the look of fear in the boy's eyes, but I had been too concerned about being caught to act and now I was sorry, deeply sorry. My hesitation had been fatal for her, but there was still the boy to worry about, that plus the fact that Fredericks had to pay the piper. On this particular cool dewy morning, the piper had come a-calling and was armed to the teeth.

I parked my campervan in one of the subdivisions that overlooked the house. The back of my camper faced his driveway. I don't usually park the campervan by itself but it was Saturday and no one was around. I prefer to park in a street where there are other parked cars as it allows me to fade into the background. I shoot from inside the van with a good pair of ear muffs, despite my most excellent homemade suppressor. There was some cover provided by the piles of building materials on pallets on the construction site. I had reversed the van up alongside a large stack of framing timber. I never take off as soon as I make the shot, any motion can give you away. This day, however, I would be gone as soon as I was done, a product of my nervousness about the position of my vehicle and my belief that I was underprepared.

I had a good look at the front of the house from where I was, even though it was over twelve hundred yards away. According to my instruments, it was 3663 feet, 1221 yards, from where his driveway met the bitumen back up to where I lay prostrate in my van. The bullet's twist and drop at that range, in this wind, is just over six feet. You needed to know the math to get the hold off right. After years of practise, I could do it in my head. I also had the advantage that he wouldn't be shooting back unless he had something that I didn't know about in that golf bag he was now hefting down his front stairs.

As I watched him struggle with the oversized golf bag, I mouthed the words *die, you fucker, die*. There is nothing like a round of golf to take your mind off your recently deceased wife, right? I lay in the back of the van, over-excited and overheated. I dropped my forehead onto my arm and wiped the sweat onto my sleeve trying to lower my heart rate. The thought of Pamela ran through my head. She was a beautiful woman. I began to tear up, which is not conducive to accurate aiming. It was early. I love it at that time of day, the crisp air and dew still on the grass. I allowed my appreciation of it to distract me while I settled and slowed my heartbeat.

I knew that dipshit had an early tee-off that morning at his club; it always pays to do your homework. He had parked his Merc out the front of his garage facing the road because his Bentley and the recently purchased Koenigsegg Agera were parked inside. People who pay one and a half million bucks for a sports car deserve to get whacked, everything else aside. He was extending the garage to fit the Merc in but it turned out he wasn't going to get the chance; his time was up.

He put his clubs in the trunk of his car and as he opened the front door to get in, something on the hill below me caught his eye. It was opportune because it caused him to pause and straighten up, looking to see what it was just long enough for me to blow his brains out. Number seven, single shot, cold bore.

Unbeknownst to me at the time, there was another shooter that day or, at least, I thought she was a shooter. I found out it was a she the following week. It must have been her that Fredericks caught a glimpse of on the hill below me. She was on the grassy knoll to my left, yeah, that's right, the grassy knoll. I didn't see who it was, but she saw me. It would have taken a professional to figure out where that shot came from, but she was in front of me, closer to the target, so that assisted her in tracking my shot's trajectory back to the campervan. I give off no muzzle flare and almost no report outside the van because my suppressor is very effective. You can hear almost nothing and certainly not from the hill where she was. But she made me nonetheless.

I was followed home that day.

I was at my desk going back over my old client list and setting up appointments on the assumption that they would follow me over to Duncan's practice when in walked the dick from Phillie that Fat Jack, Duncan's mate, had been talking about the previous Friday night when I was at Duncan's for dinner, Mark Zelenski. I knew who he was. I had been following him in the media because Fat Jack said he was looking into a long-range shooting in Philadelphia. Yeah, that's right, one of mine. I wasn't happy to see him, but I don't think it showed. *Whatever,* I said to myself under my breath, now understanding the true meaning of that word; if you don't like the heat, stay out of the campervan. I guess one of the things that started me on my crusade apart from the therapy it provided was my low regard for my own existence on this planet, that numbness I was telling you about. I wasn't frightened of this guy. I'm not sure anything frightened me anymore, except, maybe heights. I had nothing to lose except an embryonic sense of renewal and a growing suspicion that things might be about to get better, seeded that night in the pool with Pamela. Look how that turned out. This wasn't the first time I had felt those aspirations only for them to prove premature. I suspected this guy was about to scramble what was left of the fledgling Phoenix egg I was hatching in my psyche.

"Jim Jamisen?"

"Funny, that's my name." He looked puzzled. I knew who he was, so, I didn't ask.

"I'm Detective First Class Mark Zelenski and this is my assistant, Detective Joan Travis. We've got a few questions for you, if you don't mind."

Joan was an absolute honey. Tall and good-looking, with auburn hair and flawless skin. What the hell was she doing on the Phillie Force instead of being in the movies, except perhaps her aversion for working with perverts? She was looking at me as if she knew me. I'm sure I would have remembered her if we'd met before. I got lost for a moment in her blue eyes, or were they purple?

"Take a seat," I said perfunctorily, coming out of my bemusement, "always happy to help the long arm of the law. That's a Philadelphia ID, what brings you to Chicago?"

"Well…you."

"I'm flattered. What do you need?"

"We have a couple of open cases that we are looking at, both of which match the M.O. of a murder here last Saturday…one Martin James Fredericks."

"Yeah, terrible thing. His wife came in here a few weeks ago looking for a divorce lawyer. It seems it may have cost her."

I assumed he had checked the phone calls from her cell or their house back to this office. Why else would he be sitting in front of me? It's always better to stay ahead of these guys' questions. That is, if you're sure what questions they are going to ask, which isn't usually hard because they usually aren't that smart. It is, however, important not to volunteer unsought information.

"Cost her?"

"She's dead."

"Yeah, yeah. So, you think he killed her?"

"Can I say with all due respect to Fredericks and you that I don't think she fell down the stairs?"

"You knew the guy."

"Never met him." Not lying.

"She wanted to divorce him?" Joan asked. I smiled, I couldn't help it, she was so beautiful. She smiled back and her smile went through my numbness like a laser beam through my frozen cockles, as in cockles of my heart, not the other cockles, well, sure, all my cockles. We had a moment, I think, or else she was sizing me up for a pair of handcuffs. Either way, I was hers.

"Yeah, she said he used to beat her and the kid. He sounded like a real pig."

"You believed her?" she said.

"Well…again, she's dead. You're the detective."

Zelenski is younger than he looks in his photo on LinkedIn, maybe late twenties. Fit, good-looking but definitely a flatfoot. You could pick him for a copper from across a crowded room. Not so his partner. She made me feel like I should have been exercising.

"So why did she come to you if you don't do that kind of work?" Zelenski took up the questioning.

"Referral." Also true. I'm batting a thousand here.

"Did you know either of these guys?"

He put down two photos on my desk, taken before the men in the photos had been shot in the face… by me. They were Number 4 and Number 6 off my hit list.

"This guy looks familiar." I took a risk with that reply but if he had already connected me to them, which I suspected he had, a lie was going to really press his buttons.

"This guy," he was pointing to Number 4, "used to be your business partner in Grand Rapids."

"You're right, you know." I picked up the photo and pretended to examine it more closely. "Terrible picture. I didn't recognise him with the beard." That was a close call.

"And this guy sold you some investments a few years ago."

"Can't say that I recognise him."

"A dud property investment, a con job."

"Yeah, sure…I recall the investment but not this guy. I was dealing with someone else, a broker. I heard he caught a lot of people."

"Don't you think it's strange that you have a link to all three victims?"

"I know a lot of people, detective. Two of these guys I've never met before, so I would hardly say I had a link to them all. If you're collecting a list of people these guys *never met* then it's going to be a long list and you can put me on it, if you like." Careful. "Besides, everybody knows someone who knows someone related to the victim."

"Six degrees of separation?"

"Well, I think these days, social media and so on, it's closer to three degrees, isn't it? You guys are the experts."

"Don't you have a motive for wanting all these guys dead?" Miss World asks.

"Sounds like, from what I read in the papers, a lot of guys wanted this Fredericks guy dead but, as I said, I never met the man. My ex-partner in Grand Rapids was a card-carrying arsehole. He cost me a lot of money. I ended up not liking him but neither did half the population of Michigan. The conman, well I didn't know who put that scam together. I blamed my broker and he is still very much alive, last I heard."

"You would know some violent people given the job you are in, right?"

"Can't say that I do. I did some low-end crime work when I first started but it's been all commercial since then. I have met some dodgy businessmen, as you rightly point out, but no hitmen, if that's what you're asking. Why, do you have another photograph to show me?" That was two smartarse comments in a row. It doesn't usually pay to piss these guys off. Then again, why would a guilty guy smartarse a copper?

"You understand we have to follow these things through."

"Sure, anytime." I stood to shake his hand, prompting them to leave. "You and your partner can come back anytime, especially you, Detective Travis." Tread softly. But she smiled again, which puzzled me because I knew she couldn't be attracted to an overweight lawyer. I wasn't that irrational. They left amicably and apparently satisfied.

As I sat back down, I had a good think about whether I was going to ditch the Tac-50, my favourite weapon of all time, and the campervan. I went home, making sure I hadn't been tailed, and did just that with the silencer I had been so proud of and all the ammo. I took the van to be detailed, telling them an animal had died in there and stunk it out so I wanted the interior washed down with chlorine. I was thinking about gunshot residue, not animal stink. I had that van pretty well set up. I'd put in a double bunk that stood normal height and, when I lay in the top bunk and wound up the retractable top that provided head room in the van, I could get a good sighter out of the top window. I'd cut a hole about two feet long and six inches high out of the flexible plastic the manufacturer had used to connect the retractable top to the roof and kept the van weather-tight. It was perfect. I sold the van the next day. It was purchased with a false ID I'd picked up at a gun show in Missouri, as was the weapon. You can't drive around in an unregistered car with a Tac-50 in the back, so I needed the false ID to register it. I went to a dodgy cash-for-cars dealer and only got $600 for it but, right now, that was better than nothing.

Numbers 7 through 12 from my list would have to wait for a while.

CHAPTER THREE

"That was my shoot."

The sound of her voice scared the living shit out of me. I had just flicked on the light in my hotel room. I was home late, and she was already sitting there in the darkened room waiting for me wearing that wry smile I had thought was so attractive the last time I saw her.

"Detective Travis, you scared me."

"Joan, please."

I put my keys down and went directly to the open bottle of Scotch on the bench.

"I'm sorry, your shoot? Drink?"

Christ, more unstable women. This one was armed.

"You should be sorry and, no, thank you, I'd fear for my eyesight drinking that stuff."

"I make do."

"You cost me money killing Fredericks."

She didn't seem interested in the weapon in her shoulder holster, hidden by her Prada jacket. Yes, Prada, Miss Detective First Grade. What's that about?

"Is that a Glock 42 380 Auto Subcompact Slimline tucked under your arm, inside your Prada jacket? Corruption does pay off."

"You know your weapons."

"Silver plated, really. A bit abstemious, considering it's an expensive weapon. Do you intend to use it?"

"Just here for a chat."

"So…" I finished my first and poured a second. I've got to stop drinking.

"Fredericks was dirty, connected to a mob of arms dealers and with very important connections, all the way to the mayor's office, we think. I had him in my sights. I was about to get paid to retire him."

"Yes, very interesting." It was all bullshit, of course. "Why are you here? You sure you don't want a drink?" She shook her head. "Probably for the best, there's not much left."

"I've read your college file. Very bright, a boxer, a good one, regional golden glove champion, national amateur rifle champion at seventeen, and good-looking, judging from the photos. What have you done to yourself?"

"Did I mention I was a lawyer?"

"You should make a better life plan."

"I plan to finish that bottle, if that's what you mean. It helps me, you know, be a lawyer."

"I meant a little bit longer term."

"What are you doing reading my collage file?" I sat down a little more relaxed given she wasn't going to shoot me even though I now had nothing with which to shoot back.

"I'm not here in any official capacity. And you don't need to concern yourself about Zelenski, either. He was just ticking boxes."

"Did he tick yours?" I said, *tick.* I don't know why I went there, other than the fact that those jeans she was wearing were so very tight and the drink had hit its mark on my empty stomach.

Another wry smile. "That was a hell of a shot. There's probably only five people in this country who could make a shot like that. Ever miss?"

"Not lately. Grassy knoll person?"

"If you mean on the hill outside of Fredericks's place last Saturday, sure that was me."

"Ok, then." Cards on the table apparently.

"How many does Fredericks make it for you?"

"Seven." I saw no need to lie. It was against my newly minted set of values since my marriage breakup and, besides, she had seen me collect the seventh.

"Including the ones we accused you of the other day?"

"Sure. Arseholes, all of them."

"You're an amateur, right? I've never heard your name mentioned in professional circles other than the occasional *who the fuck did that job?*"

"Amateur, yes, whatever that means."

"It means you shouldn't give it away for free. Do I need to explain capitalism to you?"

"That's not my motivation."

"Make it your motivation. You're broke, judging by where you live and what you drink."

"Both do a good enough job. I don't shoot just anybody."

"Morals, interesting. You know shooting people is illegal, right?"

"So is breaking into people's hotel rooms. Are you telling me that you're a hitman…girl?"

"Sure."

"Who do you work for?"

"You won't find them on Google. Loads of dough, real money. Bill Gates wanted to cure malaria; these guys want to rid the world of arseholes."

"Seriously? It's altruistic? I call bullshit on that. There is, by the way, too large an afflicted populace for them to cure."

"Not at all, no. They don't think so."

"If it were true, which I don't think it is…" I stopped. "Wait, are you offering me a job?"

"Maybe. It was me that connected the dots with those murders of yours. I wanted the Department to find you for me."

"Thanks."

"You're welcome. The Department has lost interest in you after our meeting, so now you've only got me to contend with."

"Zelenski's lost interest?"

"He's an idiot, even when it comes to ticking boxes. I told him it couldn't be you."

"And he believed you?"

I must have looked puzzled or just numb from the booze.

"Come on. Where's my thank-you for getting rid of Zelenski, and do you want a job or not? You'd work for me exclusively. I would pay you. They would pay me, more than I pay you, you know capitalism and all that. We're encouraged to form networks like multi-tier marketing."

"So, it's Amway?"

"You can say yes or no after I brief you on each job."

"And if I say no?"

"No hard feelings, you can keep helping at the periphery, if you like, but you should get into the real game and make some money. You need some help and resources and we have plenty of both. Fredericks has friends, and they may be looking for you."

"No one knows about my relationship, such as it was, with Pamela."

"I figured it out. How many more have you got on your list?"

"Six."

"Very precise. I like a man who knows who he hates. Let's put them up for approval so you can get paid to retire them. Fifty thousand per job, no medical."

"What? I get paid to exterminate my own cockroaches?"

"If they approve the candidates."

"*Candidates*. That's an interesting term. So is *retire*."

"It's not business for them, they call themselves the Council. They use donated money."

"You must be joking, a charity?" She looked deadly serious. "A charity, really?"

"They have funds. They don't sell the service; they just decide who. But it's definitely business, for me."

"Business. You're a cop."

"I moonlight."

"You're beautiful, you know that?" My mind was wandering again. I was on my way to being drunk. "You should be modelling."

"So, now you're Harvey Weinstein."

"Want a drink?" I was getting confused, the bottle was empty anyway.

"Again, no."

"How will I contact you?"

"You're in?"

"I want to come to your next hit, insurance in case you are bullshitting me. I can't think straight right now. You've seen mine, now show me yours." That was surprisingly lucid.

"Sure. We're talking about a shoot, right? You're not back to the boxes, again, because that would be lame?"

"They must pay you a lot, given the clothes you wear. Nice jacket?"

"You have no idea how much I earn from this job." She got up and headed for the door, then turned back and said, "I'll be in touch."

She left and I went and dug out another bottle of Chateau Turpentine, the emergency reserve. Was I a killer? Well, yes. But was I that type of a killer, a professional? My head went from *yeah, that's right, baby,* to *what the fuck?* and back again. Despite what I had been doing in recent times, I never saw myself as a killer. I was just doing everybody a favour by getting rid of the deadwood as well as cleaning up the mess in my brain. I was having trouble keeping those jeans out of my head long enough to consider the proposition at hand. It wasn't entrapment. She already had me dead to rights on the Fredericks shooting. The bit about the Council had to be bullshit, surely, but did it matter? If I got paid, did it matter by whom? Well, yes. What if it was organised crime? But how was that any different? They weren't asking me to sell cookies, they wanted me to whack people. So, it was criminal regardless of how well it was organised. I sure needed that pay check. What if someone whacked me back? *I don't give a fuck* I said out loud immediately that thought popped into my head and I meant it, *I'm fucked any way,* I said, reassuring myself. The price I had placed on my own life was about the same as my next bottle of Scotch. Fifty grand was a lot more money than that.

Nearly a week later, Detective Joan turns up at my office door.

"Got a minute?"

"Sure." I followed her out the door.

We went out to her car, her Ferrari. I bet she doesn't drive that to work or wear her Prada jacket into the precinct, which I was starting to think was not the only couture she owned.

"I have a place near here, just a rental. I'm buying a place in Dallas."

"Dallas?"

"Hell of a town."

"Nothing to do with the gun laws in Texas, then?"

"You can always get what you need there, provided you have a means of driving it out of town."

"The Ferrari makes sense, now. Where are you taking me?"

"I'm going to show you something, then we've got a job to do." She smiled and hit the gas. My head hit the headrest.

She led me into a pristine penthouse with a view of the city, beautifully furnished, it had the lot. I salivated, thinking that she had done well for herself, and began to hallucinate about afternoon sex, right here, right now.

"It's not mine, it's yours," she looked at me for a reaction. I didn't have one. I was still thinking about the sex and there were too many missing details, but I think my mouth was open. "Take a look at this."

She went over to a large metal cabinet that was a three-draw safe and opened it with a code. She pulled out drawers full of the best weaponry and accessories I had ever seen. No MacMillan, but I knew how to fix that easy enough.

"Do I need to explain any of that to you?"

I could barely get out the requisite no. It was Christmas day and Santa had been very kind.

"There's a truck in the parking space for this apartment downstairs. Brand new Chevy, keys are on the bench there." She turned and faced me. "You can tell me to stop anytime you want."

I knew where she was headed but what she didn't know was that I was already there waiting for her, sitting on my new couch with a decent scotch in my hand, looking out at the city through my brand-new floor-to-ceiling windows.

She clicked her fingers in front of my face to stop me dreaming. "You want me to stop or not?"

"How do I get paid?"

"That's the spirit. There is a phone on that charger. Clean laptop there. I will only use that phone to send you jobs. There is a program on the laptop to encrypt and decrypt the texts from me and to delete them off the phone and computer when you're done. Set your own password and keep the devices synced and clean and do not connect that laptop to the net, got it? It's meant to be air-gapped, so keep it that way. You will have to set up your own bank account and advise us of the details.

You're a commercial lawyer, you figure it out. Offshore, untraceable, all that shit. So, we have a deal?"

"Sure."

"I'm gonna need a yes."

"Yes, ma'am."

"I won't be needing you to sign anything," she said, shaking my hand and giving me a look that implied she had just taken a mortgage on my life. "Get me the details of the remainder of your hit list. Give me as many details as possible so I can sell them as candidates. Use only that phone for those kinds of communications and don't use it for anything else. I'm the only pre-set contact on the phone. Understood?"

"Understood."

"The lease here is in an offshore company account but the building management has been given your name, you have full authority. Rent-free for as long as you're on the payroll. Your first bonus because I've seen you shoot." She handed me the keys.

I smiled and started to think about getting my stuff from the hotel, but then thought I would simply call them and ask them to chuck it out. My laptop was at work, I had my wallet, wristwatch, and phone with me, and I had on my best suit and underwear. That sad inventory took less than a minute to compute. There was, however, a half bottle of scotch. Ah, fuck it, a present for the janitor.

"You should think about keeping your job as a cover. It may be useful to us when you collect research without attracting attention, but be careful about who you bring here, at least for a while. Your sudden success might be hard to explain."

"You think?"

"So, come with me and I'll show you how it's supposed to be done."

The next day I found myself at the Department of Children and Family Services to see Jake. He had been placed there awaiting allocation to a foster home. Both Pamela and her husband had lost their parents and had no siblings, so Jake had fallen into this giant family services hole with no one to claim him. He was set to be a wealthy boy eventually, once the myriad of legal rabbit holes had been chased down with his stepfather's estate, complicated by Pamela dying intestate and there would of course be cross-claims from Fredericks's shoddy business dealings. Whether there would be any money left after the lawyers and trustees had finished with the estate was a whole other question. The more money available in such cases, the more legal work needs to be done, you see. I might be able to assist him with all of that, but that was not my motivation this day. I wanted to see if he was alright. I was a little concerned about bringing my association with Pamela into the open, but according to Joan Travis, I had no need to be troubled. She said she had seen to it personally that I was off the radar on the Fredericks murder, but little of that mattered to me now. I felt responsible for Jake's predicament.

"What are you doing here?"

We were in the visitor's lounge, seated together on one of the couches.

"Nice to see you, too."

"No, seriously."

"I wanted to see how you were doing. Are you comfortable?"

"Sure. The food is pretty shit but the guys in my room are OK."

"Well, that's important."

"How long will I be here, do you know?"

"No idea, but from what I can gather, they will have you out with one of their foster families pretty quick. No room here and they think you should be in a family environment."

"Sure, it worked out so well last time."

"I am sure your mother was trying her best."

"Yes, I know." Crestfallen.

"She loved you very much. I could see it when she looked at you."

Jake started to cry and I moved closer, but he didn't want any part of a hug.

"Why didn't you believe her? You should have believed her. Now she's dead."

He looked at me accusingly, angry and for good reason. It was a shit deal. I had nothing for him, no answers, and he was right, it was my fault. I think the fact that he could see the blame for it written all over my face caused him to stop accusing me. Nothing was said for a while.

Me staying after copping it from him spoke louder than anything I could say.

"So, what now, I get adopted?"

"Yeah… no idea, haven't they explained any of this to you?"

"I wasn't listening."

"Either adoption or you'll stay in foster care until you are of age."

"What about shithead's money or Mum's, for that matter?"

"It will be a while before you see any of that. Maybe I could help sort it out for you if that is something you would want, but either way, it's going to take a while."

"So, you're here looking for a job?"

That hurt and it showed.

"I'm here looking for a friend."

"So, you're planning on coming back?"

"Sure, if that's OK with you. Looking after a lost cause will be good for my soul."

A smile, thank God, he liked the honesty, I only had honesty for him.

"My stepfather was shot."

"I know."

"Do they know who did it?" I didn't answer but he pressed. "Do you know?"

"Yes."

He didn't press me on the who but instead said, "Thank him for me, will ya?"

"Amen to that, brother. Chin up, gotta go. I'll have a look into the estate, maybe get you to sign something so I can act for you. No charge, of course."

"Would you normally be worth paying?"

"I can see we're going to get on just fine."

When I left Jake, as I went outside to the car park, I had that undeniable sense of a page turning in my life, a new chapter opening. It's that feeling that makes you stop and look up to the sky as if to get fresh bearings and to remember where you were when it happened. You can almost hear the crescendo of the music as the act closes. I'm not a hundred percent sure what brought it on that day. Maybe it was because I had decided to take that new job Joan offered me, or maybe it was Jake's tacit approval of the violence I had hidden in my life, or even my fledgling relationship with him. As I got into the car, I decided to go and see an old friend of mine from my teenage years who was a gym owner, if he was still alive. It was time to move forward.

CHAPTER FOUR

A couple of weeks later, I woke up after a good night's sleep in my new abode and my growing urge to get started with hitman duties was greeted by a text from my new employer. I had done as Joan had asked and sent her the details of the people on my list, my remaining *candidates*. I synced my phone with the laptop to decipher the message and found, to my surprise, they had approved three of my six remaining to-dos. That would be $150,000 for something I would have done for nothing in a previous life, the doing of which would have been payment enough. But I was starting to realise it wasn't much of a previous life, not the last ten years of it anyway. I was now just peeking over the rim of the deep hole in which I had buried myself, looking back down the slope behind me, and I could see what a life becomes when you just let things happen to you.

I had got to a point where I was enjoying exercise again, the point where your body starts asking you to go to the gym rather than you telling it that it must go. I was eating better but still drinking most nights. The booze was pure habit as my surroundings had started to make me feel damn good about my new self. I had looked for a sparring partner at the boxing academy that I had haunted as a teenager. Old Sam, the owner, was still there and pleased to see me when I had turned up a couple of weeks back, and I was glad to see him. The certainty in his voice and his positive manner placated my devils and I noticed my walk had changed, my gait was upright and deliberate. *Stand up straight, don't mope,* he had told me constantly as a boy. I had begun to look forward to beating the shit out of the poor unfortunate fool that Sam was going to line up to spar with me. I understood that expectation was probably premature because of my current level of fitness but I had once thought that I had a future in the sport, more significantly, Sam had thought so and he would know. A boxing career, like so many other things, was passed me now but that didn't mean I couldn't work out my issues on somebody else's body rather than taking them out on my own. I have got to stop drinking.

I had bought a hard-top cover for the back tray of my new Chevy truck and had laid out two cut-down foam mattresses on the tray of the truck, one atop the other, to give me enough height when prostrate to get a sighter out of the small back windows of the tray cover. I had modified the small sealed windows to open. The manual labour needed to complete the modifications to the truck was remedial and that personal growth prompted me to go back to the rifle range. I had always used a makeshift range at a property well out of town, owned by a previous legal client and now friend of mine. He lived in New York these days and at his property I was left to my own devices. There was a small shack at my disposal away from the main house if I wanted to stay overnight, which I sometimes did to unwind. As I gazed out at the evening woodland from its small wooden porch, I could smell the country air and strove through an alcoholic haze to remember excerpts from *The Walden*.

It was unwise to join a rifle club because of the links it would create if anyone ever investigated me, particularly if I got a reputation at that club for being a good shot. That's how Jack Reacher caught his guy. In my case, I was a great shot and the members that frequent those clubs are always interested in who has the biggest dick. Anyway, there aren't many clubs with long enough ranges for me to shoot at my preferred distance. I never understood why I was so good at shooting. Practise helped, but it seemed to me to be a skill with which I was born. I only discovered it by chance as an adolescent on a hunting trip with a friend from school. Since then, I had found it therapeutic and now I would be able to afford enough ammunition to indulge myself more often in the distraction it provided.

After that first hunting trip, I joined a rifle club in the Chicago environs called the Blackstone Rifle Club. Our team was in the State final two years later, with me as its captain. I was only sixteen years of age and it was an open competition. I found myself in a shoot-off for the individual State Amateur Rifle Title with four other guys, all much older than me, I won the National Amateur championship just a year later. We were on the six-hundred-yard mound in this State competition shooting six-foot targets with an elongated black about the size of a basketball. The scoring was a combination of grouping and accuracy. I had been in the black all day. We were all lying on the mound shooting prone and there was a guy on the radio at the end of the row of shooters in contact with the scorers' bunker under the target mound. I was at the end of the row furthest away from the scorers' assistant. Halfway through the shoot-off, the guy got a call from the scorers and he yelled down the mound to me, "Will the shooter from Blackstone stop putting it through the same hole, they are having trouble scoring it." I can't describe the looks on the faces of the other four guys as they turned toward me, but in part it was the unmistakable look of resignation.

That was a good day and I thought, incorrectly, that there would be many more to come. The surprising thing about good days is that they are rare, unless you invent them; that is, you talk yourself into thinking that by doing this or that you will have, or have had, a good day. But the real ones are like diamonds; they're rare and are only produced under pressure. To create them, you need to be pressing hard at something you really want.

As a teenager, I had been asked twice to consider the Olympics. Yes, that's right, the Olympics. Once in boxing and once in shooting. It is a calling that is very easily mentioned in casual conversation but not so easily undertaken. I never gave it a second thought at the time and now it was too late. In weaker moments, I blame my parents' ignorance of the opportunities that being an Olympian would have given their nascent youngster, what such a thing would look like on a resume. But it was my fault and no one else's that I had rejected the idea. The two sports I was most keenly interested in at the time weren't part of the Olympics: girls and parties. Although, a guy I knew at college who had been to the Olympics said that screwing and drinking were the main two Olympic sports. No medals were awarded for them but he did come back with a raging dose of the clap as a memento. Back then, I thought the prospect of training or studying hard was anachronistic and there were more important things in life. It turned out there weren't; I came to that realisation as I looked out from that deep hole I was telling you about.

My doorbell rang. It was Pamela's boy, Jake.

"How did you get my address?" I asked as I let him into the apartment.

"Whoa, this is cool."

He went over to the window, schoolbag over his shoulder, to look at the view.

"Why aren't you at school?"

"Why aren't you at work?"

"Well, I was about to go…wait…"

"Sure, sure." He threw his bag on the lounge and went to the fridge.

"Why are you here?"

He was foraging through the refrigerator making himself right at home.

"Can I get you anything?"

He emerged with a bottle of orange juice.

"I never thanked you," he said as he took a swig from a half-full gallon bottle. I was going to correct him about using a glass but I couldn't be bothered.

"Thank me for what?"

"For shooting my stepfather."

"Did your mother…"

"She didn't have to. It was what she wasn't saying that gave you away. I knew why she was talking to you."

"You're mistaken."

"I want you to show me how."

"How to do what?"

"Shoot people."

"Does your guardian know you've come here?"

"Foster parents…no. I'm supposed to be at school but they let me catch the bus by myself so I can go anywhere I like."

"That's not how it works."

"They give me an allowance."

"Look, Jake…"

"Mum told me you had this no-bullshit rule. I'm not going to turn you in if you tell me you did shoot him."

I thought about it for a while.

"I'm not saying anything about your father."

"Stepfather, of course not."

"But you're right to want to know how to defend yourself."

"Sure."

"I'll introduce you to a mate of mine at the gym and next time I go to the range, I'll take you with me, see what you got. But you must get your foster parents to say yes. I want to hear it from them, OK?"

"Sure."

"I gotta get to work, not hitman work, just lawyering, you understand? I'll drop you off at school. We can talk on the way."

"So, you ready?"

Joan and I had been seated at one of Chicago's best restaurants. Joan made me feel flustered as I looked straight across the table at the low-cut Chanel that she wasn't completely wearing.

"Just about," I responded, fiddling with the silverware.

"You're looking well and you're sitting up straight. Found something that we enjoy doing, have we?"

"You know that's true. You don't look so bad yourself. What is it about you and haute couture?"

"I have the money."

"And the body. I'm having trouble breathing."

"I noticed."

I had noticed that she had noticed and that she wasn't cringing in disgust at me noticing as my insecurity would have me believe. Maybe she had shot all the guys she used to go out with and needed a replacement. Why the hell was I thinking that?

"Who the fuck are these guys, anyway?" I was annoyed with myself for feeling insecure, so I used the word *fuck* like the man I truly was. "These Council guys, I mean?"

"Can't tell you the *who* but the *why* seems pretty clear. They have a very specific view of who they want to remove from the gene pool outside of the three no-go zones: politicians, clergy, and kids."

"What? The clergy is full of arseholes."

"I used to think that it was because the Vatican was part of the Council," she explained in a whisper, leaning into the table and smiling. I had no reaction because I wouldn't have been surprised if the Vatican was involved, but I knew she was joking. Besides, I was too busy looking down her dress. She quit the melodramatics. "You don't think they would want to get out ahead of all the sinners by funding the Council?"

"I wouldn't be surprised by anything that any religious group did. But what about politicians? My God, that's a hive of…what's the collective noun for arseholes?"

"Ani, anuses, not sure. A pucker, perhaps. You don't see many political assassinations and none, as far as I can tell, that these guys were involved in. I think they want to stay right out of politics, you know, get the guys that feed the ani."

"How do you feed an ani? It's not the fucking CIA, is it?" I said in a whisper. Despite my Catholic background, I was happy befouling the Vatican but not our friends at the Agency. They have guns and keep files and, as far as I knew, the Church had given up on such things.

"The Council tends to stay away from people who are in the sights of law enforcement."

"What, no criminals, too?"

"I'm saying not necessarily criminals. They seem to figure that the police need to be left to do their job, where appropriate."

"Or is it that they see their role as social not legal? You know, there are plenty of government bodies trying to clean up the crims but no one is trying to clean up the moral degenerates." I was just playing along and she knew it.

"Maybe, I don't get to speak to any of the other shooters or killers, not all of them are shooters. As for our colleagues, it's not like we have a Christmas party or anything, but I do get the sense that it is a very large organisation."

"How large?"

"You will find after a while that you start looking at the papers, doing your own research through law enforcement channels into the background of those vics that look like they might be part of this… *process*. There are a lot of cases I think the Council has had a hand in, and I can tell you that those hits have one thing in common and it's not money or criminality, it's just that they are all dirtbags."

"You mean arseholes. Let's get the nomenclature consistent, please. Based on what or whose sense of morality?"

"Theirs. But illegal arms dealing, terrorists, and human trafficking seem to be their pet hates and those are hard cases for law enforcement to make stick."

"Relativism is a sure path to personal misery and misdirection." Yeah, that's right, I said that. An original thought, but perhaps too reminiscent of Nietzsche. Certainly too philosophical for a hitman.

"Relativism?"

Nothing from her. It seemed *relevant* to me but she looked puzzled, so I changed the subject. "I'm going to take a couple of days off next week to take care of the three guys they approved from my list. I'm going to get paid, right?"

"So, now you're worried about getting paid to do the guys that you were going to do anyway."

"No, I mean, yes. Like you, I'm a capitalist, not a communist. I'm sort of counting on the dough."

"They approved them, the money will be there. I'm counting on it, too. I got a house to buy. Go get 'em, tiger."

So, there I was, set up outside this office building on the outskirts of Detroit. The company was privately owned by a guy who was a big wig in the auto industry. Let's call the guy Bruce. Bruce had made his own way in life financially. I admired him for that, which is what drew me into his orbit, but I could never figure out how he did it, other than, as I later discovered, by fucking guys like me over. He did have one great skill that I could see: an instinct for when to cut a deal loose.

Knowing when a deal is going bad and having the guts to do something about it regardless of your sunk costs is a tremendous asset in business. Most would hang on for dear life and go down with the ship, but he had no problem putting a bullet in its ear and leaving it in a ditch, and now I knew that also applied to some of his business partners.

Bruce had been on the bones of his arse many times. Anyone who has ever made it by themselves in business has had the seat out of their pants at some point. On one such occasion, he called on my assistance. I helped him get out of probable bankruptcy and made him $160 million in the process. In return, he fucked me out of my share, simply because he could. You see, I accepted his word, silly me. There was no doubt about who should get what but, to him, it was sport. He liked to see people whinge and bitch when he fucked them, metaphorically speaking. He'd do it even when it was easier not to do it. One time, I brought a mate of mine, the CEO of one of the largest private banks in America, into Bruce's office to see him about a leasing facility for Bruce's yacht. This CEO brought an offer letter for the finance with him, basically on my say-so. The offer included a thirty-thousand-dollar acceptance fee, not unusual with finance of this type, especially considering that it was ten million bucks for a yacht and yachts sink. Anyway, Bruce jumped out of his chair when he read about the acceptance fee and called my mate a *cunt*. Yes, that word, in a business meeting with a prominent banker. Then, he gestured at me and said, "You're probably going to give that fee to this guy as a secret commission." My mate wasn't going to pay me anything. I was doing it as a favour to Bruce. My integrity aside, it is illegal to pay undeclared commissions. But Bruce went on and on and finally said he would set the dogs on my mate if he didn't leave. I said to Bruce, "You don't have any dogs," to which he replied that he was going out to buy some dogs so he could set them on my banker mate. The banker never spoke to me again and left that meeting with a speech impediment he didn't have when he walked in. Decent people don't expect other people to behave like emotional rapists and it affects them when they are assaulted. I'm sure it was just entertainment for Bruce. For everyone else in the room, it was just plain ugly, and it cost me a great contact. Bruce never got past kindergarten in school and he didn't like educated people, but as far as I could tell, he was happy to use anyone as sport. He was a liar and a cheat and he certainly qualified as an arsehole and a sociopath, which is why I assume these *Council* guys approved him as a candidate. This guy had fucked with a lot of people.

But none of that is why I wanted him whacked. He was a bully and I hated him because of it. Bruce's CFO, get this, had been to the same school as me. It was long before I got there but he had studied Latin under the same teacher as me, Brother Mac. How's that for a coincidence? Mac had been beating up boys for quite some years before he got to me. He had messed up quite a few lives and I was sorry I didn't get to him earlier than I did and, by that, I mean too late. Brother Mac was old when I put his brains onto the brick wall he had been sat up against by his carer. I probably did him a favour. It's probably why the CFO wanted to work for Bruce, you know, battered wife syndrome. Bruce was Brother Mac's clone times two, but with emotional rather than physical violence. If Bruce had ever tried to hit me, he would have ended up asleep at his desk, which he often was, but not from getting knocked out by someone who'd had a gutful of his antics. Emotional violence is a lot harder to deal with and, in the moment, it often doesn't present an obvious solution such as a punch in the mouth. The CFO had already retired by the time I circled back to Bruce this day, but I thought he had suffered enough at Brother Mac's and Bruce's hands, so I would have given him a pass in any case. But I was here to collect two IOUs.

The second guy was Bruce's current CEO, a pleasant, affable guy. I told you about those types of people, quick to smile, if you could call it a smile, hiding the arsehole within. I had thought he was my friend. More than that, I had thought he was my friend for nearly ten years. I had got him the job he'd had before working with Bruce. He, let's call him Dick, is someone who is not what he seems to be, as is the case with most sociopaths, again, the reason I think he got approved. Dick thought I had a thing for his wife. I didn't, because, unlike him, I had rules. I still remember the day he accused me of it. It was so far from my thoughts that it took me two days to figure out what the hell he was talking about. Out of the blue one day, he said, "Don't take her from me, Jim." I was on my way out the door of his office when he said it, so I kept going without replying. I thought I had misheard him. I put it together later, though, and found out exactly what he meant. There had been a dinner party at his place the weekend before his comment, when his wife had reminded me several times that Dick had gone to bed early, drunk as usual. I was unaccompanied, so it was just her and me drinking on their terrace. The rest of the guests had gone home and their niece, who was an absolute honey, had also gone to bed after providing a fine distraction with her intelligent conversation. I rejected his wife's advances that night but Dick's wife must have confessed her affection for me to Dick, probably during an argument. I didn't know that for sure but I did know he knew how she felt. Dick probably had a penis the size of a pea and she was interested to see if mine fitted her vagina any better than his; yes, I have still have the emotional age of a twelve-year-old. Women always like to line up a replacement before they dump their existing partner, especially the married ones who are otherwise unemployed, like Dick's wife. I never figured out whether she was a victim in their marriage or whether they were two peas in a pod, the analogy is intentional, and she was trying to stir up trouble because I was not mindful of her charms. Dick was my friend and she was his wife. Nothing was ever going to happen except in her mind. Shortly after that evening, out of pure spite, Dick knifed me with a large client of mine, a Korean manufacturer distributing into America. The account was worth two hundred thousand bucks a year to me and Dick invented some shit about me breaking a confidence that cost me a lucrative contract. I called him several times to tell him what I thought, but he didn't have the guts to face me. Ten years of *friendship*, I couldn't believe it. I was going to leave him a message this day that he was going to find hard to dodge.

Bruce and Dickhead were together in the car park after work, discussing something. I couldn't hear them from nearly a mile away. I got Bruce first and the other idiot turned to see where the shot came from, so I showed him. Two shots only. I haven't missed yet.

I got number ten the following day on my way home. His story was unremarkable except perhaps to me, otherwise I would share it with you. It was an old wound and it healed that day. The drive home, however, makes for an interesting tale. A case of the ever-growing occurrence of road rage.

I will tell you about the road rage incident, but let me start by saying that I've never understood why a modern motor vehicle needs a horn. Getting cattle off the road, sure, but in today's cityscape, not so sure. Some jerk sitting out front of your place honking at some love interest across the road that he's too lazy to get out of his car to go get doesn't seem to me to be a good enough reason to have a horn. The horn's role today is purely educational. A means by which to prove your self-worth as a driver to the equally incompetent moron in the next vehicle, the mating call of the feeble-minded. Somewhere in the evolution of the motor car people acquired the perverse belief that to honk was to educate. The absurdity of that proposition is emphasized by the incompetence of the educator, who usually finds himself or herself being educated a mile down the road for the same infraction by another mobile teacher using the same educational tool. The full misery of human behaviour while in control of a motor vehicle has never been adequately explained to me. Humanity made a grave error in assuming that if one rode a horse, one could drive six hundred pounds of metal at speeds of up to two hundred miles an hour. Moreover, to believe that it was somehow a person's right to do that and thereby visit carnage on one's fellow citizens, seems absurd in the extreme. The motor car has been a boon to human productivity, but it has killed close to a hundred million people, wounded ten times that many, and devastated almost every family on the planet, except those still living in the jungle, but even they will get theirs eventually. The bureaucratic lethargy with which smoking was identified as a health hazard pales into insignificance compared to the late-onset realisation of the dangers of vehicle usage. Those that assert behaviour behind the wheel is a result of innate, perhaps even primal human nature and that this explains the bad manners, road rage, spitting, honking, taunting, speeding, hooning, yelling, killing, and maiming, have no real answer as to why this behaviour doesn't arise in other human activity. People queue at the bank without yelling at each other, mostly. I propose that it is the vehicle itself that is to blame and not something inherently human that lies deep within us that needs to be vented. In the isolation of the vehicle, with the anonymity and power it provides, lies the root cause. This, combined with the need to demonstrate one's driving knowledge and superiority as a human being, has given rise to calamity. It was George Carlin who said *ever notice that anyone going slower than you is an idiot but anyone going faster is a maniac?*

So, there was this prick on the way home. He was tailgating me. I hate that. I was doing the limit but he was tailgating me anyway on a single lane two-way road with no overtaking. I can sort of understand the idiot who tailgates to force someone out of the fast lane on a multi-lane highway because he can't pass up the opportunity to educate you. You should only be in the fast lane when overtaking, you see. He doesn't want to get past you, well, not far, anyway. He just wants to educate you to ensure that you know the road rules as well as he does. So, he's going to tailgate you until you move over and succumb to the lesson he is teaching you. Then he will slow down and move into the left lane himself a few hundred yards up the road. They've usually got someone else tailgating them shortly after they have finished teaching you. In this instance, we were alone on a single-lane road doing the speed limit, so the usual excuse didn't apply. I put on my hazard lights to suggest he back off but that pissed him off. He started flashing his lights and honking. He pulled out next to me over double lines and cut me off, forcing me into the scrub at the side of the road. I ended up half in the bushes and half on the gravel of the road fringe. He came to a sliding halt in the gravel about a hundred yards ahead of me and got out of his car. He wasn't happy and looked about as rational as any idiot in a road rage. He obviously wanted to discuss the matter further and I could see the unmistakable outline of a fairly strong argument tucked into the belt of his pants. It looked like a thirty-eight, from what I could see of it as he walked toward my car. He must have been having a bad day, but unfortunately for him, it was about to get worse. I took my Glock 43X MOS out of my glove box, opened my door, put one foot on the siding gravel, and shot him in the head.

I always have a handgun in my glove box for emergencies. I carry one with me on every shoot, tucked into the back of my pants. It comforts me in case I am interrupted by someone not minding their own business. I keep it in the glove box when I'm not using it. I didn't wait for him to "pull first," as the guy in *Justified* would say. That would have been just stupid, he might have shot me. It was an isolated part of the road, so no one saw the incident. I went over to him after collecting my brass and, using his hand, pulled the gun from his belt and fired a couple of rounds into the bushes. I hoped the coppers would think it was a pair of gangsters having a shootout and not be motivated to look any further, assuming this guy wasn't someone important.

I cleaned my weapon, removed the mag, cleared the chamber, and ditched it about a hundred clicks down the road. I loved that weapon. I made a mental note to replace it with the very same model, which is why I wanted to keep the mag. I did, after all, have $150 thousand coming after today's trip. That prick was going to kill somebody sooner or later and maybe already had done, but not now… more obfuscation. But I am community-minded and I like to help out where I can. It was a freebie. My contribution to improving inter-driver relations. Maybe I should have put in an invoice to the Council.

CHAPTER FIVE

"So, keep both eyes open and measure your breathing."

"Why can't I use the Tac-50?"

"Because you're not used to the recoil. Besides, that is a great rifle you have there, respect the process."

I had bought an Enfield L42 for Jake. It uses a 303 round, a smaller calibre than the McMillan and the same calibre I started with as a teenager. Back then I used a Mark Two from the same manufacturer bought from a war surplus store. The Enfield still gave you a good kick, nonetheless, something Jake would have to learn to manage. He was lying prone with his shoulder tucked up into the rifle butt. My old Mark Two was used by most British and Australian troops in World War One. The newer model was a very effective weapon under six hundred yards, probably one of the best at that range. It made for a good starter for Jake. It was manual bolt action with a five-round clip. A back-to-basics weapon.

"Pull it back tightly into the meat of your shoulder and keep it there firmly or you'll break your collar bone when you fire. Turn your left hand clockwise a little and your right hand anticlockwise as you hold the weapon. The opposing forces of the hands will help secure the weapon and keep it steady. Not too much force with the hands; you don't want to tense up because you'll start shaking. Heels on the ground. Dig them in and spread your legs to get comfortable. Look where you want the bullet to go. Feel the weapon get you there like an extension of your arm. Squeeze the trigger, don't jerk the weapon, and don't ever close your eyes, either of them. It's like baseball, take your eyes off the ball and you have no chance of hitting it. Your brain will figure out which eye is looking through the sight and which one is looking at the target unaided. You need both sets of data to get the shot right. Don't stop breathing, it will make you too tense. Feel for the spaces between your breath and your heartbeat. It will become second nature with practise. You won't hear the shot, but you will feel the rifle recoil and the click as the hammer hits the bullet. Just let the weapon come back to the target slowly as you breathe, in one easy motion. When you're ready."

Bang. Black.

"That's pretty good for a first time."

"It's fifty yards and it's a six-foot target," he replied, "it doesn't count."

"You remind me of someone. Mate, I know experienced shooters who couldn't get black cold bore from this range. You're a natural."

"That has got to be bullshit. Now can I try the Tac-50?"

"Shut up and empty that clip. Once you get through another thousand rounds, I'll give you a go at the fifty calibre. Stop pouting and let's go. You have to put a thousand rounds through the Enfield and I'll be counting, OK? So, you've got several trips out here before you move to a larger weapon. I'm going to get a cigar from my bag."

I stood smoking and watching from behind him as he shot. He had a good eye and controlled what was a relatively heavy weapon for a boy his age, even though he was shooting with the aid of a gun stand. I would take the training wheels off at some later stage. We shot for a while, then chatted for a while. We quickly settled into being friends, rather than a surrogate Dad-type relationship. The oddity of me having whacked his old man, even for good reason, slipped into the past.

"I might buy you an automatic rifle next time before you go to the Tac-50. Something that carries a 7.62/39 round with about 123 grams of propellant. It will help you graduate. They are cheap and easy to buy, nothing exotic. Maybe one of those mutants, the CMMG MK47. A guy offered me one the other day when I was buying your Enfield."

"Graduate?"

"You need to understand how to handle the recoil."

"And you started me with a 303?"

"You're not a baby."

"Yeah, but it's still giving me a sore shoulder."

"Ok, right, sorry, you are a baby."

We had called it a day and were sitting on the porch of the shack having a drink before making our way back to the city. Well, I had a coffee and he had hot chocolate.

"Am I picking up a slight Italian accent in your voice, Jake, or am I going mad."

"Well, you are mad, let's get that on the table," he smiled, "but, yes, I do have a slight accent. My stepfather sent me away to school in Rome for two years when I was ten, when he married my mother. A Catholic school. He was a Catholic."

"Jesus, how appropriate."

"Well, Jesus was there, Mexican kid, rich parents. He became a good friend."

"You know, I thought Fredericks was your real father when…"

"You shot him. No, my real father was a drunk. He died in a car accident when I was two."

"You've had a rough trip."

"You have no idea."

"So, give me one."

He seemed reluctant to share.

"Ever lay in your bed listening to your parents shouting at each other, and I don't mean innocuous obscenities, I mean threats of violence?"

"Can't say that I have."

"Then you have no idea. Locking the door doesn't help because you can still hear it. You have nowhere to go. I can tell you the closet isn't any better. Worse still, you know someone is going to get hurt and she always tried to make sure it was her not me. He'd stand there in the hall knowing I could hear him shouting, basically having a conversation with himself, asking questions of her and providing the answers himself. Impersonating her, you know, in a smarmy voice. The mimicked answers were vile and unreal, and he would get angrier and angrier as each of his imagined characters talked back at him. My mother would cower and I would hide. Can you imagine the fear?"

"No."

"It empties your gut. Makes you wish you could get out or just die, anything that would transport you to someplace that was safe and quiet." He stopped explaining and then asked, "Why do you shoot people? I have only ever wished that I could."

I didn't see the point in lying to the boy. Our fledgling friendship seemed to warrant something better. He had been through enough.

"They were killing me. I was just shooting back. Like you, I was lying in my bed afraid, wishing I could retaliate or escape."

"And my stepfather, why him?"

"You just articulated it better than I ever could. Your mother and what he did to her, what he was doing to you."

"You were protecting me?"

"I didn't protect her. I have to face up to that reality. Your mother showed me the pictures and I should have dealt with it then. I had someone who used to beat me up at your age, a Catholic clergyman."

"I take it the clergyman guy didn't make it?"

"No. But in the end, I think I did him a favour. I was slow getting back to him. He was old."

"I want to be like you."

"No, you don't."

"You've figured it all out, you take no shit."

"Jake, listen to me. You don't want to be like me, a drunk lawyer who couldn't make a success of his opportunities or his marriage. I'm no role model, mate."

The forcefulness of my response made him hesitate and think for a while, but his expression seemed dismissive.

"Sam's a good guy."

"Now, Sam will make a good mentor. What he doesn't know about boxing doesn't matter and perhaps life as well, I suspect. You should listen to him, not me."

"Yet here you sit, talking."

"Smartarse."

I had been at my new job for nearly two months. I had been given four jobs from the Council and been paid for my own three. The three hundred and fifty thousand was handy, all paid and banked. I had no overheads except petrol and booze and I was still getting paid for my work at the practice. I was laughing. I hadn't gotten around to the last three unapproved candidates on my list; I was having too much of a good time making money. The clarity is amazing when the responsibility for deciding who is a candidate is taken off your shoulders.

I sent some money to Clara. I didn't have to and she didn't ask me for it, but I did it anyway and that was the end of it. I don't know what it is about Irish genes that makes it so hard to let go of a relationship or its imagined responsibilities. It probably served the community well for many years, especially through the potato famine and English occupation. Maybe it would serve any community well to put regard for family above all else. It can be a pain in the arse, though, to hang on to such things when the other party doesn't reciprocate those feelings or worship the same gods. I still don't know whether I would have come out of my coma if I had stayed with Clara. She would never have approved of my new job nor could she have ever known about it. The secrecy it would have required if I was in a functioning relationship with her or anyone else would have been debilitating. I will never know the answers to that question and in quiet moments, I'm sorry for not knowing.

I was in Florida having taken a week off from the law firm and had flown down on instructions from the Council. I was waiting for information on the new candidate and where I was going to get a weapon to follow their pending orders. Information on both matters had been promised, but by midday on the third day I hadn't heard anything, so, I declared it a public holiday. I was having a drink in the outdoor pool bar of my hotel when up walked Joan in a bikini. All the blood in my body went to my dick and I nearly fainted. Yeah, that's right, it takes a lot of blood. I had to sit down, both to avoid embarrassment and because I was light-headed.

"What are you doing here?"

"Hello, stranger, haven't seen you in a while."

"My God, Joan, you look amazing."

"Are those abs?"

I had been working out something fierce and boxing daily after work and on weekend afternoons, as well as eating carefully. I always said that if you get your life in good shape, your body will follow. I was wearing shorts and an open shirt and, yes, I was showing off the product of my labours.

"If you stop eating for recreation, it ain't too difficult to lose weight. Are you working?"

"Yes," she said, "but not police work. Well, actually, a bit of both."

"What, Council business?"

"Yes."

"Me, too. Well, you know that, I guess."

"We are going to do this one together."

"Why? Don't get me wrong, it sounds good, but why?"

"They are afraid the targets might shoot back."

"There's more than one?"

"Four. Ever had one shoot back?"

"I always shoot first, so…no."

"That ego of yours is a bit of a worry. I'm going to spot for you. Your reputation is following you. They are telling me you're the best shot we got, maybe the best in the country. They think you'll be okay alone but wanted insurance. Too important, apparently."

"Happy to have you. Want a drink?"

"We're on for Friday. We need to do a reconnoitre and some homework. Let's go."

"There's only three of them," I said, looking through my binoculars at midnight, peeping down from the rooftop at a restaurant from which our candidates had just emerged that Friday night. We were atop a four-story walk-up opposite the restaurant across a six-lane road and a little further south. They were standing there talking. One of them lit a cigarette.

"So, they're the guys, right? They don't look like drug dealers," I said in a reproachful whisper, without moving my gaze. "I thought you said they were drug dealers? They look more like terrorists."

"They are terrorists. I said *drug dealers or something* and, yes, that's them."

"Where's number four?"

"Look, three is good. Go."

I brought my weapon to bear, settled, slowed my breathing and released the first round. Red wall, no noise. I had a suppressor. Just the sound of a melon squelching. Well, I assumed that was the noise. I couldn't hear it from where we were, but I could see it. Definite squelching. Number two, red window, breaking glass. I love how the second guy always looks up to see where the first shot came from. Fat guy running, running, bus in the way, red wall. All clean headshots, three shots only.

"Fuck, someone told me you could shoot."

"It's three hundred yards, maybe four hundred for the fat guy. It doesn't count at that distance."

"Count?"

"As good shooting."

"Whatever you say, Rambo."

I was using a L115A3 AWM with a standard can, a hell of a rifle. British Winchester, American ammo. Similar in size to their .30.30 rounds. The .300 Magnum is impressive, but I love the .30.30 Winchester, the gun that won the West. Nostalgically my favourite weapon, thank you, Chuck Connors. This rifle was bolt-action, so I had to be dexterous reloading but it helped that it carries a five-round mag.

If you watch someone push and pull a rifle bolt, you can tell whether they have ever fired a rifle before in their life. Like an actor in the movies, if they push it with the palm of their hand, they're a fraud. If they use their thumb and forefinger to both open the breach and then push the bolt back, they know what they are doing. There's a bunch of nerves in the centre of your palm and if you were banging the nub of a rifle bolt into it all day long you would lose the use of your hand. I laugh every time I see it in those war movies. They are trying to do some serious acting while proving beyond any doubt they couldn't be the character they are playing.

This rifle is the best sniper rifle in the world at this range and it was half the size of my MacMillan. This AWM wasn't much good over a eight hundred yards with that ammo. Usually, I preferred to be more than twice that distance from the target than in this shoot. It gives me a head start if it all goes to shit. You could probably get twelve hundred yards out of this rifle with a .338 Lapua Magnum round, which I didn't have with me or need at this distance.

"Did you see how fat that guy was?" I said, as I started to pack up my rifle. I had become preoccupied with men's weight. I hoped it was a passing obsession. It had been brought on by my recent weight loss. It's an affliction suffered by people who feel they know better than the next guy because they have achieved some goal, however momentarily. Ex-smokers are the worst complainers about others who smoke where they shouldn't be smoking.

As I stood up, I heard a muffled scream behind me. I turned to see Number Four pressing Joan's gun against her temple. He cocked the weapon to punctuate his mood. He had his left arm around her neck, choking her. He was hiding behind her, watching me with his right eye from behind her head as he backed away, pulling Joan with him toward the rooftop doorway, keeping her off balance. I suspected she wouldn't make it to the stairs.

"Put the rifle down," a thickly accented voice demanded, definitely Middle Eastern.

I complied.

"Who the fuck are you two?"

As usual I had a pistol lodged in the small of my back, tucked into my belt under my tee shirt. I dropped to one knee, pulled it, and shot him in the head through that right eye he had stuck out one too many times. It was thirty-five feet at best so the shot didn't count as anything special, either.

Joan's gun flew back towards the stairwell along with the brain splatter. She fell onto her butt, struggling for breath. She was pulling at her collar but the colour was returning to her face, so I assumed she was alright as I went over to check if the guy was conscious. The right side of his head was missing, so I didn't investigate any further.

"I thought you were the spotter," I said now, full-voiced as she continued to gasp. "Did you spot him?" She gave me a look of derision with those beautiful eyes that caused me to reconsider my position. "You OK?"

"So…" She paused to get her breath, "You're good with a handgun, as well."

"It was thirty-five feet, for fuck's sake. How can you miss an eyeball at thirty-five feet?"

"Good to know. I think you got my ear."

"Probably air push."

They had given me a Walther PPK. Yeah, that's right, James Bond's gun and, less well known, it was also Hitler's choice of sidearm. I had asked them for a "short frame pistol" as a backup, preferably a SIG Sauer P226 9mm or a Pardini GT9, the latter being hard to find and not cheap. If they had given me that gun, I would have kept it and found a way to get it back to Chicago. A gift for Jake, perhaps. It's the only handgun with which I managed a two-inch grouping at fifty yards when a friend had lent me one. But they gave me the PPK-S and it was not fitted with a can, it's a very noisy little weapon, so every copper in town was now on his way to have a look. It uses .380 ammo, a little smaller than a 9mm but with about the same amount of propellant. A stubbier round but it packs a punch at that range, just ask Number 4. I always carry my handgun with a round in the chamber with the slide de-cocked. It's perhaps not the ultimate pull-and-shoot, but it's just one simple click of the safety to arm it. It sure made a mess of that guy's head. The slide bite on a PPK is a bit annoying. I've been nicked a couple of times. I think the American S&W version has a longer beaver tail, but I had the European version. It feels good in your hand and is very accurate under forty yards, sorry James, it's not possible to make the long shots that you do in the movies with that weapon. Perhaps the noise is why James Bond liked it so much, he could always scare them to death if he missed. Joan had her glove off and was pulling at her ear, looking for blood. Now standing, bent over with her other hand on her knee, she was collecting herself, rubbing her fingers together and feeling in the dark for signs of bodily fluids.

"Let me have a look." I did the perfunctory examination. It was a nice ear but it was undamaged. "There's nothing. We'd better go."

"Do you think?"

A hurried exit ensued.

Back at the hotel in her room, yeah, that's right, in her room, we were discussing why the Council hadn't sent the police after these guys rather than us. The mood was self-congratulatory and buoyant.

"As I understand it," she said, strangely apologetic, "they had tried a couple of times to alert the authorities, but Homeland Security hadn't acted, or hadn't acted visibly. The Council thinks there was something imminent with these guys, that's why they sent us. I think that's where all this Council thing started, 9/11, and they still have intelligence links into that network."

"So, they're government."

Joan laughed.

"They are private individuals acting conscientiously."

"You mean, without conscience. When do I get to meet them? Sounds like we might get on."

"That's not how it works. You get contact straight up the tree and that's it."

"And you work directly with them, not for a sponsor?"

"Yes, I am both an operative and a source, which puts me in direct contact."

I decided to let it go because of her beauty, not her logic. My mind was elsewhere. Those eyes.

"I think that was a hornet's nest we poked a stick into tonight."

"What, are you afraid?" she said, as she came over and looked me in the eye to see if I was shaking in my boots. There was no shaking but I started to feel faint again.

"I'm not the scaredy cat whinging about being shot in the ear. I thought you were going to cry."

"But I didn't cry and…yeah, thanks." The distance between us widened. I must have shrugged. I was pulled towards her. "No, really, thanks."

"No prob."

"Where did you learn to shoot like that?"

She went over to the minibar to get us a drink. I was going to stop her but I realised that this wasn't the time for frugality. Watching expenses had never been part of this girl's life.

"I was a boy scout."

"No, you weren't. I read your file."

"You with the file again?"

"Come on, where did you learn to shoot?"

"The first time I ever shot a gun, a rifle, I hit what I was aiming at. You have to learn to control your body and the Kentucky Windage thing, you know the bullet spin drift and drop bullshit, but that's just math. Understanding the physics is important but I think talent is genetic. Practise helps but it's not the key."

"You're amazing, you know that?" She had come over with our drinks and was standing awkwardly close and looking me in the eyes.

"Not possible," I retorted.

"You're not afraid of me?"

"Just the thought of you."

"What thought?"

"My own self-worth."

I took the Scotch she had brought me and clinked her glass. In my head, I made a big deal about her remembering what I drank but it was more likely the only decent thing in the fridge.

Her phone rang, her special phone. That would be right; just as I thought things were going well. The Council wanted us out of there tonight. My disappointment was quickly placated when I learned they had booked us a flight to St Kitts under two aliases. We were to pick up our papers and drop off the hardware on our way to the airport.

"Don't you just love the smell of crayfish in the morning?"

"Barbecued."

We had settled into the Sunset Cafe for breakfast. Barbecued crayfish tails with hollandaise sauce, poached eggs on toasted sourdough, and dried tomatoes. Yeah, baby. It was an amazing morning and a complete change from Chicago, night to day. We had arrived late the night before and had crashed without social pleasantries, the adrenaline having done its dash. The two of us agreed to meet for brunch to discuss a plan of action. So here we were in St Kitts, one of the most beautiful places on the planet, looking out at the ocean like newlyweds. I smiled at her.

"We're not newlyweds, so don't get carried away with this island magic shit, this is strictly business."

"Wouldn't think of it. Tell me more about our employers."

I stared out at the ocean and the beach below, not listening to her answer, allowing the scene to hypnotise me. I had come a long way from my hole in the ground. The hole in my heart was healing too, I could tell. The muscles in my stomach were relaxed, not contorted, and my ambivalence had been replaced by a sense of expectation. I turned to watch her talk, her voice was soothing, her lips...

"Don't you think?" Joan's voice became loud. "You're not listening to me. I hate that."

"Don't shoot me, please." It was a kneejerk reaction to the admonishment as I came out of my dream.

"What?"

"Sorry, I was daydreaming."

My reaction was real, as emotions often are as you come out of a dream. Business lines get blurred and it was easy to cheapen life given what we did for a living. Was I still entitled to have a life with Joan?

"Ever shoot someone you didn't like?" I had been needing that information for quite some time. "Boyfriends, workmates?"

"Jesus, man, you're damaged."

"I mean, just because you didn't like them?"

She didn't have to think about it.

"No. There are rules."

She was a little indignant and I was a little relieved but unconvinced. She was a pretty good shot.

"What rules?"

"Unlike you, they pulled me out of the police force. I had been involved in what coppers like to refer to as a non-righteous shoot. I called bullshit on that. The guy got what he deserved and that included what I had left in my clip. The Council didn't find me roaming the streets shooting up the general populace, like you."

"I wasn't...well, maybe. I was broken. It was therapy."

"They thought you were hitting the right guys, though, so they weren't that anxious to stop you. But then they thought they should bring you in before you hurt yourself or the wrong person."

"How long had they been watching?"

"They were having trouble identifying you but they were sure it was just one guy. That's when they called me."

"Were you actually there to shoot Pamela's husband that day or were you there to catch me?"

"Just to catch you."

"Thanks."

"You're welcome."

"I was being sarcastic."

"I know, but you are welcome, anyway. Her husband was a real bad guy. Connected, if you know what I mean, to arms dealing mainly. And I have no doubt that he killed his wife. I had no problem with you shooting him, but I was there for you."

"You have a thing about arms dealers."

"Sure. Who doesn't? I had already pinged you as the shooter in those other killings in Illinois, but I needed to know for sure and I needed you to know that I knew. When she was killed, I thought you were a sure thing to whack the guy. It was easy to pick where, I knew your M.O. I just needed to be patient and you didn't make me wait long."

"Bitch."

"Murderer."

We both laughed.

"So where do you think all that therapy was headed?"

"Jail, I sort of assumed. Still do. Maybe I thought someone would get back at me eventually, assuming I didn't get myself. I didn't have a bright and rosy future picked out for myself."

"Well, there is some pretty heavy-duty pull behind you now so I don't think you're going to jail anytime soon. But you might want to think about giving up on those unauthorised candidates you have left on your list. The Council doesn't like psychopaths."

"All evidence to the contrary."

"I mean it, call it square. You were hitting guys they would have paid someone to hit. You've been told the rest are not authorised. Let it alone. It's better if you let them decide from now on. They'll think you're cured or something, or at least under control."

"You're probably right. But I'm not...*cured*. I still hate those fuckers with a passion." Here was my chance. "Maybe you can cure me."

"Fuck off." No sympathy for me. "Hatred is corrosive, I should know. The hater gets the worst deal from all that hating. Revenge is the poison you drink expecting to kill someone else."

"The Buddha, really? Not in my case, not so far at least."

"I think it was Mandela. It's not over yet. Give it up. Let it ride for a while. Concentrate on this stuff and see how you go."

"It was in fact Emmett Fox, the Alcoholics Anonymous guy. He was channelling the Buddha." I hesitated to ask but there was something else I was desperate to know. "So, you don't make time for..."

"Romance?"

"No. Romance is entertainment, you can get romance on pay-per-view. I mean..."

"Sex?"

"Stop finishing my sentences. You said we aren't newlyweds…for involvement, partnership."

"Yea sure. I got someone at home. They never know where I am, I'm hardly ever home and when I am there I am totally wasted, they just love it."

"I see what you mean."

"Job at hand, my new friend, job at hand. Nothing more."

"Maybe this is not such a classy joint, after all."

We had sat down to have a pre-dinner drink in the bar of our hotel having spent the afternoon by the pool, which was difficult for me because of my Irish skin and Joan's choice of swimwear. Joan looked around to see who I was watching, the source of the opinion I had just expressed. He had a couple of thugs with him. Why didn't it surprise me that he had gone from dodgy broker to dodgy gangster? Joan looked at me for clarification.

"One of my unfinished jobs."

"You can't do it, and more importantly, you can't do it here." She became concerned that I was about to do something stupid.

"Why not?" She was right to be concerned.

"The population of this island is, what…a couple of dozen? It won't take them long to connect you to him."

"He could drown. It is an island."

"Leave it alone."

He spotted me and looked puzzled. I assumed it was because it was an expensive place and he knew he had fleeced me pretty good the last time we met. He made his way over anyway to see what else he could take from me. My dignity, perhaps. He left the two turds he had with him at the bar. He wasn't threatened by me, an opinion he based on the last time we met. He had a drink in his hand and was half smiling his usual smartarse smile.

"Jim Jamisen, as I live and breathe."

"Well, I've been busy."

I didn't bother to stand.

"What?"

"Fuck off, arsehole."

He noticed that the new me was less conciliatory than the old me. I now viewed that as weak-kneed and likely to confuse, no more polite smiles from me. You think people have passed out of your life but they haven't, not really. Karma is very real and they are always there in the background, continuing to put bad vibes about you out into the universe. Those vibes add up.

"Jim, you shouldn't be like that. It was just business, it wasn't personal."

Jesus, I hate that saying. I stood to face him.

"Fuck off, before you get hurt, you prick." One of his goons came over. Joan fidgeted.

"Nobody's going to get hurt…well, not me, anyway. This is Boris. Say hi." Boris stepped into my personal space. Dickhead took a swig of his drink thinking, as always, that he was in control. "I'm meeting friends. Let's just leave it alone, shall we?"

"You don't have any friends. You should go and flush yourself, you turd," I said, looking at Boris but aiming the remark at dickhead.

"Now, Jim, you're hurting my feelings. Boris here doesn't like it when my feelings get…hurt."

Boris didn't give a shit anymore because he was asleep at his master's feet like the dog that he was even before dickhead could finish that sentence. No Kung Fu bullshit, just a straight left. It was always my money punch.

"You never could get good people to work for you, could you, shithead?"

Boris's mate came storming over but ended up next to Boris. The second goon had a harder jaw but I'm pretty quick with my right, too. I stood there for a moment, leaning over goon number two with my right fist cocked like Ali over Foreman. Another punch would have ruined the poetry of it. He was out like a light. I always thought Foreman should have won that fight, with all due respect to the Great Man. Ali caught him with a good one when Foreman wasn't paying attention, a product of Ali's always solid right hand and Foreman's ridiculously low expectations of Ali, like Boris and his mate's of me. I straightened up and stepped over Boris and was about to beat the shit out of fatso when the hotel security intervened. An extremely well-dressed, well-spoken, middle-aged Indian man put his hand on my chest. He had brought two sidekicks, two huge south-east Islander Fijian rugby players, if I had to guess. I thought if I punched them, I would just hurt myself. They didn't seem too interested in me, though. Like I said, this guy didn't have any friends.

"We are going to have to ask you to leave, sir." He was talking to fatso.

"Me? He's the one throwing punches."

"But you're the one with the hired help."

The security manager had been paying attention. They picked up his Russian friends and escorted them all outside. I made a mental note to check the shadows on my way out. That was where this type of people resided. I learned that from a John Wayne movie, *El Dorado*, or *Rio* something. John Wayne wouldn't let the guy he was with, Alan Bourdillion Traherne, leave the salon until they could leave together because the Duke knew the shitheads that had also just been thrown out of the bar would be hiding in the shadows outside.

"Sorry for the disturbance," my newly minted Indian friend said, saluting, "the riff-raff get past us sometimes."

I decided I liked this place very much as I returned to my lounge and sat down. The look on Joan's face was gold. I hadn't seen a look like that since I was a teenager but back then it was puppy love. Joan's look was more serious, if less intense, but a hell of a lot more welcome.

"Settle down, big boy. We're supposed to be keeping a low profile."

"You can't complain, you're the one who liberated me."

"From what?"

"A life more ordinary. I have never thanked you for that…so, officially, thanks. Cheers." I had retrieved my drink.

"I didn't know I was liberating the Hulk."

I laughed. "Not green, just lean. Something is sleeping inside all of us, I guess."

"Yours is awake now it would seem." She turned to check whether the rubbish had left the building. "Is he going to be a problem?"

"Always."

"Does it matter?"

"Not a goddamn."

Joan and I walked back along the beach to the hotel after dinner. She is such a beautiful woman it was hard for me not to think of the obvious. What made it worse for me was that she was carrying her shoes. There is something about watching a woman in a flowing dress, barefoot, carrying her shoes along a beach. That is so sexy. It signals the deliberate removal of formality, an inclination to connect to her primal urges like the sand in her toes, like Jane Greer in Out of the Past. Robert Mitchum and I were both slaves to her after that scene on the beach with her carrying her shoes in the moonlight. She was so very small next to him and so beautiful.

"I'm not going to get involved with you," Joan said, sensing my mood.

"Of course not. Why would you?"

"I won't date workmates. Particularly in this type of work. It's too distracting."

"Sounds like you are speaking from experience."

"Everyone is allowed one mistake."

"Lucky guy."

"It almost got us killed. Not so lucky, it was a mistake. It was early in my police career. Don't get intoxicated with the lifestyle, if you can call what we do a lifestyle."

"A calling?"

"Yeah, maybe."

"Brutal violence?"

"Mostly."

"Lonely?"

We stopped walking.

"Always," she said, looking at me, seemingly unconvinced about the rule she had so clearly just articulated.

"You're not over that guy, are you? Mister Mistake?"

I could see by the look on her face that I was right.

"It's done," she said determinedly, turning to continue walking.

"What the fuck are you doing dicking around with this stuff, Joan? You should be in the movies or something, living in Hollywood with your friend and two little dogs, you know, the yappy type, the ones you carry in your purse."

She smiled but said nothing, so I continued.

"It's over pretty quick, even quicker given what we do. It's easy not to place enough value on the stuff that really counts."

"Listen to you, Mr Everybody Can Fuck Off. Now, it's all about relationships, is that what you are saying?"

"Well… I figure that it must be about something that I don't have."

"That's an odd way to look at it."

"Look, babe, if what you got ain't doing it for you, then it must be something you ain't got."

She looked at me as if she was going to correct my English or maybe complain about me calling her *babe*, but she didn't do either and instead shrank away from me in unrequited attachment. We didn't speak until we got back to the hotel and even then it was nonverbal and ambiguous. Thankfully, I had a decent bottle of Scotch waiting for me in my room.

> *Then wear the gold hat, if that will move her;*
> *If you can bounce high, then bounce for her too,*
> *Until she cry, "Lover, gold-hated, high-bouncing lover,*
> *I must have you!"*

Attributed to Thomas Parke D'Invilliers but it was of course F. Scott Fitzgerald. Halfway through the bottle that night, I recited that prose out loud. I have never had any problem remembering great prose, even from a single reading. I have no idea why but I remember my first encounter with Shakespeare being magnified by my ability to recite his sonnets from memory. They attribute Shakespeare with inventing hundreds of words in the English language, but no dictionary will give Fitzgerald "orgastic" except maybe Wikipedia, a word he used at the close of *The Great Gatsby*. It perfectly described the way I felt as I dragged my feet to my room after the walk on the beach. It has always bugged me that it is not officially a word and, since I digress, I have just one more complaint, directed to the Man himself, Mr Fitzgerald. You could at least have finished that last book, you prick. How can you write arguably the greatest novel in American literature and then die before you finish the next one? Hollywood has a lot to answer for, I know. Tattoos and the confounding of Mr Fitzgerald are amongst its most serious transgressions. Writing fucking movie scripts, for God's sake, what was Fitzgerald thinking. Scripts that no ignorant bastard possessed the foresight to produce. You should have gotten back to work before those no-talent arseholes made you drink yourself to death trying to escape them. I once responded aggressively to a person I had met at a social gathering with the Fitzgerald conundrum in mind. This guy was with a very good-looking young lady and I was jealous and pissed, as usual. He asked me what my favourite books were, intending, I assume, to impress his girlfriend with some pre-prepared answer. I responded instinctively, "*Don Quixote* in the original Spanish, *Madame Bovary* in the original French, *Anna Karenina* in the original Russian, and *The Great Gatsby* in the original American English." He wandered off with his drink without responding, confounded, not even thinking to challenge my knowledge of any language other than American English. Not being able to speak another language is one of the many disappointments in my life, but I had read the translated version of those books several times. If he had broken into fluent Russian or French I would have looked like an idiot but, as it was, I was left to talk to his impressed but bewildered girlfriend for the remainder of the evening. I should have asked for her number. Another regret of mine is that I am slow to seize romantic opportunities. Like with Joan earlier that night. I hate people who say they don't have any regrets; they are either brain-dead or liars.

I've got to stop drinking.

CHAPTER SIX

I was back home, a little sore from sunburn and a little sorry about Joan. Making no progress with her frustrated me and it didn't look as if anything was ever going to be possible between us. The Council, whoever they were, had kept us out of the country for a week, so I had some explaining to do to my boss on Monday morning. I wasn't that troubled by the prospect of explaining myself to Duncan, but I was troubled.

It was Saturday afternoon and I would usually have been down at Sam's place beating the shit out of something or someone and the fact that I wasn't was a bad sign. I have always said that not doing the right thing is a symptom, not a preference. Instead of boxing, I was sitting on my balcony smoking a cigar that I had bought duty-free that morning. It's a top-floor penthouse apartment, so I wasn't bothering anyone with the smell. Bothering people with the smell and the fact that I didn't have any money had been the two reasons I had given cigars up, not that I had ever smoked much. I have never smoked cigarettes, except once in a Korean karaoke bar in Seoul while I looked up the skirt of the panty-less hostess sitting opposite me. I was drinking fine Scotch with the clients Dick lied to and scared off but let's not speak ill of the dead.

I took another draw on what was an exceptional Dominican cigar, unperturbed by memories of Dick, God rest his soul. I don't like Cuban cigars all that much. That is to say, they are my second choice. I know that is heresy, but I really should have got a couple of boxes of these Fuentes. I met the grandson once, the Fuente family grandson, not

Arturo. What a family story. I was in a cigar shop on Seventh Avenue in New York. I don't think it's there anymore, given the persecution that cigar smokers have suffered over the years, the gay community think they have a problem. Imagine if you were gay and smoked cigars. Anyway, I asked the shopkeeper for Fuentes and he told me he had three boxes of the sixty rings but would only sell me one box. He wanted to keep some for his other customers, I guess. I stood there saying stuff like *I'm here now and I got legal tender, I'm a lawyer and you can't legally say no,* because I wanted all three boxes, being the arrogant prick I used to be sometimes. I got a tap on the shoulder and the guy behind me said *they're my cigars.* Bullshit, I said and told him to fuck off, I was here first. It turned out to be the grandson from the plantation, in town for a cigar conference. He made the guy sell me all three boxes and promised to priority deliver more to the shop the next day. We spent a couple of hours smoking his cigars and talking about his family. That was a good day.

I had welcomed my new life with open arms but now that I had it clenched to my bosom, I had begun to waver about what it all meant. I had shed considerable baggage, as well as body fat, and even though I didn't care about shooting Dick or anyone else, humanity had begun to creep unnoticed and unwelcome back into my soul. I wasn't all that keen to renew my membership of the human race; I was happy being the *Outsider*, thank you, Albert. But I had become uneasy about the violence and lack of certainty it brought with it. I think that's why I had leant on Joan in St Kitts. I thought she might have been the answer. But one thing is for sure with those types of questions, I reminded myself, nobody can give you that answer, you have to go find it.

If I called it quits now, I could still fade into the background, maybe start a practice somewhere now that I had a grubstake. Perhaps, Phoenix, especially if you were panning for gold in the desert, which is what you do with a grubstake. I had distracted myself with the word *grubstake* because the thought of starting another law practice repulsed me and I was fleeing the prospect through the vacant recesses of my brain, screaming no and thinking of *grubstakes.* A practice meant dealing with people, people like Dick and Bruce and, worst of all, Bob and God knows who else. Dear God, not employees again. Being a lawyer wasn't the only thing I could do. If the last year had taught me anything, it was that I could start again. A Scotch might help me think this through.

I sat back down on my balcony, fully equipped for a session of planning with an afternoon picnic of cigars, Scotch, and peanuts. Yeah, that's right, three of the four major food groups. I began to think about that prick in St. Kitts and the other two guys left on my list. I understood what Joan was saying about not biting the hand that feeds you but the guy I was saving for last was going to be hard to dislodge from my list and my psyche. He used to bully me at school, right up to the time that I learned to box. I was a pimply adolescent and the guy was relentless about my complexion. I always felt, even before I could box, that I could beat him in a fight. But I was so conflicted about what was the right thing to do that avoiding him seemed easier. We never had a defining confrontation. Like all bullies they don't have the guts if they know you could defend yourself. I minded my own business back then, as all bullied children know is a product of being bullied. But now he was sticking in my craw. I knew where he lived.

I wondered whether all lives end up spoiled and dirty like mine, like so much used linen. You start out with a fresh, clean soul but inevitably it gets ruined. Some people would have us believe they are pure and clean. Most of those people are clergy and most of them are lying or delusional. You have to wear it, the soul, you have to take it out of the box and use it every day and you can't live your life without carrying it around. So, it's going to get dirty. Is there any possible way to use it without it getting torn and battered and broken and filthy? Or can you somehow get a new one? I wanted a new one. Or do you just find a way to live with the broken one? Can you live a good life with a torn and battered soul? Maybe we have to die so that we can get re-fitted. All humans are imperfect. I assume that is why people turn to religion to cleanse themselves but does that really work? You did the things you did and lived the life you lived. A healer telling you that you are cleansed doesn't really do the job, surely. Is hiding behind hymns and mythology really going to get the laundry done or do you just have to face up to the fact that your soul is broken beyond repair?

Alejandro Jodorowsky would have us believe that the goal of life is to *create* a soul. That concept both intrigues and worries me. If he was right, I had downed tools a long time ago. There is an alternative belief that we don't have a soul, perhaps you never had one or haven't been able to build one. Whatever, I think it's just you and what you make of yourself and your life at any point in time. You just move on, trying to invent a better version of yourself without carrying forward guilt from past misadventures. Now, there's a difficult task. Bring on *Eternal Sunshine of the Spotless Mind*. Whether acquired or built, a soul is heavy baggage.

On the way back to my bar for a refill, my own phone bonged with a message. The message asked for a meet at a cafe in the city. The message said it was important and related to my work, but it didn't say which work. I thought Joan said I reported only to her?

I should have brought a red rose to identify myself, I thought, as I sat nursing my second coffee and waiting for my date. I assumed they knew what I looked like.

"Mr Jamisen?" asked a tall guy in an inconspicuous black suit, grey tie, and sunglasses. Yes, they did know what I looked like. A photocopy of him stood behind him. Don't these guys look in the mirror before they leave the house? "Come with us, please."

"Sure, why not?"

I stood and we went out to the mandatory black SUV and climbed in.

"Where are you taking me?" It was difficult not to be a living, breathing cliché but at least I was living and breathing. No answer from the guy or his photocopy.

"Look, you guys can just drop me off here if you're going to shoot me, I'm happy to do it myself, if you want." It was a disturbing remark because I meant it. Maybe I wasn't healing, just hiding. When I tried the door handle, he noticed but I didn't care. Neither did he, because it was locked.

"I'm armed, you know."

"No, you're not."

Arsehole. How did he know that given he didn't search me?

"Look…"

"Shut up, put your seatbelt on, and relax. We are going to be a while."

I took his advice. I was in this for the long haul apparently.

We pulled up at a cabin about thirty minutes outside of Algonquin on a quiet little street, a good place for a murder. It was just on dark. Hopefully, it wasn't going to be torture and rape as well. What is wrong with me? We made our way inside.

"Sit down."

It was like something out of a forty's movie. It was as though I was watching this whole scene on a small black-and-white TV. There was no colour in the shabby room except for a standalone lamp timidly dispensing a pale-yellow light. The room was furnished with two old couches separated by a slim laminated wooden coffee table with matching side tables at either end of the couches, four in all. They were there in case they served drinks and hors d'oeuvres, I presumed. My mother would have loved the ensemble when it was new.

"Mr Jamisen," a male voice came from behind me. I turned in my seat to see a young man casually dressed in jeans and a t-shirt. "Thank you for coming."

"I had a choice?"

"I'm Bill Benson from Homeland Security. Would you like something to drink? A Scotch, perhaps?"

That was unsettling, both his employer and his knowledge of my personal habits.

"I am going to assume the Scotch was a good guess and that you are who you say you are unless you ask me something important. Nothing to drink and no hors d'oeuvres, thank you."

"Good deal." He looked puzzled.

It sounded like he said *good deal* often. He sat down opposite me. The two M.I.B. goons were still standing by the door. Bill was chipper and smart and, I guessed, up-and-coming, he probably knew everything and everyone important to know and must have been promoted quickly. This guy was going to be insufferable. At least I wasn't the only cliché in the room.

"Look, Bill, can we get to it? I have washing to do. I've been away."

"Yes…St Kitts with Detective Travis." He waited for a reaction from me. I didn't have one for him. I was a recovering empty vessel that was still largely empty. The difference between coma and catharsis, I was discovering, is marginal.

"That's Travis of Travis Industries."

"What, the rich dead guy who left everything to his daughter?"

"His daughter Joan."

"She's a cop."

"A rich cop."

"Wait. How did you know…?" Stupid, stupid question. I mean, they have all my emails and everyone else's emails, and tapes of phone calls and any loudly expressed opinions.

"We had a drone on you that night in Florida."

And drones.

"The fat guy was an agent."

They had my attention. I leant forward and put my elbows on my knees and my face in my hands. I started rubbing my face, trying to erase that last remark. I said, "You should have taught him to run faster," but I wasn't listening to myself and neither was he.

"Great shot. Very unhelpful, though."

"An agent?"

"Homeland Security Agent."

"Agent."

"Yes. And a very knowledgeable agent he was, too."

"Sorry." That seemed inadequate.

"I'm not that unhappy about the other three, though. And here's the thing." He paused for effect, crossing his scrawny jean-clad legs. "They know that shooting guys is not our *modus operandi* unless they're shooting at us, of course, so we think they're assuming that you are from a rival cartel trying to push them out."

"A rival terrorist organisation?"

"They're not terrorists, they're arms dealers. For them, it's business, not personal."

Coming from Mr Cliché, that saying seemed apt. I was certain that he was about to say he was *too old for this shit*, and add that it was going to be *all touch and go from here*, and it would be a *cold day in hell if we didn't get these guys*. Thankfully, he was too young for a Vietnam war flashback.

"There is a view out there that these are the guys who killed Elias Travis, Joan's father. There was an illegal buy underway from one of his subsidiaries, Travis Technologies, when the old guy got hit. Nobody knows whether he was in on it or he was trying to stop it so they whacked him, but these guys were involved and I can tell you that it will be a cold day in hell before I let them get away with it."

I rest my case.

"Bill, are you going to arrest me or fuck me?"

He seemed taken aback.

"I mean is this business or personal?"

Now, I was on his wavelength.

"We want your help." That was a relief. "You have them rattled with that little show you put on last week in front of the restaurant. We need you to run another raid into their territory. We have got a pretty good bead on these guys but we need to flush out their competition before we do anything about it. If you irritate them enough, they will go after the other guys themselves and that will give us the intel we need. That's the theory."

"And Joan?"

"Take her with you."

"I can tell her about you?"

"Best not to."

"Well, how do I get the job?"

"We'll feed Joan some more titbits and get her to initiate it. Sit tight and wait to hear something from her."

"So, you're happy for me to keep shooting these guys?"

"Don't know what you're talking about."

"But you'll remember if I don't cooperate?"

"Something like that, yeah."

"Can I get a lift home?"

"One more thing."

"Why not?"

"We want you to help us to find out what else Joan Travis is up to. She has been implicated in a number of hits on prominent mobsters but we can't pin them on her. It looks like she trusts you."

"I don't know whether I'm comfortable..."

"So, you shoot our agent, the fat guy, and now you won't help us out."

"There is that."

"Look, let's stop pretending you have a choice here." He stood.

"Sure."

"You'll hear from us. Take him back to the cafe."

The doorbell rang early Sunday morning while I was mulling over the events of the previous evening. It was Jake, looking for another shooting lesson. I was happy to accommodate him after what had happened with the M.I.B. guys. Something more normal might provide the antidote. I had spoken with his foster carers in detail during the week before my trip and they had approved both his boxing and his shooting lessons. Early indications were that he was pretty good at both and I had been quick to mention to Jake and his foster parents that the Olympics in either sport might be a worthwhile objective. Unlike my own attitudes as a teenager, I expected to see Jake consider it should he prove to be sufficiently dedicated and me sufficiently un-killed.

We took most of the day to travel out and use the range and it was late afternoon by the time we found ourselves in the ice creamery on our way back to his place.

"So, how do you know so much about weaponry? You're a lawyer."

"I lost myself in it there for a while as a young man and that is easy to do. So many manufacturers and accessory suppliers, so many enthusiasts, and so many interesting stories. In this country, it is both art and devil worship."

"Is that a good thing?"

"It is what it is and there is no changing it now, that's for sure. If anybody ever invaded and tried to take over, they'd be in a world of hurt."

"It's got its own language, but I don't know about being an art form."

"If you spend enough time in the culture, you get to know the slang and there is a rich and extensive culture of guns in this country. Some say *sub-culture*, but there ain't no *sub* about it man, there is as much culture in this as any art form: the engineering, the design, the beauty of the weaponry."

"You've got to stop slipping into the vernacular, I can't understand you sometimes."

"Learn it, shithead, or move on."

"What's a can?"

"A suppressor."

"A rail?"

"The hand grip on a rifle."

"Brake?"

"Muzzle brake, you stick it on the end of a rifle and it directs muzzle flare and sound forward away from the shooter."

"And I don't get these calibre conversions."

"Unfortunately, we use both metric and imperial in this country. Nine millimetres is basically your .38 Special, handgun cartridges known as a '38' being .357 calibre, generally, for revolvers and rifles, .355 for autoloaders. It refers to the width of the round. But now there are so many minuscule variations of calibre and propellant, the ammo availability tends to follow the market trends in rifle or gun popularity." His eyes were glazing over. "Are you enjoying it? The shooting, not the ice cream?"

"Both."

"You're pretty good at it."

"I'm going to have to be."

"You're not still fantasizing about being a hitman, are you?"

"Of course not, who would do such a thing?"

"Smartarse."

"Killer."

"Hey…I prefer special agent."

"But you're not 007, you're a killer."

"You think there's a difference. I'm special."

"You are special, just not an agent."

There was no one close enough to hear us talk, thank goodness, and Jake was not yet at an age where one-word answers made him a cool teenager. I was thankful for the conversation.

"I guess that has to be right."

"I'm not criticising."

"Just being judgemental."

"So, do you think you will ever get caught?"

"Yes."

"For sure?"

"Yes."

"Then what happens to me?"

"You'll be looked after until you get your hands on your stepfather's loot and then you can grow a beard, own a private jet, and fly from one party to the next, fucking everything that moves."

"A beard?"

"You're happy with all that except the beard? So, you can hide until you're ready to be your real self and do something worthwhile."

"Which one are you doing? Hiding or being worthwhile?"

"I don't have a beard."

"I want to come live with you." I choked. "You're a lawyer, a respectable citizen. You could adopt me."

"So, you've thought it through. Jake, they wouldn't let a single man…would they? I'm sure they wouldn't. Besides, my lifestyle wouldn't be conducive to a stable home environment."

"We could have a nanny, as long as she was good-looking."

"What would you do with a good-looking nanny?"

"Same thing you would."

"I can see I was right about the jet and the parties."

"Look, just think about it, will ya? You're the first adult I have ever been able to have an adult conversation with."

I wasn't sure that made sense.

"I'll think about it." I was more reassuring than serious. "I'll make the relevant enquiries."

I had probably said too much but he was happy to leave it at that and I was happy to go and identify some bureaucratic nonsense to hide behind.

A couple of days later, Joan turned up at my door at about eight in the evening.

She stormed into the centre of my living room.

"Homeland Security. Really? You're talking to fucking Homeland Security."

"They had ray guns and my head doesn't grow back."

"What the fuck are you talking about?"

"Men in Black, MIB, Jack Jeebs?"

She is not into movie references. Maybe they had to be wearing black ties for that analogy to work, in my head, I mean. She didn't know what they were wearing. The ties were grey but they were armed, just not with ray guns.

"Put that cryptic movie shit aside for a minute and listen. I get this lead from my source at Homeland Security about those guys that we hit the other week, telling me where more of them are going to be tomorrow night. I know when I am being spoon-fed, so I dig a little deeper and you'll never guess whose name came up."

"Jack Jeebs?"

"No."

"I…but…" English escaped me. "They were going to tell on me."

"What are you, six years old?"

"Not physically, but I haven't been telling fibs like you, Ms Travis Industries."

That shut her up and started her puzzling.

"They knew I was with you at that shoot?"

"They had a drone." I made a flying aeroplane sign with my hand to illustrate, since I was six, but I swear I didn't make the engine noise. This all seemed a little disingenuous coming from her, so I was predisposed to ridiculing her. She slapped my hand out of the air.

"Hey, those things cost money."

"Fuuuuuck."

She started to pace, bending forward as she walked and shaking her hands on each side of her head to emphasise every word. She's a worrier, this one. It surprised me a little given what she does as a hobby.

"You might be happy to go to jail, but I am certainly not."

"Relax. They want our help. No one's going to jail."

"I thought…"

"Look, Joan, stop. Sit. You're making me giddy. Did you honestly think you could go around shooting people, on whoever's instructions, and not get noticed?" Suddenly, I was the adult and she was the spoilt rich kid. "They've got us dead to rights, including a video from the drone." I sat down and beckoned her to do the same. "All we can do is give them what they want and deal with it, or them, whenever."

"What, they use us to do their bidding?" she said derisively, still standing, "and then send us to prison while they get a gold star?"

"Maybe. Maybe not. You don't think the Council is using us?"

She stopped pacing.

"Spill it. You've got something in mind."

"This is a dirty business, Joan. Those guys, especially Doogie Howser, the head guy I met. I can't remember his real name but he was a little blonde teacher's pet know-it-all prick and looked about twelve years old. They are definitely not following the rules. Fuck, they have already broken them trying to deal with us." She sat down and calmed down. "I say we use them like the muppets they are, not the other way around. Who's to say they didn't send us to shoot those guys a couple of weeks ago? They had assets on scene and they are asking us to go shoot some more of these…arms dealers. They are in this up to their armpits. They are the crims, they made us help them, right? If we go down, they go down, and they won't let that happen. We just need some insurance."

"Insurance?"

"The guy who fed you the intel from Homeland Security, did he catch on that you were on to him?"

"Poker face," she waved her hand dismissively, shaking her head.

"Well, the Council has access to resources, right?

"Sure."

"Drones?"

"No drones."

"That's right, you broke our last one." She didn't get it. "Do we have access to the big boys at Homeland Security? Back door, hush-hush, on the QT."

"We have someone."

"Is he a lawyer?"

"How did you guess? What else?"

"Some serious shit, eyes and ears technical bullshit about which I know nothing."

"Got just the guy."

"Great. We're set. Drink?" I got up and walked over to my now extensive bar. Pamela's bar, God rest her soul, had nothing on this baby. "I am willing to bet my brand-new McMillan that Doogie isn't as smart as he thinks he is. Tell me about your dad."

She was a little taken aback by my lack of concern about the plan, but she complied.

"He was someone who other men stood aside for. A bull of a man. Intelligent, capable, successful."

"But?"

"No buts or ifs. He was the real deal."

"And these arms dealers took him from you."

"Did Doogie tell you that? Yes, it was one of those two arms-dealing groups. I strongly suspect it was the competitors of the one we hit the other night. But they can all go to hell as far as I'm concerned."

"And it's your plan to send them there. Got it. That is why you started this Council thing. It's you, isn't it? The Council, I mean. It's not some obscure group of anti-crim benefactors. It's just you, right?"

I stood there holding out her drink, jiggling it, making the ice rattle, looking her in the eye and wanting her to be honest with me. She wasn't sure how to respond but decided to hide behind the truth.

"Me and a couple of Dad's friends." She took the drink, with a guilty little girl look for making up the Council story. I sat. "I wasn't overstating it when I said there was money. There's more than enough to get this job done and cure malaria, too, if we want. We were trying to work through official channels but we kept coming up against...the Doogie Howsers. We decided to take things into our own hands."

"So, you're Batgirl."

"Look, this is troubling stuff. I know you mean well, but trivialising this isn't going to get us anywhere."

She stood up and started to walk over to the bench to put down her drink and leave.

"I'm sorry. I'm hearing this for the first time. I was just processing it. Please, don't leave. I need to know what's going on."

She sat back down without her drink. I guess she thought she owed me an explanation.

"Where would you like to start?"

"With you."

"Poor little rich girl. I did the cop thing before all this started. My father was against it but that just made it all the more important to me. He wanted me in the business, but I didn't have his brains. So, I chose something else that was the opposite of what he wanted and made out like it was important."

"It wasn't important? The police thing, I mean?"

"It seemed important. I loved him, we were friends. I think I felt I would fail in the business and he would see me fail. So, I made my new career important."

"Were you really up on charges for a wrongful shooting?"

"Yes. Well, IA was involved. No charges eventuated. That allegation was just as much bullshit as I said it was. That was around the time Dad got killed. I was suspended and couldn't do anything. I felt so useless."

"That's a big jump for a law-abiding young cop to make, from cop to the Dark Knight."

"I wasn't that young and law enforcement can be a dirty business. I think I had already crossed that line when I shot the guy that got me into strife with IA. I could have arrested him. I had him on his knees, arms up. Instead, I just emptied my clip. Couldn't have happened to a nicer guy. I planted a gun on him and claimed it was self-defence."

"Why do you need me?"

"Come on, Jim, I know you've buried yourself in booze and self-pity but there's maybe only four or five people in this whole country that can shoot as well as you do and they are all current or ex-military. None of them would be interested in working for me. I wish you'd wake up from that dream of yours. There's a hell of a guy under there and I'd like to meet him."

If that was true, my compass was awake and it was pointing directly at her.

"I'm not happy being lied to." Did I just say that?

"Jim, you kill people for a living."

"Not before I met you, not for money. There are rules, you said."

"OK, no more bullshit. It might have been the guys we hit who killed Dad or it might have been their competitors, but it was someone in one of those two organisations. I have to put it right. I'll work my way through every one of those miserable bastards if I have to."

"By *work through,* I assume you mean *kill.* That's a tall order."

"That's why I need some help."

"Doogie said something about the second group but didn't know who they were."

"No one has ever seen them surface. They work in the shadows, the biggest operators in the business, but no one has tagged them. They must be very well connected because when anyone gets a lead, it disappears into thin air. The guys we hit are not so well organised. I thought that if we started shooting up their opposition, the group we are after, would show themselves, or the guys we've been hitting would go find them for us."

"Yeah, that was Doogie's plan. You've been lecturing me about hating people, yet here you sit, telling me you're going to kill everyone in the illegal arms business."

"You, of all people, should understand. I can't move forward without redemption. I can't, and I have tried."

"You are a beautiful woman, Joan, you could be doing anything. Why waste your life on this?"

"There are so many slimebags walking around scot-free. You see it on the Force. They have a good lawyer so they think they're above it all, no offence."

"I'm not a good lawyer, so none taken."

"It just hurts me deep inside. The guy I shot that got me into trouble had been slipping out of convictions his whole life. He had made an art form of it, but he was the real deal; drugs, human trafficking, weapons. He was responsible for the death of a twelve-year-old girl in a case I was working. Part of his *cargo.* Well, he didn't *slip out* of a bullet in the head."

"But it's a tough line to cross."

"Sure, but number two was a hell of a lot easier."

"The one you hit when you were with me."

"You are very intuitive for a drunk, with affection. I couldn't be asking you to do something that I wasn't prepared to do myself."

"Your mom, what does she think about all of this?"

"She left when I was ten. Dad raised me."

"Siblings?"

"Just me."

"So, all that money..."

"All mine."

"So, you've been wearing haute couture all your life. You don't shoot people to earn it. The Ferrari was a present from..."

"Dad, yes, eighteenth birthday."

"You're finishing my sentences again...dear. So, it is two hits for you."

"I have fired my weapon in the line of duty, but two, yeah. The guy I hit with you was second-in-charge to the trafficker I got suspended for shooting. I had been lining him up for weeks before we got to him that day. He had been making noises about coming after me for shooting his boss."

"No noises now, I assume. And the guys you had me shoot?"

"Well, three of them were yours and I felt I wasn't going to be able to stop you from hitting them, anyway. So, I thought I might as well use them as bribes, maybe stop you from hitting them all. The other four guys I approved were crims."

"Unconvicted crims."

"Traffickers, with long lists of arrests and a few convictions. Some were part of that group whose boss I shot, stepping up to take charge. They were the genuine article. Frankly, I didn't know..."

"Whether I would do it."

"Yeah, something like that. That group is now so disorganised. The Force has been picking off their lieutenants one by one. You and I pretty much shut them down."

"So, now it's just the two arms dealers."

"For me, it had always been about the arms dealers, since Dad was killed. I have, in my head at least, bought into this Council shit. I think it's a great idea."

"The Joan Council. I'm still not sure why you picked me."

"Do you actually know how hard it is to do what you do? And being a long way away from these guys when you whack them is a very good idea given the weaponry they carry."

"I'm not sure I'm that great a shot, relatively speaking, I mean."

"Bullshit."

"There was this one guy, Canadian military, he's got this Taliban guy lined up in some canyon in Afghanistan over twenty-six-hundred yards away, close to a mile and a half. They say it's the longest confirmed kill shot until Craig Harrison in 2009 at twenty-seven-hundred yards, give or take. Do you know how far that is? I'm comfortable at twelve hundred yards with the best optics I can find but at a mile and a half I'm calling in an airstrike. In the summer of 2014, a Canadian sniper team in Iraq had a verified recorded kill over 3871 yards. The shooter was never named, again with a Macmillan Tac 50, my preferred weapon. The bullet took ten seconds to get from the rifle to the target."

Her eyes glazed over and she fell back on the couch. Her eyes were heavy, the adrenalin from the shock of Homeland's involvement had run out of her body. We had all been very busy. I shut up and left her to drift off. My mind went to the snipers for whom I had a high regard. I couldn't rightly claim to be a *Great Shooter*. That guy from that *American Sniper* movie, the story about Chris Kyle, he was a great shot, a prolific killer. His longest confirmed kill was around two thousand yards, seven hundred yards short of Harrison's best shot and 1800 yards short of the record. In his book, Kyle refers to himself as a *record-breaking* sniper. With all due respect to a great American, I'm not sure the records to which he was referring, either distance or number of kills. I would concede that he had the greatest number of confirmed kills in the war in Afghanistan. But Furlong and Harrison are legendary for having the longest confirmed kills. Furlong's most famous shot was at an elevation of nine thousand feet, that helped the bullet carry, but he still had to hit the guy. Furlong was also using a fifty calibre McMillan Tac-50. That was the weapon I used on Fredericks that day on the hill and that is why I picked that weapon. It took Furlong three shots to get the Taliban guy. The target saw the first shot land behind him, Furlong saw the splash in the sand. So, the target ran for cover before Furlong could get off his second round, which when delivered hit the guy's backpack and spun him around. It was over after Furlong got that sighter. He got him with his third. That's a great shot, twenty-six-hundred yards. None of mine were *great shots*. Even with a good scope, it would have been hard to see that guy from that distance, let alone blow him up, which is what would have happened when that fifty-calibre round hit him.

The story of Robert Furlong is widely known in shooting circles. Not so much the Harrison story. Six of one, a half dozen of the other perhaps, as to which was the better shot. Just fifty yards separate them, and I respect both. The remarkable thing about Harrison's shot was that he was using a .338-calibre rifle, the Arctic Warfare Magnum L115A3, which supposedly has a fifteen-hundred-yard effective range at sea level, but he was using Lapua rounds. I have told the Furlong story often in a bar if the talk turns to guns because a fifty-calibre is so much more my cup of tea. A man's weapon, with all due respect to Mr Harrison. Harrison's shot with his Artic Warfare rifle is perhaps the greatest ever shot. He got the guy with his first round and then got the guy next to him with is second shot before the first one hit its mark, two shots only, there's a guy confident with his mathematics. Amazing, too good for me. You can shoot someone through a brick wall with the fifty-calibre but not so much with a .338. Kudos, Mr Harrison.

With all of that said, and with Kyle's testimony cast in stone by the account in his book that asserted he had over 160 kills, making him *the most deadly sniper ever,* and with Mr Eastwood's movie confirming that myth, I should mention here the actual largest number of kills registered. Heroes, like Lyudmila Pavlichenko, the Ukrainian WW2 sniper with 309 kills. Ivan Sidorenko, the Russian terror of Leningrad or Simo Hayha, the Finnish *White Death* sniper from WW2 who claimed over 550 kills with no optical assistance during the Russian invasion of Finland in 1939. My personal favourite is William "Billy" Sing, a Chinese Australian, who served with the Australians trapped in Gallipoli in WW1 at the bottom of those Turkish cliffs. The Australian and New Zealand forces were there because of the insane strategies hatched by the English *"hero"* Churchill, then Lord of the Admiralty, back when Australians used to follow the British around like puppy dogs into every ill-conceived military disaster they cared to design. With great respect to the heroic Australians fallen in Gallipoli, but certainly not to their English higher-ups, fuck those fat Knighted or Lorded fuckups who put those brave men on a beach and let the Turks have a free go at them from the clifftops. One of the worst-conceived military operations of all time. Made worse by the fact that it was obvious they had fucked up a couple of days into the operation, but Churchill left them there for ten months because of his massive ego. They were slaughtered by the Turks sitting three-hundred feet above them on top of the steep cliffs rising from the beach where the Australian and New Zealand forces were trapped. Many of those brave men are still there. The Turkish soldiers felt so bad they took to throwing rations down to the Australians out of respect. Too much Scotch served at the British planning meetings, I suspect. Worse still, it has never been properly explored in the history books. That fat drunk, Churchill, has a lot to answer for but never will, such is the right of British and American authors who write the history books. *Half of written history is all about hiding the truth,* thank you, Captain Mal from Serenity.

Anyway, Corporal Sing, with over two hundred confirmed kills using an Enfield Mark 1, my first rifle, unassisted by optics, had the distinction of being shot by Turkey's number one and most feared sniper of all time, *Abdul the Terrible*. Abdul's weapon was called *The Mother of Death* by the Turkish military. Sing survived the wound and eventually killed Abdul in a later encounter with what the Australians described in dispatches as *a miraculous piece of marksmanship*. I personally think that would make a great movie about snipers, Mr Eastwood, especially if it included Churchill's fuckups, which would never happen because Churchill's a "*hero*", you see, not a war criminal. Billy, a real hero, made it off that beach. They patched him up and sent him to the Western Front in Germany where he was shot again in heroic circumstances, this time by Germans. He survived and made it home to Australia, only to die alone and in poverty in 1957. Such is our ongoing, inexplicable disregard for our returned service personnel. His only possessions were a bag of ratty clothes and a five-shilling mining claim certificate in the top drawer of his bedside table in the single room of the boarding house where he resided. The epitome of the forgotten soldier; no movie for him. Always the optimist, believing the mine would make him rich even without the strength or the equipment to excavate it. It's mainly because of Sing that I refuse to put myself in his and the others' laudable company and be marked as a *great shot.*

"So, it's just you and me, then?" I asked Joan timidly as she came out of her half-sleep, hoping it was true and that she believed I actually was a good shot.

"Plus, some contacts I made in the Force." She began to rub her eyes. "Professionals, shall we say, who don't care whether it's legal, just whether it's profitable. Plus, my father's best friend, who is a prominent lawyer. He's the guy I told you about. He went to school with the second-to-top guy at Homeland Security and he knows what I'm doing, sort of. He tacitly approves, as long as I don't tell him any details. So we are not alone, no."

"Just for completeness, I guess, what about the boyfriend you almost got killed?"

"Maybe he would help; he is still on the Force. He was too conflicted about what I wanted to do. As I said, it's a lonely path. We parted ways."

"So, you're still a virgin?"

"You're a sick puppy, you know that?"

"I'm a sick puppy, I didn't start the Killer's Kouncil. You know, that's only one capital K away from being something really bad."

"Well, for a start, you can't spell and, secondly, you said you had a plan?"

CHAPTER SEVEN

What had caught me out was my feelings for Joan. Sociopaths rarely get the girl, or is that their only road to redemption? I don't know enough about sociopathy to be sure. Would letting someone love you fix the blackness, or bring both of you into conflict through your affliction? A troubling sense of guilt was growing within me and it threatened to send me back down the slippery slope. I could see in front of me where I wanted to be but I was stranded in the shadows, looking out from a dark place, unconvinced of my progress and unmoved by the need to take the next step. I was deaf to the calls to come forward and blind to the reasons that welded me to the spot I had long since staked out for my final stand. *For in that sleep of death what dreams may come,* thank you William, I had been walking around asleep and dead inside. The dream was clawing at me like a precious belonging I had left behind in some uncertain place whilst I continued to a destination made meaningless by its absence.

They say you lose your sense of belonging before you contemplate suicide. You detach yourself from the world around you. Then you become preoccupied with the burden you have become to others. After those two stages, eventually, in that dream, you shed your fear of death. These are the three planets that need to align to make you take your own life. Before I met Joan, I had them all lined up. I had lost not only the fear of my own death but the fear of other people's deaths. Well, not people in general, just certain recalcitrant deviants. But my psychosis was never complete. I still knew it was wrong to kill even though I didn't care, at least when it came to the people who had put me in that condition. Sociopaths are not supposed to know the difference between right and wrong, but I did, and I still carried around the noble objective of wanting to protect my friends. In my head, this whole social crusade of mine was to rid the world of anyone who could harm the people I care about in the same way that they had harmed me. I should have gone and seen someone before I self-medicated, and by that I mean started shooting people.

Before I met Joan, I was sometimes preoccupied with the fantasy of returning to my youth to fix these problems, going back in time with my accumulated knowledge of life. The fantasy was based on the flawed proposition that I knew so much better now than I had before. But all you would get from fulfilling that fantasy would be a suicidal six-year-old. You wouldn't go back further than six because earlier than that you would have no self-determination; listen to me, I am still constructing that delusion. Sometimes in life, it is ignorance of consequences that permits us to act, occasionally productively and at other times recklessly, with either being better than ambivalence. If you went back in time with all you had learned to date, you would know the consequences of the decisions you had made the first time around, but what about the consequences of your new choices? I had even picked out the time and place I would return to start again. It was the first time I had been confronted at school by that bully, number twelve on my list. That discussion would have ended differently on my return visit. There would have been no discussion, not from him, anyway. So, my whole life would change. I wonder how much more valuable my life could have been from that point, how much more I could bring to it than I had the first time around, except for the occasional good investment assuming the market trends were the same, money always helps.

Logically, to get my life right, I would have to subject myself to this reincarnation many times over, as Buddha suggested, and even then I might never get a satisfactory turn on the Ferris Wheel. Instead, I might just expose myself to harsher lessons each spin. I think of Ashton Kutcher killing himself as a baby in *The Butterfly Effect*, or me killing him after he married Mila Kunis. The process worked out alright for

Bill Murray in *Groundhog Day* but we never did find out whether he married Andie MacDowell's character Rita which, by the way, would have never worked out, they were too different. Perhaps he just ran off once he got out of the time loop and became a travelling musician since he had learnt how to play the piano and seduce women. Learning how to seduce women, it seemed to me, was the whole point of the movie.

Instead of allowing return visits, Nature has locked Herself into constant renewal and perhaps for good reason. It fosters genetic diversity and restitution, not necessarily growth, just change. Geneticists assume we are always evolving, implying that humans are becoming smarter and better than they were generations before. But that is demonstrably bullshit. Evolution is random and, for humans, any positive impact resulting from natural selection is now out of the picture. If anything, we strive as a species to retain the weakest links in our genome and as a result they remain part of the general populace. We as a species favour the moron with twenty-seven kids, so we have no hope. There will be more drunks and idiots in the citizenry in three hundred years' time than there are now, the only variable being whether a comet hits the planet first. Nature rolls the dice and has a good laugh at the outcomes, let's try a forty-foot-tall lizard. We are already on the thousandth version of life on this planet. The proposition that evolution has an ultimate goal or an eventual point of perfection is delusional. The process is just random generation of flora and fauna, as has been demonstrated countless times in the past. I guess it helps us to think we are on some yellow brick road but Nature has no moral imperative to seek perfection; She only seeks change and renewal. There is a lizard on another planet contemplating this same question, writing this same diary. We need to go tag its ear, track its migratory patterns, see where it goes, or do something that passes for scientific research. Or, better still, do as Captain Kirk did and beat it to death with a rock.

Resetting all possibilities does have merit. But these idiots who persecute unwitting animals or sea life, tagging them on the ear or fin and thinking that by following a radio beacon around to monitor migration patterns they might protect them from the inadequacies in their species and postpone their date with extinction, are all deluded. The species they are studying must be inadequate because it is already struggling to avoid extinction, that's why they're being *studied* These dropkicks with the tags think they can help, but Nature is shouting *leave it alone and let's just see how this plays out.* These do-gooders only hurt the animals they study as they stick tags in their ears that make them look weird to potential mates, and it must hurt. What respectable female walrus is going to screw a male walrus with a big yellow radio beacon sticking out of its ear? Did these guys even read Darwin's *On The Origin of The Species*? The ones with the beacons get selected out of the population. These fools all forget that ninety-nine-point-nine-nine percent of all species that ever walked, swam, crawled, or flew on this earth are already extinct and those that have been lost were probably a better and more interesting lot than the ones that survived. Moreover, those species that are still around probably had something to do with making the others extinct; they are as culpable in this paradigm as we all are, so why should they get protected? Nature assures us that there is always another set of Earthly inhabitants ready to take their place, including our place. So, let's not mollycoddle the fragile ones. Instead, let's get a look at the next lot that Nature serves up. Killing off a species makes room for its replacement in that habitat, which will no doubt emerge from the plants or animals the newly extinct species had preyed on. I guess it may be my current attitude to life generally, but I don't understand why we as a species are reluctant to impose sensible curatorship on both ourselves and what remains of the species on this planet. In fact, we could create new ones when we think they might be useful or interesting. Screw this *don't touch it* mentality, *don't mess with the balance of Nature*, I call bullshit. There is no balance. It's forever out of balance. That's why it keeps changing and it's being *touched and altered* all the time by cosmic rays, viruses, and all sorts of natural genetic manipulators.

Life as we know it is not static; it is fluid, and changes imposed by the environment are random, not planned. So, I'm saying, let's step up to the plate. We have the technology, and surely, we could do a better job than chance. Nature gave us the brain that created that technology. Let's get in there and start screwing with the gene pool. She is probably looking on and wondering why we are sitting on our hands. She has passed us the ball, She showed us what can be done with the ninety-nine-point-nine-nine percent that has already come and gone. *Have a go,* She's yelling, you can hear it if you put your ear to the ground and be very quiet. *Have a go, you pricks, what's the holdup?* I have personally heard that many times whilst lying on the grass after a few scotches. I am doing my part. I am busy trying to tidy up the human gene pool and that is hard enough. Certain conservationists would say we can't whack man-eating sharks. I call bullshit on that one, too. I'd like to get a quote from one of these shark lovers just as they are being bitten in half. Oh, but they clean up the oceans. Clean it up from what? Humans? Other fish? Fuck 'em, I say. The current state of affairs is all over the place, with species popping in and out, particularly viruses. Get a grip, it's potluck, baby. Let's sort out what's left and make sure they add some value. So, we keep the cats, especially the big ones, they get in because of their beauty. Some dogs, no little yappy dogs, otters, penguins, are all okay because they are cute. Chickens and cows, no problem, anything we can eat, they stay. Remember that Nature is throwing them out there randomly, just ask Charles Darwin. If they can't survive in this environment, an environment that includes humans, then they should go. Pandas are cute but they bring nothing to the party and they seem to want to be extinct, so let them go; they won't even fuck each other if you put them in the same enclosure. When it comes to in-vitro fertilisation of animals to keep a species alive, it's time for a reality check; too many overheads, out they go. This random generation of species really came up with some zingers. Nature never thought it through properly. She has to be a comedian, surely, sloths, cockroaches, flies, fleas, and mosquitoes, yes, mosquitoes, what the hell is that about? Let's use the brains Mother Nature gave us to impose some order, someone has to do it, She is expecting us to do it, it's chaos out there. Saint Patrick got rid of all the snakes in Ireland with, guess what, no impact on the eco-structure. Let's finish the job and get rid of the rest of them worldwide, the ones that can kill you, anyway. And don't get me started on rats or wasps. I hate birds, lice-ridden, noisy bastards, even the pretty ones. They are all breathing out carbon dioxide and contributing to global warming, you see. If it was just us, the cows, the pigs, the chickens, the turkeys, pheasants, some fish and most shellfish, but no sharks, the bees, almost all plants and fungus except poisonous or spiky ones, the cats, and a few species of dog, it would be heaven.

Look, all we need to do is think about what we would take with us if we were setting up on another planet. The guy that says let's take the mosquitoes or the man-eating sharks or Ebola virus, you leave him behind along with those species on Earth. Good luck to him; he'll need it. The concept that we are not able to understand the complexities of interdependency is bullshit. We should reduce the interdependency down to something we can understand, and better still, manage. The idea that we can't possibly understand it is a product of a whole bunch of biologists trying to hang onto their jobs and trying to get themselves a place on the spaceship. But they aren't coming with us, no, that's for sure. We would take what we needed and nothing more and be the better for it. And, yes, absolutely no arseholes.

Joan and I were closeted in a van outside a warehouse in Bedford Park at midnight the following night. It was the location that Homeland Security had put us onto. We had decided to play along with Doogie and maybe take out some bad guys at the same time. We had employed the technical resources we had talked about and were with him in the mandatory black transit van about two hundred yards down the street from the location where we believed the arms dealers were… dealing. Techo Mick had electronic surveillance across the whole scene, including hacking into Doogie's communications. I was counting ammunition and reloading my gun clips because the precision of the task settled my nerves, although, my banging each clip on the bench after I had reloaded it to set the ammo up against the breach side of the clip was wearing a bit thin with my comrades in arms.

This was a difficult proposition. Our arms-dealing friends were not going to show themselves in the open again, something to do with being gunned down the last time they had made that mistake. We were going to have to go into the building after them. Now, I was happy sitting in my vehicle a mile from the target because that provided me with not only anonymity and a secure exit but also placed me at a comfortable emotional distance. It allowed me to reframe the person not as a victim but simply as a target. The splash of red mist and brain matter seemed somehow reassuring at that distance, indicative of a job well done, like a bullseye at a tournament. Going into the building after them was far too personal. Something that should be left to guys like Tom Cruise or Stone Cold Steve Austin. I just love Steve and what a nickname. One facial expression fits all and that expression is so scary; and the muscles, I wish. Techo Mick was explaining to me and Joan how to get into the upper reaches of the building without being detected. I was off thinking about the fat guy running down the footpath at our last shoot and how that was more my style, even if he was the wrong target. I wasn't sure whether I was brave enough to knock on their door. Joan realised that I wasn't listening and punched me hard in the arm.

"You up for this, or not?" she asked.

"No."

"No, as in no choice?"

"Do you want my new McMillan if I don't make it?"

"Fuck off. If you don't make it, then I'm not going to make it, and that is not an acceptable outcome."

She had gotten my attention. She should have been a General like William Wallace, thank you, Mel, great speech. I started playing it in my head. Would I be willing to trade every day from today to my inevitably miserable, alcohol-drenched death to leave this van and tell our arms-dealing friends *that they may take our lives but they will never take our freedom,* or whatever bad thing they were about to take or had already taken, including Mr Travis, may he rest in peace.

"There's a fire exit here." Techo Mick was pointing at plans he had stolen via the internet from the local council. "The top floor window here isn't alarmed, as far as I can tell." Very comforting. "If you make your way down this corridor on the top level you will get a door that leads out to a balcony where you will get a good look at the warehouse interior from the mezzanine floor, here. That top floor only extends about a quarter of the way along the building but, at the point that it finishes, you can see the whole warehouse below. You got it? They should be doing whatever arms dealers do down there on the warehouse floor."

"Thank you, Mick, most comprehensive. Do you know how to shoot an AK-47? Because I'm feeling ill."

"Shut up, let's go."

Joan didn't give the fist-in-the-air signal followed by the five-fingered spread, whatever that means, but she did exit the vehicle, so I followed her.

We shimmied up the fire escape and my confidence in Mick lifted when we discovered the designated entry window was indeed not alarmed, but it was hard to open. With all personnel and equipment inside, we made our way down the darkened hallway to a locked door that led out onto a walkway and balustrade high above the warehouse floor that was the size of a football field. We could see some activity below through the small glass window in the door, including a group of three guys standing over what looked to me like an open case of JASDF Type 91 Kai MANPADs. Yeah, that's right, I know my equipment, and I know they were not supposed to have those headbangers. I had only seen pictures as they were definitely off-limits, even at the gun shows I frequented. "Man Portable Air Defence missiles," in case you were wondering what the sexist acronym referred to. The American military is second only to the computer industry when it comes to indecipherable acronyms for equipment or systems. To me, it had to be MorWPADM, man or woman portable, or just HHRL, that is, Hand-Held Rocket Launchers, or old school RPG, Rocket-Propelled Grenades, or, even more sensibly, a SYPHICs Shit-Your-Pants-Here-It-Comes. That last one even works as a word.

There would be no worthwhile cover once we were out on the walkway so we hunched down and slipped into an empty meeting room nearby with a whiteboard, wooden chairs on chrome frames, a laminated table, and linoleum floors. I pulled up a chair to sit at the table and it made the sound that pokey little chrome-legged chairs make when you drag them along a polished floor. We both grimaced but there was no one on this level of the building to hear it. I sat, she stood.

"Well, we ain't going to do anything productive hiding in here," Joan tabled, opening the meeting with her loud and assertive whisper.

I was happy to have the opportunity to gather myself and it showed.

"They got some pretty good suppliers," I said, attempting to draw out the meeting. "The shit they are handling down there is the real deal. Didn't see any cover outside, though, did you notice?"

"You got a vest."

"My head and dick are glad to hear it."

I was a little breathless. I'm not quite sure why as we hadn't done much. Maybe it was the excitement or all the whispering, or perhaps early signs of a cardiac problem. I have got to stop drinking.

"So, what do you want to do? Bring them up here and discuss it with them?"

"I didn't bring my laptop and my PowerPoint presentation, so, no. What I'd like to do is drop a grenade into that box of MANPADs."

"You brought grenades?"

"Yeah."

I showed her a pouch that I had strapped to my belt with three grenades in it. She was impressed; I felt very manly.

"Drop them into what?"

"The box with… it's boy stuff, literally according to the acronym. They're the new model RPGs. They could make an awful mess of a passenger airliner. So, what's the plan?"

"We go out onto that walkway and blast the living shit out of them, then get out the back before the place goes up."

"Intricate."

She went out and was kicking down the door to the walkway before I could critique her proposition. She got through the door and then she just stood on the balustrade and opened up on them. I've never seen anything like it. She was an angry lady, that was for sure, what can I say?

I went out and dropped a grenade into that box of MANPADS and a second to be sure and pulled her inside just as it went up. We both went back out and emptied a couple of mags then bolted for the window before anyone returned fire. Whoever was down there was now very unhappy. We half-ran, half-stumbled down the fire escape with a release of tension as we were leaving, I laughed like a schoolboy who had just dropped a flaming bag of dog turds on his teacher's doorstep. I said something like "fuck me" when someone on the concrete below thought that was a good idea. Two guys with automatic weapons started shooting. It's not as easy when they are firing back, but I settled up against the railing and switched to single-shot then shut them up, right in the face. Two shots only. It was a hundred feet so it didn't count for much. I could have hit them in the face if I had thrown the bullets at them except that wouldn't have hurt as much.

We had nearly made it to the ground when three more guys burst out of the back door of the warehouse, now well in flames, coughing and swearing. They didn't get far. Back to automatic. Techo Mick rose further in my estimation as he pulled up at the gate with a screech and the door of the van flew open. We were less than thirty seconds out of there as the police and fire engines came screaming past us on their way to the burning warehouse.

"That was quick," Joan observed, regarding the police and fire brigade. I was too busy checking myself for bullet holes to listen.

"Doogie called them," Mick clarified, turning to look at us both for effect, "just as he saw you go in."

The realisation was inescapable.

"So, Doogie is playing some bullshit game aiming to get us hung," Joan said.

The three of us were back at my place.

"And clean up his arms dealers at the same time." Thank you, Mick.

"You got the tapes of their chatter, Mick? Doogie's' chatter? I would like a listen, if that's OK?"

Mick set up and pressed Play.

The tapes were unhelpful other than as insurance to demonstrate Doogie's involvement. Nonetheless, an unfortunate thought crept into my psychotic brain, something about what Doogie was not saying to his fellow *agents* and when he was not saying it.

"He's working for the other guys." No one knew what I meant. "Doogie. The other arms dealers." I paused for them to take in how smart I was, but they weren't buying it. "Why else would he be happy for us to shoot these guys up and then call the cops on us so we get the blame?"

"He's definitely Homeland Security," Joan piped up, "I had my lawyer friend check on him."

"He's moonlighting, probably with those two M.I.B. goons who probably aren't Homeland Security either." That struck a chord with me. "They looked dodgy, not public servants, more…public enemies. And, yeeeeeees…" the realisation of Doogie's deception washed over me, cleansing me of my sins, well at least one of my recent ones. "Of course. Saying the fat guy was an agent was bullshit just to get me on the defensive. He would never have passed the physical."

"They had a drone."

"Did they? Doogie said they did and Doogie's a lying prick."

"Maybe also a candidate, if you're right."

"Can your guy find out whether Doogie opened a case file on us at Homeland Security without, you know, making someone open a case file on us? If an agent was killed, the fat guy, I mean, it would be the biggest file they have, top priority. If he hasn't, and he has kept all this to himself, then he is a dirty little pompous prick of an arms dealer."

Mick was relaxing with a beer, searching the TV for a replay of the football game. "Any nuts?"

"I'll have my guy make the relevant enquiries, about Doogie, not the nuts," Joan said perfunctorily, more confident than she had been since I told her about my visit with Doogie.

"You're relieved, aren't you?" I said, stirring her. "Batgirl wouldn't give a shit about the cops."

"Shut up, arsehole. And, yes, that would be a good outcome if they weren't onto us and this guy is just one of the bad guys we are after."

"Hug it out?"

"Fuck off and get me a drink, and some nuts."

Her relief was palpable.

The following morning, approaching midday, Joan was banging on my door having got up in the lift without being buzzed in, as usual. She probably kept keys. I had just got back from the gym and was all sweaty, not having showered yet.

"You're a fucking genius, you know that?" she said with a huge, beaming smile as she strode confidently into my apartment. I had never seen her so happy. God, she looked beautiful.

"Doogie a baddie?" I asked, having already gleaned the answer from her demeanour.

"Yeah. Ain't life grand?"

I nearly got a kiss, I think.

"Your guy didn't ruffle any feathers, did he, when he asked about the case file?"

"Didn't need to go to him. I went through official channels."

"Are you sure? Our file might be classified."

"A friend of mine at the FBI confirmed it, a very senior friend. So, yes, I'm sure. He did not open a case file on us at Homeland Security. They have no idea what he is up to. He is doing all of this on his own time."

"So, let's whack him and be done with it." I went over to the fridge to get some water.

"No, don't you see?"

"Joan, this guy is dangerous and dirty. Water?"

"No, thanks. This is the first time anyone from that organisation has popped their head up."

"So, let's take the shot."

"Yeah, but he knows where to find the rest of them and that's more than I have ever had, thanks to you."

"He knows where to find us, too, don't forget, think about that." I took a swig of my water. "If he finds out that we are onto him he'll come after us."

"But he doesn't know, and that gives us a head start. We did a lot of damage last night, there are eight or nine dead guys, according to CSI. The final count's not in yet. Grenades and exploding munitions will do that to a head count. I'm surprised the whole place didn't go up. I would have been pissed if any of those firemen got hurt."

"How much did they find in the ammo dump?"

"We got some pretty dangerous munitions off the black market, including that Manshit you mentioned."

"MANPADs."

"They had four cases of that stuff."

"There wouldn't be an airliner in this country that was safe with those in the wrong hands."

"Well, they don't give a shit who the customer is as long as they have the money. Doogie's going to be getting a lot of thank-you notes from his people and I'm not talking about Homeland Security. The call to the police last night was an anonymous tipoff. For him, we must be the ultimate resource. Shoot up the opposition and, if it gets too hot, he just drops us in it and we have no traceable connection back to his arms-dealing mates. He's got a win-win."

"He already dropped us in it last night."

"Yeah, but that was before he knew how much damage we can do. He thought we were a pair of amateurs."

"We are a pair of amateurs. So, let's whack him before he catches on and make it a lose-lose for him and his friends." That didn't make any sense. I needed a shower and a coffee.

"He's going to keep pointing these guys out to us and we're going to keep hitting them, if there's any left, and eventually he'll lead us to his own people and we'll hit them too, it's perfect."

That was too complex a line of thought for me to follow but, on first hearing, it didn't sound perfect.

"Shower time, there's water and juice in the fridge, make yourself at home."

"So, now that we've got Mick on board, I say we use him to get a listen in on who Doogie's talking to."

We had reconvened at the coffee shop around the corner from my apartment. I was much fresher and happier having showered and finished my first cup of coffee. Now, at least, I could follow what she was saying.

"So, we give Doogie a reason to contact his people," Joan continued, still somewhat frenetically. "I can feed him some bullshit through my guy at Homeland Security and we can return the favour, so to speak."

"Look, Joan, every time you say 'Homeland Security,' my arsehole puckers," I whined, "I don't want to play Doogie's stupid games anymore." I think I actually stomped my foot. I certainly fell back in my chair and signalled the waitress for another coffee. "Let's just whack him and go catch a movie. It's Saaatuuurday."

"You're a big girl sometimes, you know that? I want these guys and this is our best chance to get them. Doogie's the ultimate resource. If we kill him, we close that door."

I didn't answer her; I didn't want to. Last night scared the living shit out of me and once the booze wore off from the after-party, I didn't sleep at all and I didn't even get a root for my trouble. Yeah, that's right, I haven't grown up yet. But, boy, did I need one. All that adrenalin. I used to go along to anti-whatever rallies when I was at college because I knew everyone got worked up so by the end of the day sex was inevitable. I was going to help Joan, of course, I just wasn't done whingeing yet.

"So, you done whingeing?"

"No. You're crazy doing all of this, you know."

"I'm crazy…me?" she said incredulously.

"Don't look at me. Insanity is my Muse."

"It's probably more likely a brain tumour."

"*It's not a tumour,*" I said, trying to imitate Arnold Schwarzenegger.

"Oh, Christ, is that from a movie? We are going to have to make it a rule that you don't use movie references when I talk to you, alright?"

"I could say, *get fucked,*" I responded playfully but truthfully.

"Where would that be from?" she said sarcastically.

"…Scarface. They say the word *fuck* 207 times in that film. I was quoting Michelle Pfeiffer."

"Michelle Pfeiffer doesn't swear."

"It's not the most prolific film for swearing but if you measure it by the number of times *fuck* was used per minute of film, about once every two minutes, it probably gets the gold. I think *Wolf of Wall Street* had more *fucks* in total, though, but it was a longer film."

"How…no, let me rephrase that, why do you know this stuff?"

"It comforts me. I was going to use *say hello to my little friend* at the warehouse, but I forgot because I was scared shitless."

"That phrase meaning…? No, I don't want to know where that is from or what it means."

"Scarface, again." She gave me a disgusted look. "He was referring to his machine gun," I continued under my breath.

"I said, I didn't want to know. I've already asked Mick to set up the surveillance. I'm going to talk to my guy Monday to feed through the intel to Homeland Security."

"I keep hearing this shit about your guy. Having someone else know what we are up to doesn't fill me with happiness. Tell me a bit more about this lawyer mentor guy of yours. He's got the drop on all of us, you know that, right?"

"Dad's friend since primary school. Smart, loyal, and extremely well-connected. He's been a great help to me through a difficult time after my father died."

"Are you going to tell me his name?"

She hesitated.

"I guess I owe you that and more. Lucas Mandrell."

"Mandrell and Thompson?"

"Yes. That it in the strictest of confidence."

"I can see what you mean when you say connected. So, you trust him?"

"Dad trusted him and, yes, so do I. He was the executor of Dad's will and oversees Travis Industries. He doesn't run it, there is a CEO, he just keeps an eye on it for me. I own it. He'll feed that intel through to his guy at Homeland Security, no questions asked."

"What, then World War Z".

"No zombies, just arms dealers with their brains blown out, assuming they show themselves."

"So, you know that movie reference?"

"Brad Pitt's in that movie."

"Got it."

"In fact, I'm up for a movie too if there is one with Brad Pitt in it."

"I'm sure we'll find something."

"Why do people fall in love?"

"It's Nature's way of getting back at us for fucking up the planet."

Jake and I had spread a jigsaw puzzle across my dining table that night after dinner.

"No, seriously."

"I am serious. Nature is forcing us to procreate, that's all. It's a raw deal and She knows it. She's a real comedian, that one, and She's laughing her head off."

The mood was relaxed. We were both happy to work our way through the puzzle as therapy, after a good dinner. I had cooked us both a steak. I know a lot about cooking steaks. I had slow-baked a couple of potatoes in their jackets to go with it, sour cream, chives, beautiful. Jake had helped and I liked that, a lot. Men with fire and steaks bring out a deep, primeval satisfaction. I had a Scotch, my fifth, it had been a long process, he had what was left of his orange juice.

"Did you love my mother?"

"We never got that far."

"Were you going to?"

"She was a beautiful woman. You never know. Love just happens, like a brain aneurism."

"You're in love with that detective, right?"

"Where did that come from?"

"Just the way you speak about her."

"Unfortunately, I suspect you're correct."

"Why, unfortunately?"

"It's not mutual. She has a detective in her life, too."

"Bummer."

"It's probably for the best. She's rich and beautiful and I'm...a lawyer."

"Fuck that," Jake flicked a piece of the puzzle he was examining back into the pile, "she'd be lucky to have you. You have got to stop putting yourself down. You're a good guy."

"Thanks, mate." I was being disingenuous, but I don't think he noticed.

"Why don't you correct me when I swear? Mrs Harper always does."

"You have to be careful around your parents and women generally, but it's okay with your mates."

"They're not my parents."

"They're doing the job, aren't they?"

"I guess."

"Respect that."

"I want to live with you."

"We've been through that. They are not going to allow a single man to adopt a twelve-year-old boy."

"Why?"

"You may as well have it straight…because they assume I might abuse you."

"Like, more than I already have been?"

"Like, sexually."

"Oh…shit, eewee, that's just wrong…"

"They don't know that we know that, it looks odd, we're not related. The law is an ass."

"Tell them how it really is."

"I'm going to try."

"Hit 'em if they don't understand."

"You know I can't do that, that's not how this works.

"Have you hit anyone lately?"

"Fuck, Jake, what is this, the Inquisition?"

"Have you?"

"Did you read this morning's paper?" Exasperated.

"No." He grabbed his phone excitedly to look it up.

"Top story."

"Fuck, that was you. Jesus, man, you are Batman. How many did you get? Who are they or were they?"

"Arms traffickers. Some of Joan's friends."

"Do they know it was you?"

"Their opposition does. Part of an intricate plan Joan has worked out to flush them all out into the open."

"So you can shoot them."

"Or them us." He didn't like that answer. "What, you think this is a one-way street? You shoot at people, chances are they're going to shoot back at some point." He didn't like that answer, either. "I've been telling you this hitman stuff is a dangerous business, not much future in it."

"I don't want…"

"Me, neither."

"Jim, can I ask you something?"

The look I gave him said *what have you been doing for the last five hours?*

"Why do you shoot people?"

"Well, I don't shoot the good people. There ain't that many of them and we need the ones we got."

"So, why do you shoot the bad guys?"

"Because they're bad. There is this pain that life gives you if things don't turn out the way they should, in part because the shitheads outnumber us. You see, people do things to you that make you sad. Sometimes, it's even things that the shitheads go out of their way to do, that's the worst. It would be easier for them in some cases if they didn't do it… at all. But they do because they are miserable bastards and you end up with this choice to do nothing and die or do something and they die instead."

"But, it's wrong to kill people."

"There's a song in *John Wick* by Marilyn Manson and Tyler Bates: *we're killing strangers so that we don't kill the ones that we love.*"

"Movie references."

"Keep up."

"It is illegal, killing people, right?"

"*What threatens our souls? It is forbidden to kill. Therefore, all murders are punished unless they kill in large numbers and to the sound of trumpets.*"

"You got me."

"Voltaire. In this country, the morality of killing is not so clear. We love the guns, oh yeah, the guns…and the violence. We revere the guys in the movies who snap their necks or break the other guys' arms or both."

"I feel like snapping necks, sometimes."

"We are taught from a very young age that violence is the answer to any problem, both personally and collectively as a nation. Over thirty-three thousand people get deliberately shot and killed every year in the US. Over one-hundred-thousand gun-related casualties each year, over three-hundred-million guns in the community."

"Like the Wild West."

"We are past the tipping point when it comes to guns. If you stopped all gun sales today you could never get all the guns that are already out there or stop illegal acquisition. It would be as useful as Prohibition. The logical solution is to arm everyone…like the Wild West, to make it a fair fight. *Passive targets,* as the terrorists call them, need to become less passive so they won't be targets at all."

"My history teacher says they didn't all carry guns in the West, like in the movies."

"They may not have strapped them on their hip, but they always had one to hand. It was a tool. You know, snakes or the occasional jihadist Native American. The gunfight at the OK Corral was all about open carry rules. Earp was trying to enforce a new Dodge City ordinance preventing open carry and slaughtered three people trying to disarm them. Go figure that out."

"So, we should open carry."

"It sure would solve a lot of disputes quickly or, maybe, prevent them. You know the old mutual destruction threat."

"So, violence is a valid response?"

"I grew up confused about that issue, mixed signals from my parents. They would belt me for getting into fights, there's some irony for you. Some people say turn the other cheek and others who would call you a coward for doing it."

"I would sure like to get clear instructions."

"I've done both, walked away and stood and fought. I think back with more satisfaction on the stand-and-fight situations. I wouldn't be a good mugging target now, that's for sure. Someone would get hurt if they tapped me on the shoulder and asked for my wallet. There is a lot to be said for the days when a boy knew what he had to do to become a man. Right or wrong, we had clarity, which relieved you of a lot of frustration over what choices you should make when confronted. God knows, teenage boys worry themselves to death over what their peers think of them. That issue worried me terribly."

"Now, it's fight, right?"

"That is the choice that I've made, yes. You'll have to make up your own mind, but consider it and make a choice. Don't fuck around with it. Feminism made us toss all the old rules out, the rules that a man could follow, but didn't replace them with new rules. We got in touch with our gentler side and lost sight of what it took to be a man."

"So, you don't have a feminine side?"

"Oh, I've got one. I just don't know whose side she's on and I don't let her do the fighting for me."

"Fighting and killing are two different things."

"Well, sure, maybe. A punch can kill as quickly as a bullet."

"How can you be sure about your targets?"

"Bitter experience."

"What if someone not so smart decides to do what you are doing?"

"*Ah! There's the rub*. Hopefully, they would get shot."

"That one was Shakespeare. I never understood why it was OK to kill some gook with Napalm but it wasn't OK to lay into some prick at school."

"Well, it's citizen of Vietnam, not gook, no racism here, there are some clear instructions for you."

"Sure."

"I'm serious, racism is just poisonous bullshit, alright?"

"OK, don't shoot me, I got it."

"War, of course, is the case in point. Our community's solution to international disputes. And, at home, the State kills people. It's mostly intellectually or socially disabled misfits with a needle in a viewing room filled with the assembled haters, so it's not as if life is sacrosanct. I think it is difficult for a society to assert that an individual can't kill anybody when they kill people themselves. Then, of course, there are *House Rules*. If someone uninvited steps inside your house, in most states, you can legally shoot the fuck out of them. Empty the clip, you may as well. If you get 'em in the yard as they are leaving, just make sure to drag 'em back into the house. The people I kill have broken into my life like thieves. Fuck 'em."

"So, back to the Wild West."

"Sure. Almost all states allow open carry now and in those who don't allow it with the relevant permit, it's concealed carry they seemed to be worried about, go figure that one out."

"It's just not a fashionable accessory."

"Yeah, but wait till Armani gets hold of it or Gucci. Screw handbags. A holster for your piece with a slot for your mobile phone."

"The pop stars will lead the way."

"Anything for some press coverage. People should take responsibility for the damage they do to other people even if they are using modern ways of doing damage, business or internet or double-dealing. Let's see them fuck with you on the internet if they know you carry a .38 around with you. Go ahead, post it, *make my day*. Let's see what your brains look like spread all over your new laptop. The hackers talk about imposing a *Life Ruin* on you as a penalty for doing something they don't like, a .38 can sure ruin your life."

"Life Ruin?"

"You know, they fuck with your phone, spam you, hack your credit accounts. Well, brain matter on the monitor qualifies, for sure. It would be a better world if that was the rule, be responsible for what you say or do, including those internet fuckers, because there will be consequences. In the good old days, and I'm not talking about the Wild West, if someone insulted you, then you would go get the guns or the swords and have it out. If you had the guns on you, then you could sort it out then and there."

"Some of the guys you shoot aren't armed."

"Well, if they are acting like arseholes then they should have armed themselves."

"Clint Eastwood in *Unforgiven*, sort of. Love that movie."

"About time you got one. Besides, it's hard to say if they are armed. The guys at the warehouse were shooting back. There's nothing wrong with shooting first, just ask Burt Lancaster. If they have knowingly fucked you up then they should arm themselves. *Trespass not on his solitude* for yee will be trespassed upon."

"I don't think Emerson would approve of you bastardising his essay on educating children."

"Smartarse. I like that you know that. That's worth two points, so we're square. I like the cadence of that sentence, so I stole it. Been reading, haven't we?"

"Only the good stuff."

"I would have thought his more recent work would be more your speed, you know, *Where's Waldo.*"

"Yours would be more like *Wreck it Ralph?*"

"That last one is a little too obvious but I like the way you think, boy, working in the movie reference. And you can keep up and stay on point, Ralph Waldo Emerson, very good."

"It's you who's going to have to learn to keep up, my old friend."

"Hey, no ageism either."

"You need someone to keep you in shape, guide you."

"And you're up to it, sensei? You're twelve."

"And you're lost."

I guess it is important for the preservation of the species that twelve-year-olds are optimistic, so I acquiesced.

"Range tomorrow?"

"Sure."

CHAPTER EIGHT

Whatever Joan now had in mind was going to be perilous. These traffickers had been smart enough to stay out of the limelight for years yet build, according to her, a very large and successful business. That meant that they were organised and connected and, more importantly, they had professional personnel and all of that added up to trouble. I understood her desire to make right what they had done to her father, but the problem with many such propositions is that making it right often leads to making another wrong. I started to think that I was finally going to get what I deserved. For the first time since primary school, I wondered whether there was some kind of accounting for your deeds in this life, karmic or spiritual or even double-entry, someone or something that divvies up what each of us gets according to what each of us does? That was now a truly important question for me, compared with the *Hitchhikers Guide to The Galaxy's* question of what *is the answer to life?* 42 is as good a number as any, thank you to the mice for divining the solution. At a deeper level, it is an issue that haunts us all, including the question of whether the proceeds of your deeds, good or bad, are distributed fairly in the next life if there is one. I have a great deal of respect for people who follow a religion with a God who preoccupies himself or herself with that very personal task. If there is such cosmic tallying, then there appears to be a lot of people with their fingers on the scale. Why would any God allow certain people to fix that game?

I watched a documentary once about a nun working in Sudan. There was only one Sudan back then and only one nun in this documentary. She was trying to introduce fertility controls into local tribal communities as well as working to stop domestic violence. She was a woman in a misogynistic community, God bless her, whoever God is for her. She had little or no funding and was selfless. She operated alone and my impression was that even her religious affiliates didn't know she was there. If every dollar that goes into charities could go to people like her the world would be a better place. She deserves to be rewarded and some would say that our nun will get what she deserves in the afterlife. But that is as relevant to me, and I assume to all poverty-ravaged Sudanese, as what happens to my pot plants after I'm dead. I suggest her Sudanese friends wouldn't be spending too much time thinking about the next life, more likely they would be counting the seconds until this one ended.

Even so, I do believe in karma, but apparently it only works if you believe in it and not as a ubiquitous universal force. I am certain we all put out and receive perceptibly good or bad vibes and it is an absolute fact that we attract our fears. Whether the two are the same I don't know, but if you worry about something intensely enough, I know you will wake up one morning and have to confront it. In the end, does karma create a process where good attracts good, and evil attracts evil? If all the brownie-point-scoring in your life does aggregate, who or what counts it and if that is indeed happening, why are they doing such a shit job of the math? Why are the arseholes ruling the world? The absence of an answer to that question is why I decided to do my own math and enact my own karma. That all sounds horribly like obfuscation. I know self-justification is the preoccupation of the small-minded but, in my case, I don't care. It is what it is. I told you that already and arseholes do really, you know, rule the world.

It was that frame of mind that caused me this morning to check my Belize bank account balance to see what I had left. I was thinking that my days as a hired killer might be over now that I knew that there was no Council, just Joan and her friends. I was wondering whether I should have sent that money to Clara but then I saw that there was a new credit entry for $450,000 from the usual source. I rang Joan to ask her what that was and she sheepishly suggested we have dinner that night to discuss it and our plans given that the next few steps were going to be hazardous.

"It's your money."

"Joan, it doesn't feel right, me taking money from you," I said, having got very used to my surroundings. This night, I was surrounded by the best restaurant in Chicago.

"Nine guys at $50,000 each. Nine was the final count from the warehouse."

"You were there, too, Joan. Who says who got who?"

"Come on, you got the guys in the yard. That's five, and I suspect the grenades got the rest. I can't shoot straight with those fucking AK-47s."

"The gas ejection does push the gun around, especially firing multiple bursts, but I do know you can shoot." As I complimented her on her ability to kill people, it struck me that this wasn't your usual date night conversation. Then I started to wonder whether this was a date. "I'm not comfortable now that I know the money is coming out of your pocket."

"Do you have any idea how much Travis Industries is worth? Shitloads, with a capital SHIT."

I hesitated to respond, betraying my desire to keep the money. Half a million bucks would buy a lot of whiskey if I was headed back to my hole in the ground.

"You see, you hesitated. You do want the money and I would be unhappy if you didn't take it. We had a deal. So, I'll have to go easy in fashion week in Paris this year, so what. Truth is, it's not a lot of money to me."

"Where are we going with this, Joan?"

She looked perplexed because she thought I knew the Plan and then embarrassed as she started to think I was back on the relationship bandwagon, which I was, and screaming *yee-hah* to the horses.

"Well, we are going to find these guys and we are going to end them."

She ignored the personal undertone of my question. I watched her eyes evade mine. I was in a weird way pleased to be having an effect, any effect, on such a beautiful woman, but it wasn't the effect I wanted.

"And after we end them?"

"I go back to my job and try not to shoot the bad guys unless I'm allowed to, and you..."

"And me?"

"And you retire early to Belize or wherever you want, given the money you will earn."

There it was. She was already using the money as a substitute for anything more substantial in our relationship than my services. That took the wind out of my sails. I was just the hired help because…I had just agreed to be. I sat back in my chair, prepared to leave it at that but not wanting to. Instead, I settled for calling the waiter over and asking him to bring the most expensive bottle of wine that they had on the premises, not knowing what it was nor how much it cost. Very James Bond.

"The wine's on you, to celebrate our arrangement."

She didn't flinch. In this place, asking for their best bottle of wine was dangerous. It could have had the price tag of a small house. I'm not saying it would be worth a small house, just that it might have that price tag. Luckily, they must have been out of the really good stuff because it only cost six grand. Yeah, that's right, *only*. And it tasted the same as the one we had just finished that cost sixty bucks. I'm not going to ask the forgiveness of every pretentious wine aficionado that ever lived for expressing that opinion. Yeah, yeah, settle down. I've tried the Premier Grand Cru French reds to great delight but six grand, pass. Ordering the wine was a knee-jerk reaction from the expensive prostitute in the room: me. I had always had an unanalysed affiliation with prostitutes, though I had never hired one. I assumed it was something from a previous life but now I knew why; it was because I was one. There was silence while the parties evaluated the ground just staked out. For me, it was like watching a puppy drown as I saw the prospect of our embryonic sexual relationship die while Joan pigeon-holed me as accounts payable. James Bond would not have cared. I have no idea why that mattered because I was the opposite of James Bond, except for the body count. Maybe I should buy a tuxedo. Wearing one might have improved the taste of the wine.

"So, what's on tomorrow?" I asked.

The banality of that question seemed to appropriately punctuate the mood at the table. It was dismissive and I meant it to be.

"Well, hopefully, we get something from Mick." She didn't care that it was dismissive. "I already laid the bait. We might get something tonight. Then we can figure out how to expose these guys enough so that we can get at them."

I wasn't listening. I had decided I was going to quit. Her indifference was killing me, so she could shoot her own bad guys from now on. It was a schoolboy tactic, for sure, but appropriate. A hissy fit was definitely called for, I thought. I formed the words in my head but noticed I wasn't saying anything. I let it wash over me and allowed it to be replaced by concern for her safety if she decided to proceed alone. Yeah, that's right, concern for her, not the money.

"I want a raise." I wanted to punish her.

"Fuck off."

That seemed definitive.

"Ok. What about some more information?"

"Like what?"

"Why is this so important that you would risk your own life or freedom? I know you loved your dad, but frankly, that doesn't seem to be enough."

"Can you hear yourself? Just remind me what you were doing when I found you."

"Yeah, but you're…you."

"You really have to do something about your self-esteem issues, Jim. You're a good-looking guy, smart, a great shot, probably the best in the country, and you've got a hell of a straight left. What is your problem?"

I was stunned.

"What, you find me attractive?"

"I didn't say that."

"You do find me attractive."

There was a revealing silence.

"What the hell are we doing, Joan? Let's get the fuck out of here. Let's go get that Ferrari of yours and put this shit in the rear-view. I got so much I want to talk to you about."

"That's not going to happen. It ain't over. My father was a good man. When my mother left, it was just him and me and he did a good job of looking after me. We weren't just close, we were friends. He got in the way of a deal these guys had lined up and they killed him for it."

"And the guy who set it up?"

"Not sure he set it up. He was arrested but they didn't have enough on him or enough to chase down his associates. That's the way these guys do business, from the shadows. That all made me realise how pathetic I was fighting crime with a badge and a gun I wasn't allowed to use when the system could never get the job done. These guys arm terrorists and get away with it because they can afford the right lawyer or the right hitman. I know you adore hackneyed phrases but *it's me or them*."

"I guess that means it's us or them."

Despite my return of serve on the cliché, the look she gave me made me forgive her for not running away with me. I was in love with her and there was no going back. It wasn't the money or the terrorists; it was her. She had lifted me out of a hole and now it was my turn to help her, even though I know I wasn't good enough to either save her or be her equal. I got lucky at the warehouse, but from here it was going to take more than a little luck and a lot more courage than I could bring to bear. The problem with self-doubt is that it leaks into everything. I wasn't just a lousy lawyer and husband; I was a lousy hitman as well.

What is it about relationships that makes us crave them when we don't have them and crave the opposite when we do? Even the sincerest loner will confess in a moment of honesty that having someone else on your side makes a disproportionate amount of difference when considering the question of whether you are a worthwhile human being. When I was living with Clara, I had persuaded myself I didn't need that second vote as my marriage atrophied. But I confess, I miss it now. The misfortune of being in an adult relationship when you aren't yet an adult is that it becomes part of your emotional furniture. I was twenty-one when I married Clara. Her abandonment of our relationship represented an amputation of something that had been embedded in me as I tried to grow up with her. Teenagers should never marry because when they inevitably lose that relationship, it brings them to a screaming halt in their development. An intrinsic part of what has become their adult self is taken away, whether it's one year or twenty years. In my case, I now had to start again as a teenager, become a fully formed adult first, then take on a long-term relationship. We parted ways with Clara when I was forty-two, God forbid it happened at sixty, then I would have had nowhere to run and no time to rebuild.

It often happens in a marriage that he ends up in the shed outside, shouting obscenities and drinking while she tidies the house, fulfilling her stereotypical wifely duties. When that was inflicted on me, I became psychotic and convinced myself that I could live in the same house with her as a dead relationship stank up our lives. During that time, I focussed on the past rather than what could happen in the future. Many of the skills I had acquired at great cost had also atrophied: my education, my license to practice law, my ability at the gym, and my social skills, for what they were worth. All had withered in concert with my relationship with Clara. I still wanted to text her about my feelings and sometimes did, usually drunk. I hate the immediacy of social media. I think we are all guilty of projecting our desires onto our partners and often they reflect it back to fulfil the demands of a society designed around couples. If your partner is alert to that social contract, they pretend to be who you wish them to be.

I never understood where the line was with Clara, where she finished and my perception of her started. In the end, I guess it didn't matter because relationships are just a state of mind. In a relationship, you must let go of the failures and the stereotypes that society prescribes for those failures. I'm no expert, but that observation seems inescapable. Learn and move on, the learning is optional but moving on is compulsory if you want to stay together. But what you don't need is someone constantly reminding you that you didn't measure up calling you a liar or a cheat or another form of failure. Be aware, they only play the cheater card if they don't want the relationship any more. You cheat to get out and they eat biscuits and refuse sex for the same reason. *Once a biscuit eater, always a biscuit eater.* Your partner apparently doesn't have to provide love and affection or renewal in the relationship, you see. It is alright to just get fat and ignore you and their position as the legitimate wife will be protected by social rules like *no cheating*. The truth of the matter is that such lazy people, male or female, deserve to get cheated on and they need to be discarded preferably before it gets to the cheating part. Just don't wait until you are sixty to figure that all out is all I'm saying.

It's withering when your partner uses those things you screwed up in the past as an excuse to deny you the engagement you deserve in the present. It saddens me when I realised how long it took me to see that for what it was with Clara, poison. I used to think that Hollywood was to blame, that it was their romantic notion of perfect love that kept couples apart once one or both had inevitably screwed up. But it is really just about whether both partners are willing to move on after failures and rebuild the relationship. However, you need to watch out for reassurance from your partner made under duress. You need to make sure that your partner is truly willing to forgive and forget because one of the characteristics of poisoners like Clara is that they are always up for more misery. They hang on to it and drag your mistakes out every now and then like a dead cat to stink up the house. Put those people in the rear-view as soon as you can find your car keys regardless of the value you place on the relationship. My problem was I waited ten years too long and that nearly, perhaps actually, drove me insane.

Fortunately, I didn't get too much time to study those issues discussed with Joan at dinner as I looked through the informative lens provided by the bottom of the whiskey bottle because by morning, we had a nibble from Mick's surveillance. Some lawyer in New York saying stuff to Doogie that could definitely be interpreted in a bad way. What is it with lawyers? They were setting up a meeting between Doogie and one of his informants and some other guy he referred to as *Chook*. Other than being an Australian euphemism for chicken, that name wasn't familiar to me, nor did it fill me with fear and trepidation. Why would someone want to call themselves a chicken unless they didn't know the vernacular? Gigantor or Big Dick or Stone Cold, maybe, but Chook? Anyway, Chook and Doogie and his informant, referred to as D1 in the telephone conversation, were going to meet that night at a diner in Chicago and we all felt that a listen-in would be appropriate.

Mike had done the thing he does and from our van we had good visibility through the windows of the diner and surround sound provided by a sensitive directional microphone on the roof of his van. Mick had disguised the microphone in a circular air conditioner casing with vents running around its exterior that gave it 360-degree rotation. It had the added benefit of not being detectable on a local bug sweep inside the restaurant. Mick knew his stuff. All we needed was the participants, so we chatted and waited. Joan had been called into a raid at her precinct so it was just me and Mick sitting uncomfortably in the back of the transit van with just enough headroom to sit but not stand. I looked at an impressive array of monitors and lite buttons, some of which were blinking. It seemed comfortingly comprehensive to my eye.

"She's out of your league, you know."

I guess Mick wasn't as socially inept as I had made him out to be.

"Who, Joan? You noticed."

"She's beautiful. You're a lawyer."

"I get it, thanks"

"No, you won't."

Smartarse.

"You married, Mick, girlfriend?"

"I'm a geek, second only to lawyers in the sexual food chain."

"Second from the bottom, you mean."

"I like the ladies, but they don't like me. I've considered the guys, but you have to be a homosexual, apparently."

"Yeah, that's a state of being, not a preference. What do you think of all this? Do you think we can crack these guys?"

"Sure."

"No, you don't." He gave me a look of ambivalence and shrugged as if he was happy to tell me whatever I wanted to hear. He stopped what he was fiddling with and looked at me. "And if we do crack them? I don't think being a good shot is going to be enough."

"Yeah, that's what I figured. So, where do you stand?"

"I'm no crime fighter, if that's what you mean. I'm the tech guy. If this gets ugly, I'll find the nearest exit."

"You were pretty quick to pick us up at the warehouse."

"You forget the warehouse gate was on my way out. Don't expect me to come in after you."

"This is supposed to be a big organisation. Successful enough for us to assume they know what they are doing and well-connected enough to have Doogie and some New York lawyer involved. Sadly, I don't think whacking a couple of them from my truck is going to satisfy Joan. She wants to shut them down."

"Well, good luck with that. I can tell you the *where* and perhaps the *who,* but I can't tell you the *how* or help you do it. What if this is just the local branch..."

"Shut up, here we go."

Two guys sat down with Doogie at the corner booth in the diner. I guessed that D1 was the guy who looked like an A1 drug addict. Chook was all Armani suit and immaculate grooming, early sixties perhaps, fit, good-looking I think, I'd have to ask Mick.

"You got 'em?" I asked in a whisper.

"You don't have to whisper and, yes, I got 'em. Take a listen."

Mick flicked a switch and the audio played in the van.

Chook: That show at the warehouse drew an awful lot of attention from the authorities.

Doogie: Yeah, but it has basically shut the Mustafa brothers down. It will take them at least a year to put their American operation back together. We can charge whatever we like in a monopoly, right?

Chook: Your guys swept the diner here for bugs?

Doogie: This afternoon.

Chook: Davis, you're sure your brother got the details on that next shipment, correct?

"I guess that's where the D1 comes from, his brother is probably D2," I suggested to Mick, "maybe R2D2."

"Shut up."

D1 (Davis): Yeah, my brother says that the info is good.

Chook: And your brother wouldn't lie to us.

D1 (Davis): He knows what's at stake.

Doogie: I'm not sure I want to keep using the dynamic duo for this hit-and-run shit."

Chook: Why not? It's perfect. They get it done, that's for sure. They sure made a mess of that warehouse. When you're finished with them, just arrest them. I've even used Joan to clean up some of my shit.

Chook started to laugh out loud.

Chook: That stupid little crime-fighting bitch has got no idea what's going on. It's hilarious.

He continued to be amused with himself.

"Are you recording this?" I asked Mick.

"Sure."

Chook: I'll let you know if they're onto you. Right now, they are shitting themselves thinking that Homeland Security has got 'em by the balls. I had Joan in my office the other day asking me what her options were. She's as misguided as her father.

"Ah, Mr Mandrell, I presume."

"Who?"

"A very dear friend of Detective Travis and her father in whom she confides everything. You're recording the visual as well, right?"

"Sure. I got an SLR here if you'd like a couple of high-res photos."

"Do that. Mandrell and Davis. Joan is going to have trouble believing this and it might help us track down this Davis guy."

Mick clambered over me to go to the front window of the truck with his camera.

Doogie: You sure you got Batgirl under control? Because I wouldn't want them turning their attention to us.

Chook (Mandrell): It's under control.

D1 (Davis): So, I'm telling my brother we got a deal, right?

Chook (Mandrell): Yes. Saturday night.

Mandrell passed Davis a package that I assumed was a payoff. Mandrell was obviously the money man and apparently not happy to have anyone else handle it. That might end up being his first mistake. I guessed that was what had brought him to the diner personally and, in so doing, into the open.

They all got up to leave. I slumped back in my chair and wondered what Joan had told her lifelong friend. I assumed everything. She had used her own resources to check on whether we were under investigation by Homeland Security, that much I knew. That was why Mandrell was still under the impression that we were afraid of Doogie, but it was pure luck that she hadn't wanted to bother Mandrell with that enquiry. If he knew that we knew Doogie was a bad guy, my story would probably end here.

"They didn't say where the location was on Saturday night, did they?"

"No."

"Let's stay on Davis. I think we know enough about the other two, at least enough to cry ourselves to sleep tonight."

"We got a problem with this Mandrell guy?"

"I'm going to say yes," I said in a strained voice, ducking my head as I crouched to waddle toward the front of the van and get into the passenger's seat.

Mick started the van and we waited to follow Davis.

Later that night, I printed off the photos from the meeting at the diner and placed them in a manila folder on my coffee table. Mick had gone home in a huff after I teased him about losing Davis just one block from the diner. Joan was perusing the file with the AV of the meeting running on my television. I could see she was devastated, mechanical in her movements, pale and traumatised. She kept picking up the photos to flick through them before putting them down again to listen to the video, rewinding it to the bit where Mandrell laughed at her. I think she was trying to find some reason to believe that Mandrell wasn't involved. There was none.

She switched the video off and threw the remote onto the chair opposite so hard it bounced back onto the coffee table with a clatter and then onto the floor, the batteries flew everywhere as she fell back onto the lounge, covering her face with her hands and groaning as she rubbed her eyes.

"Want a drink?"

"Sure," she said, uncovering her face and sitting up. She started to run her hands up and down her thighs. "I'm starting to see why you drink. What the fuck is this guy's PROBLEM?" she said, her voice rising to a near scream. "How much money does one person need? My father went to school with this...PRICK. He must have known him for forty years."

I said nothing. She wasn't talking to me. Besides, I had nothing to offer her about identifying arseholes before they get you. I did, however, know how to fix the problem, if she was interested. Well, maybe not the problem, but certainly the arsehole. I could probably get it done in the morning if she wanted.

"Here," I gave her a Scotch and she finished it in one swallow, so I gave her mine and went back to the bar to pour myself another. "Let's whack him and call it square. You got your guy." I sat down opposite her thinking that was pretty good advice.

"That's your solution to everything, isn't it?"

"Not everything, just things of this nature."

"What did he mean when he said that I had cleaned up some of his shit?"

"I assume one or more of the guys I hit for you were chosen by him for reasons that were commercial, not altruistic. I assume he played you. I assume that..."

"Alright, alright, I get it." She stood; here it comes. "This guy knows everything that I have been up to. I relied on him for support and he's been playing me." She started to pace.

"And, probably, he had something to do with having your father killed."

That made her stop pacing.

"Why would you say that? Why?"

"Were you listening to what he said about your father? He is up to his neck with those guys. Your father got in his way."

"So, you think he's running that show?"

"Not enough info to have a view on it. He's no mug, so I assume he's there or there abouts. Money man, partner, don't know, maybe he's the boss. You need to be more than a lawyer to run an illegal international arms-dealing business. You need to be something a lot worse, a salesman. Can you remove him from Travis Industries?"

"Sure, sure, I own the shares, so I have ultimate control. I can't remember what is in his contract. He drafted it, so it's probably pretty good for him. I never read it."

"You never read it?"

"Fuck off." She wasn't quite ready for my critique of her business practices.

"If you fire him, he will know something's up. But fuck knows what he's doing with your company. I'm assuming you don't."

"I pay Mandrell as non-executive Chairman, not CEO, why *buy a dog and bark yourself?*"

"Maybe to make sure it doesn't bite you. I know a guy, a forensic accountant. We should give him all your documents, including Mandrell's contract and recent board minutes and get him to give us the bad news. All the key company communications to see if he can get a feel for what this guy's been doing, on the quiet, of course. I assume you have all that stuff?"

She sat thinking, now not ranting.

"Sure. Dad gave me all his logins and I get copies of all key correspondence."

"Which you don't read." That got me another nasty look. "At the very least, my guy can come up with a way to extricate Mandrell from the business when the time is right. All the necessary paperwork. You have to protect that asset."

"You sound like a lawyer."

"As it happens…"

"You're right, though. Let's brief him in the morning."

"Who controls the money?"

"The usual financial controls are in place at the company. Mandrell is not a cheque signatory. Dad insisted on keeping him out of the money controls, he was very cautious. I can get into all the bank accounts online but, if I move money, they will know, except for my monthly stipend and yearly dividend."

"No money moving. A look-see is all we need." I stood. I think better when I stand because my brains are in my arse. Now I was pacing. "We need to find out if it's Mandrell running the arms business. If not him, then who?"

"How…?"

"So, you go to Mandrell in the morning and tell him you want to draw these guys out into the open by offering them a deal for the technology they were wanting to buy when they killed your father."

"He knows I would never sell them that."

"Yeah, but he thinks he's smarter than you and he thinks you're scared. So, he's going to set it up, but he will be planning to get you to go through with it so that he can dump the blame on you."

"So, I act like I trust him implicitly."

"You have, so far, so that shouldn't be hard for him to believe. He's going to be happy to set up a meeting for you with the head guy, which will be one of your conditions for doing a deal."

"But he'll know that I'll be wanting to whack the guy."

"Of course, but he won't know that we know what he's up to, if that makes sense. It certainly makes a hell of a difference. It was never going to be easy to get the head guy to show himself, but if Mandrell says he should meet you, and assures him that he has it all under control, then I think it will work, assuming they want this technology bad enough."

"Oh! They'll still want it."

"In a strange way, Mandrell has given us the key to getting at this guy."

"You know, he's just arrogant enough to buy it."

"It'll work, alright, but maybe Mandrell is smarter than us and will have all ends covered."

"Meaning?"

"Our goose is cooked, not theirs."

"Let's turn on the oven and find out who ends up basting who."

CHAPTER NINE

I never did find out exactly what it was that this clandestine group had attempted to steal from Travis Technology, save that it was important, and therefore, I assume, valuable. The size of that importance was underlined by the fact that the Head Researcher Joan said was implicated in the sale had died in a car accident a week after the police released him on bail. An unfortunate turn of events for him. I never bothered to seek further clarification because the exact nature of the technology and its function and relevance would most likely have been beyond my ability to understand. It had, however, piqued my interest in how the control and reporting systems were structured at Travis Technology and its parent Travis Industries. Internal personnel must have been involved in Mr Travis's murder as no alarm bells had been set off running up to his murder. I assumed the police had investigated who knew what and how they got access to information about the technology, but I had no idea how thorough they had been. There is looking and then there are specialists who look. Understanding the strengths and weaknesses of the corporate control systems might shed some light on who had the opportunity to access those secrets and whether there was any discernible link between them and Mandrell.

Joan had, of course, retained a seat on the company's Board, but only attended meetings irregularly. As it happened, there was one scheduled for the next day. I had convinced Joan to show up and propose a full system controls audit by a reputable firm. Not their current audit firm, in case Mandrell had a connection with them. She would propose that a fresh set of eyes was required. It was hardly something that an earnest Board member could refuse and most of them were reputable independent non-executive directors.

As it turned out, the audit proposal was passed unanimously. The firm Joan put forward was headed up by an old college friend of mine, Fred Thomas, the one who went to the Olympics. That firm had the added benefit of having no obvious links to Joan. This day, I was sitting in my old friend's meeting room with Joan, waiting to brief him on the audit.

"I spoke to Mandrell yesterday," Joan said, talking softly. The two of us were alone in the meeting room, seated at a twenty-four-seat boardroom table with views of the city and a bar at the end that would rival my own. Business must have been good.

"Speak in generalities, you never know who's listening in these places. Mick's ability to listen in from just about anywhere has put the wind up me."

"I told Mandrell I had come up with a plan to get these guys out in the open," she continued in a whisper. "After the occasional emotional outburst to prove my own instability, he bought into it. He'll be back to us tomorrow with a proposal."

"He admitted to knowing them?"

"No. He said he had contacts *who might know how to get to them.* Arsehole."

"Jim, how are you?" Fred said, as he entered the room with an assistant.

"You're looking well. This is my boss, Joan Travis, owner of Travis Industries. You're not swimming again, are you? You look very fit. I thought you would have had enough of that when you were training."

"Always swimming. Take a seat. My assistant, Jenny. I was troubled by your father's death, if I may say, Ms Travis, he was quite a loss."

"Thank you, please call me Joan."

"How can I help? Jim here tells me you want us to take a look at Travis Industries' control systems."

"Yeah, Fred, I need to be very blunt here," I took up the briefing because, I could be very blunt, here, "we need to know that this is confidential."

"Always."

"Always is not good enough," Joan emphasised. "We believe that there are problems afoot. Illegalities linked to my father's death. Can you assure us that this can be dealt with discreetly and in confidence?"

"Jenny, can you excuse us, please?" There was a pause whilst she left the room. "Whatever you need."

"What we need is for you to look into what is happening at Travis Industries, but we need it to look like a standard system and security audit," I took up the briefing again, "even produce your standard report, you know: change the locks, lengthen the passwords, and avoid concentrations of authority. The one you've got sitting on your PC that you give all your clients."

"Jim, we do more than…"

"Of course, of course, that's why we're here. It has to look basic, with all the standard questions being asked by all the standard auditors and with the standard report issued so that we don't scare the chickens. I have a list here of all the things we actually want you to look at and it boils down to this: who knew about the technology they tried to steal when Mr Travis was killed? Who could have actually accessed it? And who might they have been working for when the deal was proposed to steal it?"

"Tall order."

"No, it's not, not with our help. Stop selling and start listening, you will have carte blanche."

"And you have me," Joan chirped up, "I have access to everything and I mean everything, passwords, accounts, IP servers, the works. Dad ensured that I got access to all of the data spines, everything."

"And there's more," I continued, "there is one guy, and this can't go past you, strictly no one else hears about this, there's this one guy that we want you to look at. The guy Mr Travis put in charge of his legal affairs, the company Chairman, Lucas Mandrell."

"Jesus, you think Mandrell's involved? No wonder you're nervous. He's seriously connected. We need to be very careful here."

"Well, yea. Look, have you got the balls to do some real investigative auditing or do you only do tick-a-box?" Joan cut to the chase.

There was no answer, so I pushed.

"We need an answer."

"I'm in," Fred responded after serious thought. "That guy is an arsehole. I always wondered about him, so damned arrogant. And quick to litigate. If he thinks you're onto him, he'll push back... hard."

"Time to grab your balls, Fred," Joan added for colour.

"We want him out of the company regardless of what you find, so we need you to prepare paperwork to disconnect him from the position he holds. I'll give you a copy of his contract and you can start from there. But we only want to act when we are ready. Up until then, he can't know that you are looking at him or it will jeopardise something we have going."

"Ok. I'll stuff and mount him if you guys are right."

"We got that bit covered, Fred, we just need to know what he's been up to, what damage he may have caused and what or who he has put in place inside the company that might do us harm if...*we stuff and mount him.*"

"When do you need it?"

"About a week ago," I said, then added obliquely, "at least before the meeting in the diner." Joan knew what I meant. She smiled an *only if* kind of smile. Fred didn't get it or care, a rush job meant a bigger invoice.

"Show me your list?"

Almost a week passed and we hadn't gotten anything concrete from Mandrell about a meeting. Joan had spoken to him again but he was, he said, having difficulty making the relevant connections. We guessed he wanted to make sure that Fred's audit wasn't going to yield anything special. Bad guys don't like coincidences and it was a bit odd that a security audit was underway just after we had asked him to hook us up with his arms-dealing friends. We thought he was giving it some time to see if anything emerged from the audit. Fred was being appropriately duplicitous. Everything on the audit seemed...like an audit.

Joan had come around to my place to get a progress report from Fred. Mick had set up a secure electronic hook-up, a video conference call because we didn't want Fred turning up at my door or us at his again. The audit was board-approved but we didn't want Joan to be seen to be taking a special interest. Mick had found the two bugs they had hidden in my apartment and was regularly scanning to see if they had planted any others. Instead of destroying the bugs and alerting them, he had set them up with an endless loop of randomly selected banal conversation between me and Joan, including mindless sex. I could turn on the tapes just as she walked in the door and it all hung together, beginning as always with a giant wet kiss. All, unfortunately, fake. Sadly, it was only audio, so I didn't get to make the requisite sex tape with Joan in the production of which I would have gladly acquiesced.

"So, I think we can close out the official audit tomorrow and give the Board our report Friday. We'll put some good stuff in there but nothing that is going to rattle Mandrell's cage."

"That's good. I think it's making him nervous. But did you get what we really wanted?"

"Yes. Mandrell's up to his neck in it. He was tight with that dead research guy. We were able to pull deleted emails off the server. He influenced the Personnel Department to hire the replacement researcher, who's been there almost a month now. We think he's setting up for another crack at the technology but he put things on hold about three weeks ago."

"Around the time you had that conversation with him about doing a deal," I said, as an aside to Joan that Fred couldn't hear.

"We have more than enough to fire him, if that is where you were headed."

"We need to know all of the linkages he has created in the company. It's no good firing him if he can just keep doing what he's been doing from the outside."

"Sure. We have cloned the email server and our forensics guy is going over it with a fine-toothed comb. One more thing, and it's not good."

Fred paused for effect and made us ask "What?" in unison.

"The night your father was killed, it was Mandrell who set up the meeting."

There was a momentary silence while realisation made its way from Joan's ears to her heart.

"Fucking arsehole, I knew it." Joan was up and yelling. "Do we know where he is now? Right this fucking minute? I say we take that brand new McMillan of yours out for a spin."

"Joan, settle yourself."

"Sorry, who?" Fred asks.

"My new motorbike, Fred. The ride calms her nerves. She's going to SIT DOWN now and CALM herself." Joan didn't sit down, but she shut up and went out of shot of the computer cam.

"Look, our guys have got the paperwork ready to go, including a show-cause demand for Mandrell and an immediate termination letter, change of chairmanship, relevant minutes and notices, and the basics of a lawsuit against him. We can't pin the murder on him, well, not yet, but we can say that he was having conversations with the researcher. At a minimum, that represents a conflict of interest."

"Fred, thanks, keep going on those emails and whatever else you've got. We'll talk again in a couple of days, OK?"

"Sure."

He hung up.

"Jesus, Joan, you can't say stuff like that in front of guys like him."

"Sorry." She was rubbing her forehead. "I think I want to do it now, fuck the other guys. The thought of Mandrell getting one more good night's sleep shits me to tears."

"OK, we go hit him now and head back to the Caribbean." I had pulled up a dining chair and was sitting backwards on it, directly opposite her and looking into those eyes of hers. Jesus, those eyes. "We'll get some cocktails and relax by the pool, you can put that bikini back on, and I can watch you wear it..."

"Oh, shut up, you fucker. You know I can't relax 'till we get them all...at least the guy running it. Then we take care of Mandrell. Oh yeah, Mandrell."

She started to cry. She wasn't sobbing, but her eyes welled up as she tried to hide it. I'd never seen her cry.

"Fred will submit his report the day after tomorrow. I'll bet Mandrell is on the phone to you a minute after he realises there is nothing in it that compromises him."

I got her the tissue box and gestured for her to sit down. She complied. I had been disconnected from the human race for so long I didn't know what to think or feel, let alone do. I just let her process it.

Joan had fallen asleep on my lounge. It was nearly three in the morning and I was out on my balcony with a cigar, drinking a seventeen-year-old Green Spot. Yeah, baby, James Joyce's favourite whiskey. I was a fellow Irishmen and, like him, a hell of a drinker. I must have read *Ulysses* a dozen times. I guess you probably need to read it a dozen times, at least once when you're drunk. I like the density of Irish prose. It comes from the Irish weather, I'm sure, and the complexity of our history, putting up with all that shit from the English.

"What are you doing?" the sound of a grumpy child came from behind me. Joan was standing at the balcony door with her hair dishevelled rubbing her eyes. I had to look away. She was killing me with cuteness. "I didn't realise how close you were to the lake here."

"*When anxious, uneasy, or bad thoughts come, I go to the sea and the sea drowns them out with its great wide sounds. It cleanses me with its noise and imposes a rhythm upon everything in me that is bewildered and confused.* It's one of the reasons I love this place."

"Poetry? At this time in the morning?"

"Rainer Maria Rilke. A German with access to his inner thoughts. Not the first one. Translated it myself years ago, word for word. I don't speak the language but I almost became fluent as a teenager because of their literature and poetry… and art, for that matter. That work spoke to me. *Wenn ängstliche, unruhige und schlechte Gedanken kommen, gehe ich zum Meer, und das Meer übertönt sie mit seinen großen, weiten Geräuschen, reinigt mich mit seinen Geräuschen und drängt alles in mir, das verwirrt und verwirrt ist, in einen Rhythmus.* I'm surprised I still remember it."

"German, really?"

"You want something?" I asked the void in front of me with the Chicago CBD behind it. I didn't stand or stop smoking. I didn't want to make a big deal of her vulnerability. I thought it might embarrass her. "It's too early for eggs and a bit late for Scotch for you."

"It's starting to get cold again." She shivered as she sat on the chair next to me and looked at me as if she was impressed by my rudimentary knowledge of German poetry.

"It's Chicago." I stood and politely suggested I'd get her a blanket.

"Thank you…for…"

"For?"

"For knowing when to shut up."

"I'm good at not talking. Except for quoting someone else."

"I've noticed."

I went and got her a blanket and a glass. The bottle was still out on the balcony coffee table. One of the things about beautiful women is that they don't mind, or even notice, you doing things for them, not at all, not ever. Their sense of entitlement is palpable and I don't know any heterosexual male or lesbian woman who would give a shit about that fact with Joan. We're always happy to help.

"No, nothing, thanks," she said with a dismissive glance at the extra glass but she took the blanket and pulled her knees up in front of her on the chair to surround herself with it. I sat back down and picked up where I had left off. She turned toward me, putting her head on her blanket-covered knees.

"You're a good man, Charlie Brown."

I looked at her but didn't say anything. Charlie Brown never owned a McMillan and Peggy Jean never got fucked.

"Why are you here, Jim? You seem so at peace with what we are doing."

"When your options run out and you routinely accept the poverty of your existence, coming out the other side is illuminating."

"So, this is meaningless to you?"

"Mark Twain said that the two most important days in your life are the day you were born and the day you find out why."

"And the why is?"

"Well… you are why… us. But I'm not alive enough to believe that this is anything but transitory."

She was complimented, I think, but now she knew that she had me hooked as she played Don Quixote and I played Dapple the donkey or was it Rocinante? No, Rocinante was the horse. I can't remember. I have got to stop drinking.

"So, it's about me?"

For fuck's sake, are you blind? "Well, you as the manifestation of my fight against ordinariness."

"That's a word?"

"If it isn't, it should be. My life with you is orgastic."

"Is orgastic a word?"

"Don't go there."

"I want to go to the Caribbean."

I noticed she didn't say *with you*. She meant nothing by the omission. It's only a guy like me who would pick it up.

"I want this to be over," she continued.

"The way we're going, that will be soon, I think."

"I never thought it would come to this. I never thought Mandrell would betray Dad. I guess, I never…thought." Her forehead dropped onto her knees.

"We're here, it is what it is, and it's going to be what it's going to be," I said out loud, I think for the first time. "Oscar Wilde, I'm not that articulate."

"You put yourself down too much." Her voice was soft and husky.

"With good reason." She didn't like that answer, so I changed the subject. "You have to let Mandrell come to you, you know. Don't push it or you'll lose him."

"Yeah."

"And when he does, pull back. Tell him you have changed your mind, sink the hook."

"Yeah."

"Tell him…"

"Leave it. I want to know why you don't think that much of yourself. You're a hell of a guy walking around like you're in a dream or something, like some zombie."

"You said no…"

"No zombies, enough with the movie references. Why are you so detached?"

I wasn't ready to answer her.

"No better reason than anyone else, I guess. Life didn't work out. I met people, bad people. Suddenly, I was forty-two, fat and a zombie. My life would not make a good Broadway musical."

"I thought you only did movie references."

"I do it all, baby, including vaudeville." She looked puzzled. "This Irish guy walks into a building site and the foreman says, I'll give you a job if you can tell me the difference between a joist and a girder. The Irish guy says one wrote Ulysses and the other wrote Faustus."

"How is that relevant? Ahhh, yeah, I just got it, very funny, but still not relevant."

"I'm Irish, we are literate, we don't only do movie references and we worry about our friends."

"You were born in Chicago, right?"

"Do you know what the largest Irish city in the world is?"

"I'm guessing Chicago."

"That wonderful town."

"Back to Broadway."

"I've got one for you. More of a Greek tragedy than a Broadway play."

"Shoot."

"I'm in love with you, Joan, and I don't know what to do about it."

"Jim, that is a compliment to me and I know you don't think I mean it, but I do. The thing is, I've got nothing for you. At least, you've had a life. I'm thirty, a spoilt kid who never grew up, pretended I was a cop, lost my dad, felt impotent to do anything about his murder, even though I was second in my class at the academy, and was soooo good at judging character that I partnered up with some useless lawyer prick, I mean Mandrell, not you, the very guy who got my dad killed and who just used me..."

"You should put that to music. You'd need a cello, so forlorn, so soulful. Yoyo Ma, I love you, man." I took a long draw on my cigar. "You forgot, of course, rich and beautiful."

"That doesn't give you a pass on this shit, it makes it worse."

"Money never makes it worse. But one thing I can tell you for sure and certain is that judging character is not within the realm of human capability. Until they develop a vaccine, we are all going to keep getting infected with these fucking arseholes. I'm starting to think you can't shoot them all, either. You definitely can't spot them coming, you just can't. Anyone who says they can is delusional. Sociopathy is rampant and getting worse. There must be something in the water. Maybe it's because of the loss of religion, or national service, or any sense of service. Maybe booze or fast food, whatever the fuck." I had to stop, I was rambling and it sounded too much like I knew what I was talking about. "What I'm actually saying is, don't blame yourself for misjudging Mandrell." She didn't seem convinced. "Are we going to whack these guys or turn them in?"

"That's new. Getting cold feet on the *kill 'em all* plan? I sort of felt vindicated when I had Chicago's top lawyer telling me it was OK, but it turns out he was just using me. Chalk one up for the arseholes. I'm not so sure, now."

"My approval isn't sufficient? I'm a lawyer."

She gave me a smile with a warmth that I hadn't seen from her before.

"The fuse is burning, baby."

"It is."

"I say, let's see who's still standing after the bomb goes off." I looked at her with some concern. "You know, it's going to go off, right, and it may not be us who survives it, so we may not have to decide what to do… after."

"That's what I'm saying. If we turn over Fred's stuff to the authorities, then we can avoid this showdown and put Mandrell in jail."

The look I gave her communicated my firm opinion that Mandrell would not be prosecuted, he would not under any circumstances spend any time in jail, and the yet-to-be-identified head of the arms organisation would not show his face, let alone face the courts. Still, I was reluctant to argue against pulling out. It was what I had wanted to do for some time.

"I am happy to pull the plug, if that's what you want. Say the word. Me and you, Texas, the big country, the oil, all the social benefits of being wealthy. They know who's who down there, that's for sure. Do you like to golf?"

"Tell me about your wife."

"Way to change the subject. No golf for you. Where did that come from?"

She waited for an answer.

"Ex-wife. Clara. Sweet girl."

"No bullshit, no movies, no Broadway plays. Why did you break up with her?"

"The question is, why did I stay with her for so long."

"So, *you* ended it with her?"

"It was a draw. Why does anyone stay in a relationship after it dies? It's hard to leave, I guess. For me, at least. She was a mean girl, though. When the numbers didn't stack up, when I stopped being a good provider, it was over. I was slow to act because I don't favour making change for the sake of change, you just end up where you were, but geographically somewhere else."

"So, why did you leave in the end?"

"I was dying and she didn't care. It was my fault that I was dying but her lack of interest wasn't helping. We were living under a contract of love and support but were doing neither. I had known her my whole adult life. She was the vessel that carried the history of my life to that point. I was very much aware of that. You don't re-format the hard drive when everything you are, or ever were, is on it. The problem was, the relationship didn't amount to a hill of beans, so I had to hit delete. She saw the faults and the mistakes and didn't respect the rest of me. Do you know how hard that is, to realise that the person you have spent so much time with has no respect for your story? That, my beautiful friend, will kill you quicker than a .50 calibre bullet. She was probably right about me, though."

"Jesus, Jim," her voice was raised, "a champion shooter at seventeen, an elite boxer in college, admitted to practice law, a licensed professional, how much more do you think a guy should achieve in one lifetime?"

"A failed businessman and husband, broke, fat, drunk. I didn't need more achievements, just more life, more love."

"You're not fat, now."

"That's right, baby."

She laughed and went back to being philosophical. "What is the meaning of life then?"

I nearly said "42," but she would have got up and left, for sure.

"Personal respect and affection, the chance to give those two things and the chance to earn them from someone in return, especially one particular person. If you want it from a crowd, then you are an egomaniac."

That seemed to resonate with her. She sat and thought about it. I didn't think I should disturb her. I was just happy she was here and I could look at her.

"My father was a smart man, a loving man, but he surrounded himself with pricks like Mandrell."

"Easy to do. Story of my life. Those people are always out there, Joan, like diseases. Some kill you quickly, like Ebola. Some take years, like cancer. But they get you in the end. What happened to your dad wasn't unusual or your fault."

"I know what you mean about respect and affection. My home was full of both giving and receiving, and you're right, you flourish in that environment. I think I immediately started looking for it with Mandrell after Dad died."

"Killing Mandrell for his betrayal won't bring your father back."

She sort of laughed at the irony of who was preaching that sermon.

"How did it work out for you? Killing people, I mean?"

"I have been thinking about that recently, a lot. The answer I keep circling back to is…you. It brought me to you." I'll keep the look she gave me. "Not that I think I deserve you. I'm a murderous bastard. I'm certainly not going to ride my bike into a truck like Jacks. Fuck that, he should have shaved his beard off, tossed the gang leather, and gone to become a shopkeeper in Frisco like William Munny."

"Who the fuck is…? No, no, not even going to try to figure that one out. You are not a bastard, but don't give up on the murderous just yet. We've got work to do."

"So, it's kill 'em all, then?"

"I like your plan. Let's see where the bodies fall, shall we?"

"Let God sort 'em out."

"Movie reference?"

"No, historical. The Crusades, somewhat appropriately. Arnald Amalric *kill them all for the Lord knows his Own*, he wrote."

"How do you remember that shit?"

"It's appropriate. We are not the only violent sons of bitches that ever lived."

"You think."

"That quote from Amalric comes from the sacking of a town called Beziers in southern France in 1209 where there was an enclave of Christian Cathars who didn't want to follow the Pope. About half of the town was Cathar, the other was Catholic. The problem was that the army of Crusaders the Pope sent to educate them didn't know which half was which. Hence, the quote. They killed every man, woman, and child in that town, some 20,000 souls, and left it to their God to sort them out in the afterlife. You know, the name of the Pope that sent them? Pope Innocent the Third."

Joan got up.

"I worry about you, I truly do. You should stop drinking, you rant too much about religion when you do. Do you have a hairbrush?"

I pointed her to the bathroom. I thought Joan was a little naïve for a killer. My mind went to the multitude of conflicts in my own ancestral home.

> *"The old for her*
> *The new that made me think*
> *On Ireland dearly*
> *While soft the wind*
> *Blew down the glen*
> *And shook the golden barley*
> *Twas hard the woeful words to frame*
> *To break the ties that bound us*
> *But harder still to bear the shame*
> *Of foreign chains around us*
> *And so I said the mountain glen*
> *I'll seek at morning early*
> *While soft the wind blew down the glen*
> *And shook the golden barley."*
>
> *The Clancy Brothers*

CHAPTER TEN

Every day, from this moment to the moment that you die. That was the price Mel was proposing that his troops should pay at Stirling in *Braveheart*, the subvention they had to contribute for Scotland. Just conceptualising that payment draws feelings from within your soul, either aspirations or dread depending on your state of mind and the state of your health. What would that time be worth if you were to trade it for something? What value would the *rest of your life* have or what would you ask for it if you had to make that bargain? Mel was telling his men that the time they had left on Earth had less value than the bequest those brave Scots could, and in large numbers did, make that day at Stirling. Yet, to this day, Scotland remains part of England, later Britain, despite their sacrifice. Their ancestors recently voted for union with England. I heard William Wallace and his troops spinning in their graves when the result of the vote was announced. I'm not sure Mel's movie would carry the same impact now that we know the Scots really do want to be British. The sacrifice those men made was, in the end, meaningless.

That is often the case with wars fought over nationalism or religion because borders or deities often over time become inconsequential. My ancestors, the Irish, and the Scots have suffered the English together. Perhaps often not together enough to reach critical mass to see them off. So, both nations endured their tyranny, each in isolation. I look at the Northern Ireland conflict with a combination of understanding and remorse.

To this day the English send documentary makers to various parts of the world to make cultural or cooking biographies of countries so the modern-day Poms can sit back in their lounge chairs in front of the *telly* with their tea and be comforted by the fact that the English are still bringing civilisation to the world, or at least observing and cataloguing it with appropriate dignity. *Here you see the Turk scurry about their everyday activity. Are they not splendid to watch as they undertake their meaningless non-British endeavours? But they do, indeed, make a good manti.* English textbooks still claim that many of the lands they *discovered* were uninhabited, leaving the indigenous populations of those lands wondering whether they were invisible. Clearly, they meant uninhabited by Poms, not by humans.

But the Scottish or English predispositions were not what I was rolling around my Irish head this day. It was the value that could be placed on the remainder of *my* life, the value that the remaining years of one life is worth. The size of the residual is, I guess, pertinent to that analysis. The value represented by a seventy-year-old's residual life is less than that of, say, a ten-year-old, mathematically at least. That is certainly the impression you get from news commentary and films. *Women and children first,* they scream as the boat sinks, the value also varying by gender apparently. I always wondered why that was so. Is it because women are the mothers of the children? I'm not sure that the *fairer sex* paradigm cuts it anymore, thanks to Germaine Greer. You can't open the door for a woman but you can stay behind and drown with the orchestra. In the same way, the value of any given child's life varies depending on where the ten-year-old lives, what the racial ancestry of the child is, and whether the child or the seventy-year-old suffers any impairment, assuming your valuation is based on the quality of the remaining life rather than its quantity as measured in years. Let's not pretend that Americans care as much about a ten-year-old Sudanese boy as they do about a blond-haired, blue-eyed kid from Scarsdale or that they value the life of an intellectually impaired ten-year-old as much as an average ten-year-old. Don't shoot the messenger, I'm just making the observation.

Putting that aside, is the amount of time left on Earth holistically pertinent when assessing the value of the life that is left or is it all about the quality of the life that would be sacrificed? I am forty-two. I have less value than that ten-year-old but more value than a seventy-year-old according to the *how many years left* mathematical schema. Is it indeed the quantity of your life left to you that counts or is it the quality you bring to other people's lives that is more pertinent. If the cost of installing a safety program in the United States exceeds five million dollars per person likely to be protected by that initiative, it won't be approved by the regulators in charge of public safety. That is the cut-off value of human life, after which they won't pay to take the necessary precautions to save you. By extension, I presume that is what they think you are worth regardless of your age, gender, ethnicity, or IQ. In the eyes of the American military, William Wallace take note, the cost of every soldier was about six hundred thousand dollars, which was what the US paid the families of soldiers killed in Iraq One. If that sounds disrespectful to those wonderful men and women who have fallen, I apologise. I am again just making the observation. Insurance companies have a whole other set of math. About one hundred and thirty thousand dollars, on average, per death and a bunch of tables showing what each part of the human body is worth should you lose it. Peculiarly, the sum of those parts does not equal the whole. In my case, the price of an arsehole's life was fifty thousand dollars to me but, as you are discovering, using dollar values leads you nowhere in evaluating this question.

There remains an underlying assumption that human life actually has an intrinsic value no matter how much of an arsehole you are, how much pain you are suffering, how much time you have left on Earth, what shade of skin you might have, or what intellectual capacity you might carry around. According to most people's beliefs, the life of all other creatures and plants is there for the taking without remorse except what you might get for it in the local produce market unless it is cute in which case one needs to show a modicum of regret at its passing. What is it about human life that gives it higher value? If the answer to that question is that it is because humans are capable of considering whether their life has value, then that is circular logic that leads us nowhere, again except to conclude that, if you adopt that paradigm, the higher your level of consciousness, then the higher the value of your life. I know some idiots who wouldn't think that was true. If it were true, then why aren't sinking boats evacuated based on educational qualifications as opposed to whether you are a woman or a child? *Let the smart guys move to the front please and you other dumb fucks step back,* doesn't have the same ring to it. And don't get me started on those courageous people who face life with a disability. In the film *When Worlds Collide,* as people evacuated the Earth to escape imminent global destruction, the only guy with a ticket who got tossed off the spaceship leaving Earth was the one in a wheelchair even though he had paid to build the ship. Apparently, that was OK at the time the film was made, no doubt a product of the social assumption that he would have been a burden *as are all cripples.* Messenger. There'll be *no cripples on Earth Two* I presume was written on the ship as part of its insignia, in Latin, of course. *Claudus non hominibus super terram nouam* written in a circle like on a stamp on the side of the ship with a picture of an erect penis with a face drawn on it in the centre, smiling, pointing to a better place *sans* cripples. I laugh at that proposition because if the ship crashed while landing on the new world and they were all left crippled, they'd be wishing they had that wheelchair as well as the organisational skill of the guy who paid to build the ship.

There is Spock's affirmation that *the needs of the many outweigh the needs of the few or the one* as he gives his life to save the Enterprise. Of course, they dig him up again for the next film, so perhaps Spock's life can be valued based on what his character contributes to the revenue of the franchise. But can we measure the value of one life in multiples of other people's lives? If Spock was right, two lives are worth more than one. Too bad if you're the one. The other two guys better be able to defend themselves if they intend to throw me out of the boat. How old and fit or even smart are the two guys you count as being worth more than me? What if the life you were valuing was that of Mother Theresa? Wouldn't you be more inclined to value her by the number of lives she saved rather than the number of lives that were about to be terminated before you gave her up as a trade?

Most of the Scots at Stirling were killed because William Wallace's girlfriend got whacked by some English lord. Her death was what sent him on his crusade. How does that math work? All of them for her?

Sixty million people died in the Second World War, yet Poland wasn't liberated and Stalin kept killing the Polish and East European Jews. America handed back what was left of Japan after they had bombed the crap out of it. If Churchill had said yes to Rudolf Hess when he flew over to Britain to sue for peace rather than locking him up and telling everyone he had gone mad, twenty million lives would have been saved in the European war alone. So, what value did Churchill place on each of those lives he traded for his vision of Europe? Hitler would have been left to rule the German-speaking peoples of Middle Europe but they are now combined under one union anyway. So, twenty million lives, most of Europe and England in rubble, I'm not sure I can process the math that gives the answer that it was worth stopping Hitler and promoting Stalin. Who knows what could have been achieved by offering Hitler what he wanted say, for example, freeing German and Polish Jews and creating a Jewish state in the Middle Eastern colonies then so coveted by the British. The fact is that neither Churchill nor the Americans gave a flying fuck about what was happening to Jewish people in Europe except to glibly use them as an *ex post facto* excuse for the carnage wrought on Germany and Europe as they expended those twenty million lives. Stalin, Churchill's best friend, killed twelve million Ukrainians when he took their entire wheat harvest in 1933 to sell to the Americans to buy guns. What value did anyone in the international community at the time place on those Ukrainian lives, including the Americans who purchased the wheat crop and sold them the guns? Now the US is paying billions to help the Ukrainians kill Russians. Either that is a bit late or demonstrative of the futility of that expenditure.

OK, if you are one of the many people who deify Churchill, and English and French history books would certainly support your view, then replace that analogy with that of Vietnam, and perhaps reread your history books on the Second World War. So, in the Vietnam analogy, you would need to consider about one-and-a-half million Vietnamese deaths, five-hundred-thousand Cambodian and Laotian deaths, and about seventy-thousand foreign military deaths, sixty-four-thousand of which were American military. All sacrificed to achieve... what, with all due respect to the fallen. Perhaps you would have to ask William

Westmoreland, who wanted to increase the American military presence there until there would have been more Americans in Vietnam than Vietnamese, by which time you could have resolved the dispute with a vote. Or ask Nixon, who let it go on for six years after the Americans knew it was a war of independence, not a domino in the red advance, and that it was none of their business being there. Presumably because the Yanks had stockpiles of World War Two munitions they wanted to get rid of and, of course, once you run out of that stuff you need to buy new stuff, right? Looking at it from the other side, I guess Ho Chi Minh would say that the Vietnamese achieved independence but I'm not sure you could find a relative of any American soldier killed there to agree with him. The discussion of the value of that *independence* for the Vietnamese brings with it a whole other set of conundrums, including whether Vietnam would have been better off as an American-friendly satellite state rather than what they are today that being an economic backwater unable to fully feed and educate its citizenry. Apparently, independence is better than a well-informed and well-fed populace with iPhones and American work visas. Obtaining independence was well worth the two million lives it took to achieve…right? The answer to that depends on the value you place on those lives, which brings me back to my initial thoughts on the matter.

You can't talk about mass violence without considering religious purges. Many religions suggest that the value of a life depends on the individual's belief system and how well they follow it. The worthlessness of a non-believer or barbarian life makes it permissible to not only kill them but to prey on them financially and emotionally as the slaves they were born to be, a slave to the higher-minded, more worthy conquering class, including the slavery called *natural* by Aristotle based on the same concepts of moral and genetic superiority that infected America. Having a social or religious philosophy that embraces the concept that certain races or non-believers are without worth and can, therefore, be enslaved or killed, has turned out to be economically handy when believers had the military strength to enslave the heathens. Not so good if the non-believers had the upper hand and the authority to write the textbooks and the new religious scripts after the fighting and killing when their religion became more worthy than the one embraced by those poor bastards who lost the war. The concept of religious or social superiority has also been more than handy for geeing up the troops when you want to send them to their slaughter by assuring them that they are acting for some higher cause, that you Mel, or some deity against an evil and less worthy enemy who didn't have the ear of the Almighty. Throughout the Dark Ages, life wasn't worth much at all if you were not a Catholic. In some religions today, to be considered a person you have to be part of the religion. Some religions even think your life is so worthless if you aren't part of their religion or their version of that religion, that it can be snatched from you whenever they deem fit. I know we all wish we could rid the world of those fanatical arseholes, but I seem to be the only one I know who is doing it on a personal level. If the body count from religious purges was resurrected today, like Spock, we would have billions of more mouths to feed. Billions of people killed or their progeny extinguished because one group believed you should pray on your knees and the other believed you should be prostrate. A *billion* people killed in the name of God, their God, not yours, but insanely often the same God. Whether you're a Christian who doesn't want to be ruled by the Pope or a Christian who does, or a peace-loving Muslim as opposed to those who think it is OK to cut off your head. The Buddha, the ultimate pacifist, suggested we could live one life and be reincarnated as a rat or live another and be reincarnated as a Deva. So, if you do the math as a Buddhist, you come up with the answer that one life equals a rat and another life equals Oprah. Sorry, that's Deva, not diva.

It might seem like I am digressing, but all this comes back to my view about killing arseholes and the value of their lives and, by comparison, my own. I had been valuing the lives of the arseholes at around the level of a rat, but I was conscious that I wasn't the official Buddhist actuary. If I subvert Spock's hypothesis, I could ask how much of an arsehole do you have to be before the needs of the many kick in? I confess I am a bit of a *needs-of-the-many* kind of guy, therefore, I assert that there is a point where you become such a handbrake on society that the rest of us should have you whacked. We already do that in those states that have capital punishment but, of course, that action is sanctioned by the State after due process and certainly not by me independently assessing the situation. However, the guys on death row might question how *due* the legal *process* is, but it is official and, once again, I realise that I'm not supposed to be the *official* who does the *processing.*

Unlike some of the arseholes on my list, these arms dealers were killing people or facilitating their deaths, so I had few qualms about what we were doing. I refer you to religious and political purges for which someone had to have sold the righteous the means to wreak the havoc they inflicted. I wasn't morally troubled by the prospect of having it out with them but I was troubled by the thought that my death, not theirs, might be the outcome of that confrontation. And all of that led me to this whole *what is it worth* thing. So, I was facing up to the fact that I didn't want to get shot, which was new data for me in a life where I had shot other people and had even got momentarily to the point of seriously planning suicide. I didn't doubt my acceptance of my own death but rather my view of life had changed while I wasn't looking. I didn't want to be a lab rat for Nietzsche anymore. I wanted to understand what it was that I was giving up and what I was taking from someone else. An egocentric perspective can take you only so far and the loss of an objective or universal perspective confuses such assessments no matter how smart or religious you are. Nietzsche was right when he proposed that life leads only to a constant, even fluid, reassessment of the rules. *The individual has always had to struggle to keep from being overwhelmed by the tribe. If you try it, you will be lonely often, and sometimes frightened. But no price is too high to pay for the privilege of owning yourself.* I had been happy to make my own rules up to this point but now I had a new tribe: Joan and Jake.

We found ourselves on a lounge in the back of a jazz club in the city. I watched untroubled civilians walk past concerned only about where their next date was coming from or their next rent payment. Not that any of that is trivial, stress has killed more people than Burt Lancaster. I had wanted to own one of these jazz bars ever since I saw that movie with Robert De Niro and the ever-so-fat Marlon Brando. My God, what an actor, both of them. Imagine Brando's career if he hadn't developed a penchant for Twinkies and a disdain for the Hollywood establishment. But I suspect the shine would go off the dream of owning a club like this the first time I had to clean the vomit off the floor. Nonetheless, being called Mr Jamisen by everyone as I walked down the long line of people waiting on the red carpet to get into my ever-so-popular bar would fully compensate me.

We hadn't heard from Mandrell and it had been nearly a week since Fred submitted his audit findings.

"I got me a mess and I haven't got enough long boot to step out of it."

"Jesus, Jim, I assume that's a movie reference. Can't you talk about your feelings without quoting movies?" Joan said.

"Mandrell thinks he is a good man with a gun, he's a big mouth who thinks he's a good man with a gun and there's a cold hole in the ground between the two."

"Jim, for fuck sake, English, please."

"Both Robert Ryan in *Lawman*. I was thinking about that movie the other night, dreaming about it, in fact. About how cold and matter-of-fact Burt Lancaster was as he gunned everybody down in some God-forsaken Western cattle town."

"The relevance being?"

"I don't know how to process our situation but I do know that I'm not as cool as Burt Lancaster, under fire or at any other time."

"You're welcome to have out, if you want, with thanks."

"Not going to happen. It's you and me from here, that much I know."

"I appreciate what you're doing, Jim, and I've seen you under fire. I'm glad you're on my side."

"Nice of you to say but I am a coward at heart."

"We all are. It's not whether you are or are not a coward, it's what you do when the chips are down and everyone else is cowering in fright."

That was perceptive and true. Burt would have been proud.

"There is no courage without fear."

"Brilliant, yes."

"The platoon sergeant in *Edge of Tomorrow*."

"Right, of course, not you."

"I got lucky at the warehouse."

"You're forgetting that I was there."

"This is not a date, right? Because, when you give me a compliment, I just have to keep reminding a part of myself that it's not."

"Which part…? No, it's a strategy session."

A tall, very good-looking guy intruded on our conversation.

"Joan?"

"Daaaave?"

The look she gave him was unmistakable; it had to be Mr Mistake. I had seen that look in high school. I was walking to class with my first real girlfriend, I was smitten, and she stopped dead in her tracks to talk to some passing jock with whom I later found out she was equally smitten. I walked twenty paces before I noticed I was talking to myself. I looked back to see her staring devotedly as she listened intently to him telling her, I imagine, about his latest fungal infection. I left them to it. She didn't notice and no one was noticing me here, either.

"Joan, you look…"

"Dave Morgan, this is Jim Jamisen, a friend of mine." It was a no-look pass from her and I waved at him.

"Detective First Class Dave Morgan, right?" I yelled, seated because the music had started up again.

"Lieutenant, actually, how did you…?"

"I looked you up. Joan mentioned you a couple of times."

"Is that right?" His attention returned back to her and so did mine.

"You here by yourself, Dave? Want to join us?" Joan asked.

"No, I'm with someone."

Dave looked over to the bar and our eyes followed his gaze. Great legs, short black dress, blonde.

"How are you doing, Joan? Things were getting a bit hairy the last time I saw you."

"Yeah, all that settled down, just pounding the beat now."

"Sure. Listen, Joan, can I talk to you, privately?"

He pulled her aside out of my earshot. I watched her face pale. When he left, she sat and watched him walk away.

"So, that was Mr Wonderful? Good-looking guy."

No answer. I let her ponder on it as I called the waiter over. I relaxed back into my chair and watched Mr America leave the bar, black dress in tow.

"Doogie's dead, he got shot," she said. "Long-range, .50 calibre, they think."

I didn't want to keep the glancing look she gave me, not this time. "Dave suspect someone?"

"No. But Mandrell is going to. Dave knows that I had some dealings with the guy. It was just a heads up," she said without looking at me.

I said nothing. She turned. I confessed.

"I caught his two goons following me the other day. They made me nervous," I explained. I was exasperated and looking for approval but none was forthcoming. "He could have ended us at any time, Joan. I was sick of looking over my shoulder." That was no good either, apparently.

"Who are you?"

"The devil, a man, and everything in between. I'll whack Mandrell too if he says boo to me, and by that I mean doesn't prove useful. If he wants to kill me or us or turn us in to the authorities, which he has already tried to do once, then he can come get some. Right in the face."

I meant it with a passion. I'd had a gutful of these arseholes and the cowering. I hadn't been healing, I'd been maturing as a killer. There was no love in my eyes when I returned her gaze, just hatred for Mandrell and his friends. "These fucking arseholes ruling the world, fuck 'em. Let's stop pussy-footing around, Joan. Doogie was their stooge, disguising himself as a lawman. Burt Lancaster came to me in a dream and said, whack the fucker, so I did. Not a fast draw in a street where he had a chance, just a good shot from a safe distance. Burt shot his girlfriend's husband in the back in that movie. At least, Doogie was facing me when I introduced him to my McMillan. *From my cold dead hands,* I screamed when I shot him and, yeah, I know that was Charlton Heston, not Burt, but I love my McMillan too."

"Why didn't you consult me? You're exposing us. You are jeopardising the operation."

It was an operation now.

"I'm protecting us. Doogie had us cold. Mandrell will think it's his competitors responding to the warehouse hit. No way he'll think it's us. We're on his side, remember?"

"You think?"

"He thinks so, and he thinks we believe that Doogie was Homeland Security. He doesn't believe that we will hit law enforcement. Doogie was with Davis so I got Davis as well, so that's two more of Mandrell's flunkies out of the picture. They were at the docks to pick up that shipment we couldn't identify. Mick and I finally figured out where it was. I called the cops anonymously. It will make it look bad for Doogie, getting shot in the company of gangsters supervising the unloading of a shipment of illegal arms."

"Have you hit anyone else I should know about?"

"Not yet, but Mandrell is next. What the fuck happened to *kill 'em all*?"

"No wonder Mandrell hasn't contacted us. He's probably hiding in his basement."

"Don't think so. Firstly, he's not the type, and, secondly, he thinks you're an idiot *like your father* so I doubt he's doing anything other than planning another hit on his competition in retaliation for Doogie. Doogie was killed in the line of duty, he thinks, duty to him. But now he hasn't got Doogie to do his dirty work, so he definitely needs you."

"Homeland Security is going to be all over Doogie's death."

"Drop a few clues, link him to the Davis brothers. You've got the tapes from the diner, pass them in and say you were watching Davis at the diner. Edit Mandrell out, if you want, or, better still, leave him in."

She got up to leave.

"You're a dangerous man," she said, jabbing her finger at me. I don't think she meant it as a compliment.

The legs came back and sat down at the bar a couple of minutes after Joan left. There was no sign of Dave. I waited a little while to see if he showed but went over to the bar when he didn't. I suspected Dave had left with Joan.

"Jim Jamisen." I stuck out my hand.

"Dave's friend." She took my hand without shaking, more like she expected me to kiss it, but I didn't, though I think I gave an indiscernible bow towards it and rubbed it a little with my thumb. It was a pretty hand.

"No, Joan's friend."

"Ah, yes, Joan of Arc."

"So, you know her?"

"Only by reputation."

"Dave's erected a few monuments to her at his place?"

"All over his house, yes, very perceptive."

"I'm a perceptive guy. I perceive that you have the best arse I've ever seen. Buy you a drink?"

"Just an old-fashioned boy, are you?"

"Yes, ma'am." I had a bit of a chuckle to myself and got a quizzical look. "Just an old story about one of the Marx brothers, you just reminded me of it."

"Do tell."

"It's rude."

"So was your remark about my arse."

She knew it was a fine arse.

"Chico," I began with some hesitation, "had a reputation with the ladies and he got it by being very direct. He was very successful using that approach and it used to drive Groucho mad with jealousy, even though Groucho was married, mostly." The bartender came past, so I ordered a Scotch and silently offered her a drink, waving my finger over her glass. She accepted with a nod and the bartender nodded back, so everyone knew the secret language from the Bond movies, or was it Clooney in *Ocean's Eleven*? The barman went about his business. "Chico was introduced by a couple of nervous friends to a very young Tallulah Bankhead, actress, sophisticate, and niece of an important and wealthy politician. Chico had wanted to meet her ever since he'd seen her photo in the papers, which happened a lot. She was something of a media favourite and a very good-looking one. They warned him to behave himself as they took him over to introduce him to her. The conversation was travelling along traditional lines until Chico pipes up with *you know I really want to fuck you*. To which Tallulah responded without hesitation and to the surprise of all assembled, *and so you shall, you dear, old-fashioned boy*."

She laughed. We never did get that drink.

"So, what's the story with Captain America?" I asked.

"You mean, Lieutenant America."

She reached across me to get a pack of cigarettes and a lighter that were sitting next to the alarm clock on her bedside table. Her bare breasts pressed against my naked chest as she leaned over. I was alive again and at peace, transported there by a woman's body pressed against mine, all reassuring me that I was both a male and a person. I guess all that unresolved sexual tension with Joan had consequences. I didn't help her retrieve the pack as a gentleman might because she was doing such a fine job of it herself. My arm had gone to sleep from her lying on it and I had disappeared into a mammary infused wonderland having entered that coma that all men enter when juxtaposed skin to skin with breasts. In this case, real breasts, beautiful young real breasts, mummy, the ultimate weapon of mass distraction. She showed me the pack as if to offer me one and I shook my head. She extracted one and lit it, then lay back down on her side, facing me and putting the pack and lighter on the bed behind her. She was polite enough to hold the burning cigarette in the hand resting on her head, not the one on my chest.

"I never did ask your name."

"Brittany."

"Christ, you weren't born in the nineties?"

"Just."

"I hope that means just at the beginning."

"You don't like nineties women?"

"From a sample of one, I would have to say that I do like them, yes."

"You're pretty ripped for an old guy."

"I box."

"Why?"

"So I can beat the shit out of arseholes."

"Do you do that often?"

"Not as often as I would like. Speaking of arseholes, how long have you known Dave?"

"Three or four months. My uncle introduced us. Can't say that I know him, though. He's wound up pretty tight and still in love with your friend. He's probably over at her place now."

That sent a shiver up my spine but who was I to shiver? She noticed. Evidently, she wasn't emotionally stupid.

"Is that why you're here with me?" I asked, before she could.

"No, I'm a nineties woman, we are sexually liberated. You're a take-charge kind of guy, I like that. You want something to drink?"

She got up without me answering and slowly extinguished her cigarette in the ashtray on her bedside table, slow enough for me to get another look at why I was there. She put on her robe and headed for the kitchen. I pulled on my t-shirt and boxers. There is something so stimulating about being in a single girl's home, specifically the bedroom, unspoilt by a live-in man, her sanctum. You are invading a damsel's private abode. It is somehow primal, exploratory, like there was no woman before her in your life, just the promise of a new adventure, a new beginning, a garden full of new smells and new excitement. It makes you wish for more time and, just for a moment, you are alive again. I felt like smelling and touching things, looking for the revered present I had never given her. Every secret garden is different, it is filled with flavours and aromas that are both magical and confronting. Tonight, I was lost in her garden. She was lovely. I still had her smell on my breath.

"I'll have a coffee," I said, as I caught up with her in the kitchen.

I touched her hair as we met up in front of the coffee machine, our bodies together and me finding a tenderness that I was surprised I still possessed. It was about three in the morning. I always feel strange at that time, mindless and paranoid. I think it's got something to do with the creative side of your brain being awake and the logical side still rebooting, so you start to imagine things that aren't real. Things like monsters in the closet or relationships in the kitchen, and you can't defend yourself against the imagining of them because the other side of your brain still has that little hourglass going round and round indicating that it's not yet available, but working on it. She set up the filtered coffee machine, definitely a nineties girl.

"You wear a t-shirt?"

"Yeah, it comforts me, and I don't have Frank Capra trying to get the scene cadence right."

"OK, I love movie references but what the fuck?"

"Clarke Gable, *It Happened One Night,* doing a scene with Claudette Colbert. He was taking his clothes off to frighten her out of his part of the hotel room because he wanted to go to bed and she wanted to yak. The director couldn't get the timing of the scene right because Gable had too many clothes on to match the dialogue. The director made him ditch the t-shirt he wore under his shirt so the continuity of the scene worked the way Capra wanted it to and started to shoot the scene again with Gable not wearing a t-shirt under his business shirt. The sale of t-shirts in America dropped eighty percent the day after the movie was released because the male populace concluded that if Gable didn't wear a t-shirt, then neither did they. I am starting a new trend, I think it's time. The t-shirt industry needs guys like me."

"Got it, I think. I'm going to have to see that movie now. You're crazy, you know that?"

"You have no idea."

"I would like to have some idea."

"Worth the effort, you think? The movie was probably the best thing Gable ever did."

"I meant with you. You're staring at me," she said modestly.

"I am. I didn't notice how beautiful you were in the bar. And you like movies."

"Maybe you were too busy looking at my arse to notice anything else?"

"No, I was too busy wondering where Dave was."

"I find honesty very attractive."

"You have a nice place. What do you do for a living?" I went over and sat on one of the kitchen stools.

"I'm a high-end prostitute."

"No, you're not."

"That was a quick response. How do you know I'm not?"

"By the way you move."

"I'm sorry?"

"Entitled, high self-esteem, plus you have family pictures plastered all over the walls, wealthy family by the look of some of those locations. I think I know that fat guy there from some show on TV. This is not the lair of a prostitute. Do you work at all?"

"I used to, but it's too boring. I'm not qualified to do anything interesting."

She put down a jug of milk on the bench and went back to get me a black coffee from the drippings. She came back with an overly small coffee cup half filled with coffee and put it in front of me on a saucer with the cup offset from the centre. She had been to Italy, but there were no biscotti and she was using the wrong equipment. She lit another cigarette. The machine continued to gurgle.

"You don't mind me smoking."

"I don't mind anything about you, otherwise I'd be on my way home."

"More honesty. And you…" she wandered over to one of the lounges that looked out from the large room through floor-to-ceiling fourteen-foot penthouse windows to the city which looked like a carnival from the darkened room. "What do you do?"

She flopped into one of the plush chairs, those legs escaping from her robe, those legs.

"I kill people for a living," I said, following her with my coffee.

"No, you don't, you're a lawyer. Dave told me at the bar."

"How would Dave know?"

"He knows a lawyer who knows you. I met him once."

"And who would that be?"

"Manfred, Mansfield…"

"Mandrell?"

"Yeah, that's the guy."

CHAPTER ELEVEN

I watched Dave get into his car outside Joan's place. I hadn't been there long, having come straight from Brittany's apartment after discovering Dave's link to Mandrell. It was 4:40am by my truck's clock. They had obviously been having a long talk or something, and despite my attraction to Brittany and the hopelessness of any relationship aspirations with Joan, I hoped that it wasn't *something*. Given his association with Mandrell, I also hoped that the discussion with Joan hadn't been about anything important. I had to assume, however, that Dave now knew our Plan with Mandrell and that Mandrell was about to know. Dave may have already had the opportunity to alert Mandrell, so shooting him here would be pointless. Besides, for all I knew, he was a decent policeman. I had no real concept of what his relationship with Mandrell was other than that it existed. He hadn't done anything wrong that I knew of, aside from spending time with Joan into the early hours. I followed him home.

I noticed he was on the phone on his drive home. "You shouldn't drive and talk on the phone, Dave," I said out loud, wondering who he could be talking to at this time in the morning but believing he was briefing Mandrell. It obviously couldn't wait. I assumed Mandrell had expected an update regardless of the hour. I was not inclined to phone Joan and warn her about Dave's involvement with Mandrell, partly because the damage was already done and partly because she would, no doubt, find it intrusive. Despite my interest in getting one up on him, I was concerned about how she might take Dave's betrayal especially coming right on the heels of discovering Mandrell's duplicity. I actually cared for her, I noted. I started to wonder what Brittany and I could possibly have in common and why Brittany would find me attractive at all. I was weighing the two girls as potential partners but my logical brain was now awake and telling me that neither relationship was possible. I watched the light come on in Dave's building, fourth floor at the front. I knew where to find him if I needed to, so I started home. Streeterville wasn't far from here, a walk along the lake with the city lit up like a Christmas tree seemed like a good idea.

I had cigars in the glove compartment. The weather was cool but not cold enough to stop me having a stroll ever so slowly along the newly constructed walkway as I lit my cigar. I wasn't going to bother anyone with the smell at this time in the morning; I had the place to myself. They had done a good job with the path and gardens, very pleasant, I pondered, avoiding the reason I had decided to have a walk and to have a think. When you set yourself to cogitate, the smallest distraction is enough to divert your gaze. The hour and clear weather heightened my senses and I forced myself to consider the facts. The likelihood of Mandrell exposing his role in all of this was now non-existent because Dave had told him what we had in mind. Our Plan had failed. That also meant our lives were now in imminent danger. Having seen the look on Joan's face tonight in the club, I knew she was still in love with Dave, so my Plan with her had also failed. Doogie had been dealt with, that arms shipment was now in the hands of the authorities, and we'd put the other arms dealers out of business, at least for a while. With the loss of Doogie and Davis, Mandrell's organisation had been dealt a blow, though miscreants like Davis were a dime a dozen. Mandrell was about to lose his job at Travis Industries and perhaps face criminal charges. So, all of that added up to what? Was it good enough and was it time to leave? There was Jake to consider.

Brittany was a lovely girl and my mind went momentarily to the sex, but she was a child, nearly twenty years younger than me, and a one-night stand does not a summer make. In any case, if we were to go on with it the chances of me keeping up with her social schedule and meeting with the approval of her friends were nothing short of fanciful. As always, I thought it was best to drop it now to save myself the embarrassment and misery that lay beyond tonight's excitement.

I loved my apartment but it smelt of and belonged to Joan. That realisation reminded me that I would struggle to get over her. Dave had once been her reluctant crime-fighting partner and he could perhaps talk her out of taking things any further with Mandrell, a proposition that was surely more easily sold without me being there. My phone rang. It was Joan and she wanted to come over. I said yes without hesitating. Old habit. I would tell her that it was over.

We arrived at my place about the same time, so I let her into the garage. I have two spaces; well, she has…forget it. In the lift on the way up, I waited to be asked but it took a while.

"So, where…?"

"Brittany's place." I couldn't even wait for her to finish the question.

"Who…?"

"Dave's friend at the bar." Yeah, that's right, baby, you heard me, I'm a dog. "She came back after you left. I assumed you had gone with Dave."

"Well, I passed your friend headed back to the bar. Dave was outside waiting for the valet and said he wanted to talk. Wait…you dog."

"And did you *talk* to Dave?"

"Yeah, he's been at my place the whole time."

She knew what that would do to me, but she didn't know I already knew. Now I had a new question. We got out of the lift. I didn't ask her; I was going to play it cool.

"So, did you fuck him?" Did I just say that out loud?

"Dave is Mandrell's stepson. I meant to tell you. When he showed up at the bar, I assumed he had something for me from Mandrell."

"So, all that *oh here's Dave, isn't Dave wonderful* shit," I put on a smarmy voice, "was just for show?"

She laughed. "It isn't hard, he's pretty good-looking, but he's also a real goodie-two-shoes."

"Is he in on it?"

"No, God, no. He's too straightlaced to get involved in anything crooked. But you need to be careful about what you say to him; he is a bigmouth."

I pushed the door open and let her through first, happy with that answer. *I'm the only real accomplice you got, baby,* I sent telepathically into the back of her head as she went past. Suddenly, I had become Shaft, so why did I still feel like Shrek?

"Brittany let it slip that he knew Mandrell," I updated her. "I thought it was important. I was going to call you, I wasn't going to leave…or anything."

"What?" She wasn't listening. "So, here's the deal. He took a lot of convincing that we knew nothing about Mandrell's role in this. He didn't ask me directly what we knew because he knows nothing himself, he just kept asking how things were in a thousand different ways. Mandrell had obviously asked him to make sure we were focused on all things not associated with him. He would not have told Dave why and Dave wouldn't have even asked. Dave would have just run off like the puppy dog that he is to get the answers Mandrell wanted."

That's right, puppy dog, remember that. "Drink?"

"Well, coffee, I gotta be at work in a couple of hours."

I had a cappuccino machine. It was better than Brittany's and, yes, I still revert to childish comparisons, especially at this time of the morning. The knot in my stomach had disappeared now that I knew Joan's real agenda with Dave so I was suddenly ready for my blankee, no coffee for me, just a straight Scotch. Ever notice how quickly we discard the remedial plan once we realise that more of the same will do? I'm not really dying of cancer… yet. So, where's my cigar box?

"So, we going to meet Mandrell's buddies?"

"I hope so. Dave thinks the sun shines out of Mandrell's arse, so he would have reported back on our conversation by now." I knew that was true. "I expect to hear from Mandrell tomorrow about a meeting."

"What's the plan?"

"I say I have that meeting, then decide. Don't expect them to agree to any al fresco dining though."

"One could only hope. Where's the line with this, Joan? Does getting this guy and Mandrell give you closure?"

"Close."

Good enough.

There is a tide in the affairs of men which, taken at the flood, leads on to fortune. Omitted, all the voyage of their life is bound in shallows and in miseries, so Brutus said of Julius Caesar, thank you William. In recent years, I had charted those shallows extensively and been intimate with those miseries. Having missed my first tide as a young man, I now wondered whether there would come another which, this time, would carry me out to sea and to my destiny. Would it be Mandrell who'd open the floodgate?

There was an ugly alternative. It might indeed be me who provided Mandrell with his tidal surge. With Joan dead, Mandrell would be left in at least temporary control of Travis Industries while they sorted out who should own the shares she left. Mandrell, by now, had ample proof that Joan had been playing in the shadows, sufficient at least to explain her untimely death at the hands of the terrorists she had hoped to thwart. Perhaps Dave's ill-fated courtship of her was aimed at providing the answer to who got what shares. Dare I even suggest such a cynical interpretation of Dave's attentions at Mandrell's urging? If it were so, it would be no different than his stepfather's feigned patriarchal connivance. Had I been in the shallows so long that it had made me irreparably cynical or are there that many scheming self-interested arseholes out there with no regard for their fellow humans as to make such expectations reasonable? I was surprised that I even asked myself the question.

"What is it about life that makes us feel inadequate?" I asked.

"We are defined by our humanity, so we can see the possibilities but we are always inadequately compared to what we could have done," Brittany said.

We were lying naked on the floor of her lounge room, propped up by lounge cushions, smoking and looking out over the city. We had a picnic of strawberries and champagne like in *Pretty Woman,* but I wasn't as prudish as Richard Gere; I helped the lady drink the booze. I had gone to her apartment that afternoon to suggest that we take our dalliance no further, yet here we lay, my dick still pointing north, though now not angrily. I hadn't smoked a cigar inside since…I couldn't remember when. Cigar smokers have been *persona non grata* for much longer than cigarette smokers. I was enjoying the perversion. Better still, it was the middle of the day. Sex is always better in the early afternoon. I didn't know why and have never sought to find out; it just is. Brittany had called when she woke up from our coquetry the night before and wanted a repeat performance. I had gone at her request and I had gone to end it, but her idea turned out to be better than mine. She was right, of course, with her surprisingly insightful observation about our inadequacy which I attempted to elaborate further.

"Let me be clear, you're not inadequate in any way. Gorgeous, rich, did I mention your arse at any point last night?"

"You did, and I appreciate the sentiment, but I am useless."

"I have the sneaking suspicion that you could do anything you turned your mind to."

"Yeah, maybe, but, if that's true, it just makes it worse. A dullard by design, purposeless by preference."

"Charming by choice. Beautiful at birth. We were doing alliteration, right?"

"You're good with that stuff, aren't you?" She pinched my cheek like an approving parent. "The use of language, I mean."

"I think we all choose to be inadequate, never the best possible version of ourselves. I don't know why that is and I don't know anyone who has tried to be at their best all the time. Joan, maybe."

"Fuck, are you in love with her, too?" She wasn't excited, it was just a matter-of-fact statement. There was no commitment between us so there was no line for me to cross. Intimacy and attraction without confinement make for interesting conversation. "What, am I the second prize in the Joan lottery?"

"I was taken by her, at one point," an obfuscation which, as I have explained, is a favoured pastime. "And, no, you're not second prize in anybody's lottery, baby." I kissed her slowly and I meant it, both the kiss and the sentiment. "You're too young for me, though. No way I can keep up with you."

"More inadequacy?"

"Maybe. Your mother and best friend won't approve of me."

"That's true."

"The world is driven by the *good enough approach* to life," I returned to my train of thought. "I boxed in college until I reached the top level, then lost interest. There was a friend of mine that topped my final year academically but I believed I was smarter than him and still believe that to this day. Yet, I made no effort to beat him because my ranking was good enough. I am sure it sits well on his resume to be top of the class. For me, there's always something else to do. Another party, another phone call. I was a good enough lawyer. I wonder, sometimes, about the damage good-enough does to a person."

"Are you smarter than me?"

"I have no idea how smart you are, other than to say that I think you're smart and insightful about the human condition. If you were an eighties woman you might have trouble getting rid of me."

"You mean, seventies."

"How old do you think I am? If you were twenty-eight, maybe, so what's that, 1986?"

"Twenty-eight, really. So, you're sexist and ageist."

"I try to be well-rounded."

"What, a fourteen-year age difference is OK but a twenty-year age difference is off limits?"

"Maybe. Half the man's age plus seven." I truly wasn't sure.

"I call bullshit on that math. But here's the thing. I could easily waste four or five years of my life with you and still have plenty of time to go hook the guy to raise my kids and leave you behind to die of emphysema. Therein lies the advantage of dating someone as old as you."

"Nice of you to say and thank you for dumping me in my hour of need. That would be a hell of a bargain, though, if you don't mind me contradicting your sarcasm."

"Sarcastic is something I never am."

"Five years with you in some of the best spots in the world..."

"Sure, the best."

"I have money, as well, I'm no bludger, but don't interrupt when I'm painting a picture."

"Sorry."

"Five years with you, best spots, etc, emphysema, which I have the cure for, by the way, in the glove box of my truck so it wouldn't be slow and painful. By then, you would be getting increasingly bored..."

"Shsss." She put her finger on my lips. "Skip the inadequacy part."

"OK. Five years, best spots, great sex, best restaurants, falling in love, beating up some arseholes, living like James Bond with you on my arm, then dead. Write that up for me, will you, and make three copies for me to sign."

She laughed. I didn't. She noticed. She actually wasn't sure about it now that it was in writing.

"You sound like a lawyer."

"I am a fucking lawyer..."

She got up. I didn't want to get up but did.

"It wouldn't work. I already dumped one guy this week because he was in love with Joan."

"Hey," I went over to her. Both of us were now in the kitchen. "Joan and I never were, never could be." I wasn't sure why I was selling her because she was right, it wouldn't work. "I didn't know you back then, now I do."

She bought it and I wasn't sure whether I wanted to make the sale. She was twenty-three years of age, whichever way you did the math that doesn't add up to a productive relationship. Was there anything about this woman that would be the same in a year, let alone five?

"I got a thing tonight," she explained, "a soiree. Very high brow. Got a tux?"

"Soiree, you say. Free booze, I assume. No tux, not for at least ten years."

"I got a guy who can tux you."

"Know a lot of guys that need a tux, do we?"

She went over to her phone and made a call. I listened to her explain the urgency of getting me fitted out to the guy on the other end of the line. I assumed she had some pull. Suddenly, she was Richard Gere and I was Julia Roberts.

"OK. Set," she said as she hung up. "I'll drop you off in town at Dobsons to get you sorted and pick you up at your place about eight.

You can leave your truck here. We'll come back afterwards for another fuck."

I liked the way the girl thought.

The marble and prominent American art added to the formality of the venue as we entered the Rice Building at the Art Institute of Chicago for a charity reception put on by the Mayor. Sculpture and fifty-foot ceilings punctuated the ostensible importance of the assembled personae, all appropriately attired in black tie and ball gowns, the affectation made large by chamber music and the pretentious looks worn by the patrons.

"They did a nice job with your tux, James," Brittany said as we fronted the bar.

"What, as in Bond?"

"No, as in Jim, I don't like Jim. I think you have more presence than a *Jim.*"

"You sound like my mother. Why are we here again?"

"My uncle invited us."

"You, not us. Meeting the family already. I'm feeling pressured."

"No, you're not."

She was right. I was feeling surprisingly at home and comfortable in my new tux.

"You make that dress look expensive."

"You have no idea."

"It's giving me an idea."

"Brittany?" We turned to see Dave with Joan alongside him. I'm pretty sure I faltered as my heart skipped a couple of beats. I hoped Brittany didn't notice. It was all I could do not to tell Joan how beautiful she looked, which would not have gone down well with my date. "What are you doing here? And with...?"

"Jim Jamisen," I stuck out my hand, "we met at the jazz club the other night."

"Yes. Joan's friend. You two know each other." We sort of shook hands.

"We do now, thanks to you," I said, and he stopped shaking.

"My uncle invited us," Brittany explained.

"You mean *us*," Dave clarified.

"There is no *us*, Dave, you might recall. Joan, nice to finally meet you. You look...cold in that dress."

"I'm hot-blooded, so it compensates. Jim, nice to see you. Or is it James?"

"It is James, apparently, yes." I knew what Joan meant but I had already done that movie reference and I drew a smile of approval from Brittany for not repeating it, instead assenting to my new cognomen. There was a pause while the women sorted out the social hierarchy.

"Is your uncle here yet?" Dave asked.

"I haven't...well, speak of the devil."

"Sweetheart." A large, gregarious man with a polished head and arms out in front of him pierced the space between Dave and Joan to gain access to his niece. "I hope I'm not intruding," he continued after giving Brittany a hug.

"Not at all, Mr Mayor," Dave said, adopting a submissive posture. I thought the guy in Brittany's family photos had looked familiar and somehow it fitted with my impression of her that she was the niece of a prominent public figure, just like Tallulah Bankhead. No wonder that story struck a chord with her.

"And this would be...?" the Mayor looked to his niece for introductions.

"Mayor Bridgewater, this is James, a local lawyer," we shook hands, "and Joan Travis, one of Chicago's finest."

"Well, what a pleasure, Detective Travis," he took Joan's hand and kissed it, yeah, that's right, kissed it. "I knew your father. What a terrible loss to the city. Thank you for coming tonight." I was going to say that he was welcome implying that it was me he was thanking for coming, but I thought better of it. "Dave, can I see you for a minute, please?" The Mayor pulled Dave aside.

"Did he just grab your arse?" I asked Brittany.

"He's been grabbing things since I was five. But he owns the apartment I live in so I don't object."

"Got it."

"I'm not sure you do get it, I am understating the problem. Are you being protective?" Brittany added.

"Too early to say."

Despite the Mayor's dismissal of my presence, I found myself very happy to be there and *very happy* was a welcome feeling. Here at the Mayor's charity function, in my new tux, which I was assuming I didn't have to give back because it was fitted for me, standing with the two most beautiful women in the room. Well, in Chicago. No, I'm going to say in the Great Lakes area. My thoughts went back ever so briefly to my study in suburbia with my whiskey picnic. I could see the Mayor's thumb coming back over his shoulder in my direction as he reamed Dave out over something I assumed was related to why I was there with his niece and Dave wasn't or, at least, that's what it looked like to me. I was happy to settle on that interpretation.

"Dave and your uncle close?" Joan asked.

"Don't know. I met Dave at one of the Mayor's things. I guess he uses him sometimes as a sounding board on police matters. You and Dave hooked up again, I see."

"Well, not really. He said he had been left without a date for tonight after you dumped him."

"Dave's sharing our little secrets, is he? You must be close."

"Used to be. I see you've moved on pretty quickly yourself."

"You mean James. How could I resist?" Brittany grabbed my arm. "He's quite a catch." She looked up at me admiringly. I didn't know what the hell was going on but I knew it wasn't about me. I didn't give a fuck because, apparently, I was the prize pig at the fair. I was just taking it all in like the special agent that I was dressed up to be. "I never could get Dave's attention, he was always talking about you," Brittany continued. "Besides, this one is a great fuck, I can hardly walk."

She looked at Joan for a reaction and she got a beauty, bullseye. To my surprise Joan had no comeback. I was happy to be labelled the swinging dick of the group given that it included Dave.

"I miss something?" Dave said casually as he returned to the group. The ladies were still trying to kill each other in a stare down.

"Dance with me," Joan said to Dave, dragging him off by the arm without breaking her gaze with Brittany and not waiting for Dave's acquiescence.

"I think that's one nil in favour of the younger," I said after the happy couple left for the dance floor. "I assume all that was for her benefit."

"Not at all," she smiled, "it was for your benefit. I think I got a pretty good trade."

"Nice of you to say. Dance?"

On the dance floor, things had deteriorated into one of those ridiculous Mister and Missus Smith things until uncle came over to cut in for a dance with his niece. Joan saw me leave the floor and followed me leaving Dave to fend for himself. I didn't see his reaction, I'm sorry to say, because I was headed for the bar thinking about a double Scotch neat from that bottle of Yamazaki Single Malt I saw on the shelf behind the barman.

"You don't have to fuck everything that moves, you know, just to get my attention," Joan said under her breath as she caught up with me.

"I'm proving nothing to no one, except maybe how old I am. I'm stiff as a board and not in a good way." I stopped walking to face her. "Besides," I was going to berate her about Dave but then wasn't able to look at her. Instead, I walked away. "…she's gorgeous…and rich."

"So, you're a gold digger now." She followed me.

"Always have been. That's why I was interested in you." We reached the bar with that lie. "Scotch, that Yamazaki, and make it large and neat, please."

"You arrogant arse." Joan was now full-voiced and she wasn't talking about my choice of Scotch. "You'd still be picking flies out of dud lawsuits if you hadn't met me."

"What the fuck does that mean?" The guy who gave me my drink grimaced in discomfort so I walked a safe distance away from the bar out of his earshot. Joan followed and we lowered our voices.

"It means you're on my payroll, buddy."

"So, that's all I am to you? Hired help."

"I'm trying to get a job done, here, and you're chasing teenagers around a dance floor."

"She's twenty-three."

"Yeah, like that's any different. It would have been good if we did some planning for tonight instead of pissing Dave off by fucking his girlfriend."

"Poor Dave, he looks like he's got a fragile temperament too."

"And you haven't? You're so insecure it's a wonder you can look yourself in the face shaving. Why couldn't I get hold of you this afternoon?"

"I have to ask for a leave of absence now, is that it?"

"Look, you can do what you fucking well like. I came here to meet up with Mandrell and set up our meeting with…whoever, only to find that you've reverted to adolescence." I smiled. I was comfortable with that regression. "Fine, I'll do this myself."

She stormed off. I shut up shop, emotionally that is, I don't like being yelled at, especially by someone I care about. I knew exactly what Jake was talking about when he described his trauma, huddled under the blankets as his father yelled the house down. This wasn't quite the same but it's in that same phylum of feelings. It has happened far too much in my life, often enough to be pretty sure that there must be something wrong with me. So, I pulled the shutters down and started to tell myself that none of it mattered. I went back to the bar and retrieved my Scotch. I wasn't sure where all that came from but it flicked off a lot of switches for me. I gave Brittany a *what's up* across the dance floor. She came and I finished the Scotch intending to leave.

"We need to stay until Uncle finishes his speech, otherwise he'll get the shits."

"You two close?"

"No, he left my aunt when I was two, my mother's sister. Her family was pretty well off, that's why he married her. She died a couple of years ago of ovarian cancer. He's sort of drifted back into my orbit since then, but I've never liked him. He always had his hands all over me."

"You care what he thinks."

"I just don't want him to get the shits, bad for his heart and my bank balance."

"So, money changes hands?"

"I do some PR work for him."

We stayed and she mingled a bit. Joan never looked my way. The Mayor spoke about the need for greater police numbers in the city and some other bullshit. I drank while not listening and then we left. It was a strange feeling as I stood there watching that crowd while I waited for Brittany. Lots of flashbacks, reassessments of what I wanted, one-sided un-opposed views of what the hell I was doing here and what the hell I felt about Joan. Like so many things in life, I wasn't equipped intellectually or emotionally to draw any accurate conclusions, only more obfuscation. In the end, my compass decided the direction I would go that night.

CHAPTER TWELVE

"**I**'m going to have to figure out something else to call you," I said playfully.

"OK. How about, Bree?"

"Dare I say, too cheesy."

We were lounging by the pool in Cabo San Lucas. Yeah, that's right, Cabo. Brittany's uncle owned a place down there and a private jet, both of which we had availed ourselves of in a fit of hedonism. We left for Cabo on the night of the gala. I said I had the shits and she said she had the cure, so here we were. It was hot, she was sweaty, and she had her bikini top off. It was a private residence and we were the only ones there, no staff. I was relaxed, very relaxed, for the first time in a while and happy to be out of all that drama in Chicago. Nothing turns me off quicker than a shouting match with a woman, if you're being shouted at by a man there's an easy fix. The most emotionally debilitating thing in life is a shouting match with anyone, even a stranger, and worse still with someone you respect. It's hard to come back from, regardless of the state of your self-esteem. I had none, but even if I had the effects of those confrontations always diminish me. I wondered whether I could ever be a partner to anyone again given my zero tolerance for emotional drama. I switched off so quickly with Joan as soon as she started yelling. You must allow some emotional venting in a relationship. It follows that I can't sustain a relationship of any value because when the venting begins, I would be looking for the exit or the Scotch, probably both in that order. So, here we were, the two of us, me and Brittany, drinking tequila and flipping the bird to all things conventional.

"You can call me sweetheart."

"Sure, but I mean socially. I'm serious, Brittany sounds like you're too young for me."

"I am too young for you."

"Yeah, but I would prefer not to be reminded of it every time I say your name."

"I had a nickname at school…Annie."

"As in Hall?"

"Who?"

"Movie reference."

"Of course."

"I like it…Annie."

"So, you glad you came, James?" She rolled over onto her side on her lounger and put her hand on my chest.

"A bit lower, if that's what you've got in mind."

"So, you glad you came?" she said in a lower tone. I rolled my eyes and said that joke was older than her. She pushed for an answer regardless.

"Jesus, Annie, look at you. Those tits are real, your arse is tiny, you're drop-dead gorgeous, a great fuck, and look at this place…so, no, not really, I'd rather be at the office."

"Arsehole."

She got up and dove into the pool in feigned admonishment. I followed her and we came to the surface together facing each other, yeah, that's right, just like in the movies.

"Remind me to tell you where I was and what I was doing eighteen months ago." I kissed her.

"I get your point."

"Where exactly are you getting it?"

"Pretty close to the right spot." She wrapped her legs around my waist and reached into my bathers. "That's better. Be careful with that thing," she said disingenuously, manipulating both her swimwear and mine out of the way without losing her hold on my neck with her other arm. "Ahh, now I get it."

"You're a very rude girl."

"You're about to find out how rude. Welcome aboard."

That went on for hours that afternoon and into the early evening. I don't think I had ever been that sexually free in my life. I ended up lying on my stomach on the bed, half asleep. We had made our way there via several other places, including the kitchen and a lazy snooze tied together on the lounge. Now she had gotten out of bed and I was watching her walk toward the bathroom. Everything else in my life up to that point had been replaced by the sight of her arse, tiny waist, and small shoulders, silhouetted in the light as she walked away from me toward the ensuite. There was absolutely no other thought in my brain other than the enjoyment of watching her move.

I was old enough to know that nothing ever surpasses the feeling of a burgeoning relationship for intensity and fulfilment. I don't think it is the same for women, but men will do just about anything to recapture such moments once found. But in reconstructing them, often at great cost to their marriages, they usually find only a shallow forgery of the original. But even for a pale imitation men will allow their lives to be destroyed, betray any confidence, discard any vow, to replay an afternoon like the one that had just been burned into my brain. My relationship with Annie had become very real, very quickly.

In a short forty-eight hours, I had left behind Joan's murderous pursuit of arms-dealing bad guys and replaced it with every adolescent boy's dream. I'd had more than enough of that cloak-and-dagger bullshit and Joan's disinterest in me. Even if things with Annie failed tomorrow, I had enough money stashed away to lead a pretty good life, especially in this part of the world. Drinking myself to death could not be done in finer style than in Cabo or at least it would be in better style than I had once envisaged. Conflicting with that sentiment was a re-found taste for life that I discovered, with some surprise, was displacing my disdain for it. The shape of Annie's body against the bathroom light regained its prominence in my head as I drifted off to sleep.

"Hey, no more sleeping. Dinner time. I know a great place. Get dressed."

I woke to the sight of Annie flitting around in a light cotton dressing gown putting on some earrings. I rose without thought, acting on instruction alone, and stumbled to the bathroom for a shower. Where I was and what I was doing there began to reappear as I let the water flow over my head. The sting of the hot water on my skin informed me that I was sunburnt and the rawness of my dick told me I had been a very bad boy. "No wonder," I said to myself out loud as the details of the afternoon came flooding back to me. Momentary ex-Catholic guilt was pushed aside by the anticipation of a good meal. I was hungry.

"That was quite a day," I said, stating the obvious, "and you are quite a girl."

We had been seated for dinner.

"Your dick is a bit big for my tiny little pussy," she said cheekily, knowing what that statement would do to me. I certainly appreciated the sentiment, though, and the reminder of how it felt.

"You're very rude in a monumentally attractive kind of way."

"I know. You're pretty cute yourself for an old guy."

"So, do we have a plan or are you just going to fuck me to death?"

"You can't live without a plan?"

"I guess I have been for a while. Can you?"

"Jesus, James."

"Just James."

"I don't give a fuck about what we do tomorrow or the next day as long as it's fun."

"So, you have absolutely no time constraints. You could stay here forever…if you wanted to?"

"If I wanted to."

"Fine. That gives me a timeframe. Somewhere between now and forever."

I have no idea why I was pushing.

"How's the Mayor?"

"Do you mean, how's Joan?"

"I meant, Uncle Mayor."

"I haven't spoken to him."

"Dave?"

"No."

One of those denials was a lie.

"How close were you and Dave?"

"Enough to know that he'll want me back, despite how good a fuck Joan is. How good a fuck is she?"

"No clue."

"But you'd like to know."

"Of course. I'm not as old as you think."

"Joan and Dave are probably rekindling the old flame right about now. How does that make you feel?"

"Sorry, Joan who?"

"Correct." She fed me part of her appetiser as a reward like the trained seal I had become. "But you have a thing for her. Dave did. She must be quite a girl."

"How did you get to be such an expert at twenty-three?"

"Because I'm in tune with my sexuality."

"Tell me what that's like."

"Well, you should know by now. It's knowing what makes me cum and not being afraid to cum as many times as I can and, by extension, knowing what makes you cum and getting you off."

"That is some powerful information and irrefutably right, probably, how did you acquire these skills?"

"Well, I started at a young age, just masturbation, not any boy-girl stuff."

"How young?"

"Six."

I choked on my food.

"What's wrong with six?" she continued, "those early years are the best. And an early start means that your body develops properly, everything gets hooked up the way it should be and you don't miss out."

"Miss out?"

"Yeah, the person who dies having had the most orgasms, wins. It's a rule. Catholic boys like you never win. To win you have to..."

"Start early, yeah. Telling a young child they will go to hell for getting themself off is child abuse, but it will make you think twice about doing it. It is, you are quite correct to say, the number one best thing you can do."

"Look, I understand why it has been taboo, but a distinction must be drawn between self-pleasure and sex."

"I agree. Underage sex brings with it too many problems and too many exposures, excuse the analogy, most of which are uncontrollable. It's just wrong, but not so with wanking. Do girls wank? You were telling me why you are so sexually aware."

"Yeah, that and I guess it comes naturally. I'm a very open person."

"What about other women, sexually, I mean."

"I know what you mean. It's always what men mean. I'd do Joan in a heartbeat. That is why I know you are feigning disinterest."

"So, you've been with another woman?"

"Yes, but I'm not gay. Women look at that a little differently than men. It's just pleasure. There are gay women, of course, but a sexually aware hetero woman is happy to go there once in a while, sure."

"Threesome?"

"No. No interest, I don't share well. Don't get the wrong impression. I'm not promiscuous." I didn't believe her. "I'm just sexually active."

"So…"

"Twenty questions."

"No, just a depth sound. So, how many times do you get off in, say, a week?"

"Depends on the time of the month but today was about right. How many was that…five? If I was home alone four or five would be about right."

"Most weeks."

"Most days. Not every day, though."

"Do you think that is normal?"

"I am a healthy girl with far too much time on her hands. Tell me about your first time with a woman."

"Boring."

"How old were you."

"Nineteen. I told you, boring. I was a practicing Catholic up until about then."

"Alright, tell me about the first time you could have had sex but didn't."

"Eleven. Two girls in my fifth-grade class reckoned they were doing it with boys. I still remember their names because that was pretty exciting information for a boy of that age. I wonder whether they were actually doing anything except being smartarses."

"Possibly. I think it was about the same in my class. So, you could have done it with one of them?"

"I have no idea. I never approached them or they me. All information was second-hand."

"So, yeah, probably bullshit."

"There was a girl that transferred from another school that year. She was absolutely gorgeous. Long, straight blonde hair and everything about her was feminine, even the way she ran. She was quiet and withdrawn but she was definitely a woman. I didn't figure that out until much later. I had no clue at eleven years of age what a sexually active girl looked like."

"So, what happened?"

"It was after church one Sunday. Her stepmom, she was adopted, suggested that I come over to their place play that afternoon and by *suggested* I mean insisted with my parents. So, I climbed into the back seat of their car, her daughter was in the back seat with me, short dress. I can still see her legs to this day. I could see her mom looking back occasionally but not with disapproval, sort of more like expectation."

"Jesus, she was in on it?"

"I've rolled it around in my head so many times. I had no idea back then, just fear of doing the wrong thing. But yeah, I'm pretty sure now it was a set-up."

"So, what happened at home?"

"Well, they tried to leave us alone in her room but my dad showed up out of the blue to pay his respects and pick me up. He kept a pretty good eye on things. He had good instincts it seems to me now."

"Not even a kiss."

"No."

"You were probably imagining that it was a sexual opportunity."

"She left school three months later, pregnant. The family said she'd been raped by a bikie. Very original."

"Uh! It was the stepdad."

"I think so and I was going to be the fall guy or boy. At least, I think that was it. I didn't put all the pieces together until years later."

"That is a sad story."

"I tried to look her up a couple of years ago. I had something in mind for her stepdad, an unexpected gift. But I couldn't find her or him. And you?"

"My first boss. I was nineteen. Awkward, messy. I fell pretty hard, though."

"So, not such a rule breaker, either. You like older guys."

"Father figure. He was older than you."

That night, I sat on the beach just down from the house having a cigar. It was after midnight and Annie had fallen asleep on the lounge while we watched a movie, the youngsters need their sleep. All that sex talk over dinner had got me stirred up again, but apparently, Annie had reached her quota for the day. It is a fact that the more sex you get, the more you want. It's beautiful there at night. Warm, with a nice breeze off the sea. I was happy, I guess, but not completely. Matters with Joan had left me feeling a bit empty.

"I love the smell of those things," a voice came over my shoulder, "my husband used to smoke out here, God rest his soul."

I started to get up, being polite.

"Don't get up. Mind if I join you...? Gwen." She sat.

"James."

She had brought two glasses and a very fine bottle of Scotch, so she had my attention and my friendship. She was from the house next door and when I say next door, I mean about one hundred and fifty yards up the beach. A sixty-something woman who had been beautiful in her youth and still was in this light. Classily dressed in a full-length chiffon pool gown.

"Mind if I have one?" she said, referring to my cigar as she poured me a drink.

"Of course not, they're fairly strong." I only had double chateaus.

"I used to smoke them with Eric. If I pass out, just leave me, it's fairly safe here."

I cut and lit her cigar. She had indeed smoked them before, you can always tell.

"Isn't it beautiful?" she said, puffing on the cigar as competently as Groucho Marx, "the beach, I mean, the sea."

"I was just thinking the same thing as you arrived. Even better now, cheers."

"Nice of you to say. Is Mayor Bridgewater down? I usually notice his entourage."

"No, just his niece, Brittany."

"Ok…OOOH. Congrats, she's very pretty, though, she always did like older men."

"So, she was telling me at dinner."

The conversation was easy. We stopped talking for a while to smoke and enjoy the evening and the booze. Some people just fit like a glove, like you've known them forever and she knew just when to shut up.

"You live here?"

"Yes, Eric and I bought it as a holiday home but I can't seem to leave."

"Good for you."

"So, Brittany's given up on that old goat she brought with her the last few times? Nasty man. I thought she was pretty tight with him."

"She brought Dave down here?"

"No, that's the stepson. Eric knew the family. Brittany was tied up with Lucas."

"Lucas Mandrell?"

"Yes, that's him. Big shot in Chicago. He always seemed a bit shady to me. Had her wrapped around his little finger. She used to work for him, then got a promotion to gangster moll. I'm sorry, that is a bit nasty. She's a lovely girl. That was my husband's private joke."

As I have said before, I never react badly to confronting situations or news. It always brings a calm over me, for some reason, but I'm not good company after things right themselves and the trauma catches up with me. I lay back on the sand, making a hole for my glass of Scotch. I didn't want to spill any, I needed it. I took another long draw on my cigar.

"I see," I said out loud. "So, he's a gangster, you think, this Mandrell guy?" I already knew. However, the news of Brittany's involvement with him was new.

"Eric thought so. I hope I'm not treading on any toes. I'm too old to bother about that, one of the reasons I stay here."

"No, no, I appreciate the clarification. Brittany doesn't talk about them much at all. So, when was Mandrell here last?"

"It was only three weeks ago, I think, just him and Brittany. So how did she end up with you in such a short time? They must have had a cracker of a fight. They were overdue."

"Yeah, that must have been it." Sadly, there was a more likely alternative, she wasn't Dave's ex-girlfriend but Mandrell's current one. I paused while the brightness of the last forty-eight hours faded to black. "So, Bridgewater and Mandrell must be close, then?"

"Long-term friends. I think Lucas uses him for his connections. Listen to me, the cigar has gone to my head."

"Did Eric know where Mandrell's business was based?"

"Yes, he was a nosy buggar. He had a file. He started out as a reporter but made his money in property. When he retired, he used to poke around investigating stuff that interested him. The gangster lawyer with the young moll and the connection to the Mayor of Chicago was far too much for him to resist."

"Would you mind if I got those details off you, Eric's file?"

"It's back at the house. Going up there might be a bit dangerous, though."

I looked over her shoulder to what looked like a pretty well-maintained path.

"To give me the file or negotiate the path?"

"Neither. With all this Scotch and cigars, I'm likely to try and fuck you. It's been a while."

Jesus, it never rains but it pours. That is true with sex, though, as soon as you've got plenty, there's plenty more available. Something to do with the vibes you put out, I think.

"I'll take my chances."

I saw no need to wait until we got back to the house. Her Scotch got spilt. She didn't have anything on under that Momo. I surprised myself. For some reason, fucking her seemed like a very good idea, something to do with Brittany's duplicity. Gwen was beautiful. It was a fuck-you to Brittany, I think, as much as it was a fuck for Gwen. I came harder that night on the beach than any time since I got to Cabo. I got my file and an invite back.

The next morning, I invented a reason to return to Chicago, a serious family matter. I saw no reason to confront Brittany about Mandrell and alert them to the fact that I was onto their plan to keep me out of town or to pump me for information, whatever it was that they were up to. Maybe to convert me to their cause. Now, that would be profitable. So far, it was just the pumping. As I sat in the kitchen with my coffee that morning, I had been wondering why they didn't just whack me, if I was that important to them. Maybe they did want to hire me. Who knows and I didn't care. In any case, there was no real reason to discuss it with Brittany. Whatever Brittany's reasons were for the deception she couldn't justify it to me or placate my hurt at her betrayal. We had no commitment but another lying, conniving arsehole had slipped under my guard and I wasn't happy about not improving on my hit rate for spotting them. Twenty-three, drop-dead gorgeous, and rich, might have been a clue. The male ego is a terribly debilitating thing. I forgave myself and her, in this instance, it had been a great few days.

I watched her walking towards me bleary-eyed from the bedroom, rubbing her head and wearing one of my shirts as a nightgown. It is just so compelling when a woman does that. I assumed it was one of my shirts, not Mandrell's. I started to wonder if I shouldn't prolong the fantasy.

"Why are you up?"

"Gotta go."

"Where?"

"Back to Chicago. My ex-wife has had a car accident and I'm needed there."

I think I saw a look of genuine disappointment. My imagination, I assumed.

"You don't have to come. I've booked a commercial flight."

"What's the problem?"

"They couldn't say."

"But…OK." She stopped and turned back. "James, there was something I've been meaning to ask you." Here we go. "What do you think of Dave's stepfather?"

"One of Chicago's finest lawyers."

"That's what I thought. Some people think he's a bit shady."

"He's Joan's mentor and I think she's a good judge. Why?"

"He still handles my affairs, just checking."

Perhaps that was all she had been asked to confirm. Perhaps they didn't want me out of the way, they just needed to know what I knew. I didn't care. I'd had an absolute gutful of connivance and misdirection in my life and now she was part of that hatred.

As the taxi drove past Gwen's place, I felt like going in to say goodbye and tell her that I appreciated her honesty.

CHAPTER THIRTEEN

I had been back in Chicago less than twenty-four hours and was lying prostrate on my lounge procrastinating and sadly still alliterating. I was a little surprised that Joan hadn't changed the locks on me but I assumed she had more class than that and would let me know before she threw me out. That would probably be soon. The thought of finding other digs washed in and out of my mind like suage along with the question of whether I really wanted to take up the hitman cudgel again. Leaving Joan to her own devices didn't sit well with me when I was in Cabo, but going back to shooting people, regardless of the risk, didn't appeal either, even though Mandrell was now top of my list, if I still had a list.

I had told Brittany I would be tied up for a few days, sorting matters out with my family, so I didn't have to explain my sudden lack of interest. It wasn't really a problem, though, because I was still interested in her, despite her deceit. On the trip back to Chicago, I had replayed parts of the last few days in my head, looking for tell-tale signs of her dishonesty, but I could not find anything that should have alerted me to the fact that she was acting on instructions. Perhaps she just really enjoyed her work. It didn't seem right, in any case, to continue to get sex and affection from her under false pretences, even though that was precisely what she had done to me. I hadn't yet fixed a point on my battered moral compass for that one. She was a very beautiful girl and she was playing me, but did that mean I could take advantage of her? Even as I mulled it over, the answer revealed itself. The words *take advantage* when talking about a young girl gave it away.

An old friend of mine once told me there was a reset button for the brain. What you needed to do was go somewhere that no one knew you and where you had nothing to do except feed yourself. So, you needed to have some money put aside. No stressing about money, maybe go for a walk, do easy regular tasks. A garden would help, he said, and a pair of cats. He described it like it was witches' alchemy, eye of toad, shell of snake egg, and he believed it. He spoke like he was sharing a secret. Best do it without the cats because that's a fifteen-year commitment, he suggested. So, no cats, but they did bring an indifference to all things that was infectious. The process happened quicker if you had the cats. They know what they know, do what they do, and help you understand that the world is what it is and will be the same without you. What happens eventually, with or without the cats, is that indifference swallows you. It is the first step of the restart, you just shut down. Nothing matters. It gets you, eventually, and you have to wait for it to happen, he said. You must wait long enough for it to happen. It is difficult for a busy person to realise, he explained, that if they stop being busy, the world keeps turning. Once you get to that point, there is a realisation that you could stay that way forever and everyone you know and everything you would have done moves forward without you. That is the *reset*. Then the brain reboots. It comes up with the same programming, of course, just like your computer, but with all the crap cleaned out of your head. All the caches are empty, you've got more room on your hard drive to process your life, and the priorities become clearer. I was lying there thinking about hitting reset. I had the money and sufficient cause. I have no fucking idea why I let the program in my head keep running instead of packing a bag.

Eric's file had proven much more comprehensive than Gwen had indicated. It looked as though he was preparing some sort of exposé on Mandrell and his political connections. Gwen was adamant that Eric's death was from a heart attack and that Mandrell had no idea that Eric was investigating him but, still, his death seemed awfully coincidental. The file had dates and times of meetings and noted suspicious attendees at those meetings, but contained nothing substantial as to what their subject matter had been. He had no electronic surveillance. He had identified a warehouse at Naperville about forty minutes out of town as the place he believed they stored their ill-gotten gains. Notes indicated he had intended to infiltrate the building to see what it contained. He had floor plans. What was particularly useful were the names and contact details for people that Mandrell had been meeting in the lead-up to what Eric had identified as being a major transaction. The timing meant that it had to be the Travis Technology deal. I was prepared to assume that Mandrell was still dealing with the same group of people, at least, that would be a decent starting point. Doogie had made Eric's list, but Eric hadn't identified him as a Homeland Security agent or defined his role in the criminal enterprise. There was one guy that Eric seemed to think was key to the operation, a guy he listed as Patrick Kenneth Ames. He had an address for him at a business on State Street and the next morning I went over there to poke it with a stick and see what I could stir up.

This guy wouldn't know me from a bar of soap and I didn't intend to use my real name. I'd met a guy at the Wanenmacher, the gun show in Tulsa, who was a big shot, excuse the pun. One of the largest gun dealers in the North East. I had done some legal work for him on a barter basis so I knew a little about his business. His name was Joe Wesley and he was mainly into wholesaling, so I thought it was an acceptable risk to use his name and company to see if I could get this guy out into the open.

"Mr Wesley?"

"Joe, please. Mr Ames?"

"Mr Ames is busy. So, Joe, my assistant tells me you're one of the biggest wholesalers of firearms in the North East."

It was Ames, alright. Eric had a picture of Ames in his file. Ames wanted to play silly-buggars with me. I played along.

"The biggest, I think, at least the biggest legit wholesaler."

"Yes, illegal arms trafficking is big business these days."

It was a women's clothing store, a big one. We were on the main floor of the three-level store, standing in the women's casual wear section. I had waited half an hour to see this guy. I assumed they were checking me out.

"It was hard to find you on the net, you a bit gun-shy of publicity, Joe? In the end, I had to ring a friend."

"Yeah, gun-shy, that's a good one. Of course, I'm gun-shy. There are a lot of nutters out there with some gripe and they're armed. I know, because I probably armed them. Besides, this business is almost always about who you know, not what you can find on the net."

"And who do you know, Joe."

"I know that you are a man who can get things. I have a very large distribution database who want to buy those things, things I can't get through the usual channels. I thought we should talk."

"So, you just turn up here out of the blue."

"Like you would have accepted my phone call."

"No, I wouldn't have, but an introduction would have been nice."

"Well, now you have one from your friend, I assume, the guy you phoned."

"So, it would seem. As it happens, we are trying to expand our network. Our competition seems to have lost their way a bit and we have recently expanded our supply lines as a consequence. What sort of *things* were you looking for?"

"Some of the weaponry I'm after is hard to come by. Can you help me or are we just going to dance around?"

He thought about it, seriously.

"You see, I don't know you and I don't care that you think you are a big dick in Hicksville. I think I am going to say fuck off, but let's not close the door on it. If you can find someone we know who can vouch for you, we will review it. Bye."

Eric was right. He had the guns or at least he had something he didn't want me to know about. The look on his face when I asked about the guns, and the goons standing in the doorway to his office, were a dead giveaway. You didn't need that kind of muscle to control the ladies looking for clothing at sale time. I didn't expect to get anywhere with him, I just wanted to take a sniff and he had that unmistakable stink of hubris and invincibility. What I was going to do with that information I had no idea but I felt more informed as I left as instructed.

I now thought I had all the important parts of the business hierarchy figured out. This Ames guy was the boss, Mandrell was the money man and fixer, with all the necessary contacts, and Doogie provided the muscle and intel. All I needed was sales and marketing and I had me a real live corporation. Perhaps the other parts of Eric's file would provide me with more of the organisational chart. The secret business that Joan had been so hot and sweaty to uncover didn't seem to be so secret anymore. Mandrell had the political connections and everything that goes with them, including the unions with control of movement across the ports. And he had the legal connections, perhaps with influence over certain parts of the judiciary, to obtain the necessary permits and get-out-of-jail-free cards. It was a sweet setup; it put the organised back into organised crime. Going against these guys and missing would look bad on my tombstone.

Back home, I packed unenthusiastically, mulling. It was just clothes, nothing else here was mine, including the weaponry, except my new MacMillan. Joan had said the place was mine as long as I worked for her, or for the Council, as she had me believe back then. It wasn't right to stay. I didn't work for her any longer and I had decided that I wouldn't in future. I had at least made that decision and I needed to let her know. What I hadn't decided was whether or not I was going to help her. If I got out of here and got my own place it would give me a different, perhaps clearer perspective. But I didn't want to get a place in Chicago again. I wanted to move on, but what about Jake?

Cabo looked real good. Maybe rent a room from Gwen, my dick for her room. I was reverting to adolescence again and that wasn't a good sign. Maybe New Mexico outside of Santa Fe. Set up a studio. Yeah, that's right, I always wanted to paint. I remember walking down Canyon Road there once, wall-to-wall owner-operated studios, many with shop fronts. They seemed happy people and some of them were really good at their craft. It was a Thoreau kind of moment for me: *we need to witness our own limitations transgressed and some life pasturing freely where we never wander*. A lot of things ran through my head, I was all over the place. I had come to the end of my time as a paid assassin. The remaining transgressors on my list would be left to pasture freely wherever they wanted to wander. I had, without noticing, let go. I felt a bigger man because of my newfound capacity to evolve, not forgiving or forgetting, just prepared to leave it in the past. The thing about life is that you have to keep something on your bucket list, doing the whole list means that you come to the end of the list and then what? My mood was sanguine and deliberate. No rush, just clarity, finally. Not clarity of purpose, just clarity of being, *unbearable lightness* or otherwise.

It had been a long road for me and quite a ride. I could see now how desperate my circumstances had been when I lived with Clara, how dead I was inside. It was no wonder I had started dreaming. I was right about one thing back then, better to be dead than stay in that state. I had been dragged back from that dark realisation by circumstance. *I came here to die with you or live with you,* Josie Wales told Ten Bears, *dying ain't so hard for men like you and me it's livin' that's hard… you don't always get a fair word or a fair fight, well, I've come here to give you either one.* Ten Bears chose life for him and Josie, I had chosen life for me.

I would go get a coffee, then come back and finish packing.

"Jake, what are you doing here?"

I had given him a key to my place. I had only been gone an hour but he had made himself very much at home.

"Doing my homework."

"No, you're not."

"I brought it with me," he gestured to his bag on the lounge. "You haven't been around much."

"I was in Cabo with a hot chick. You would have liked her. She was about your age."

I went to the fridge to get myself some water.

"Yeah, where have you been the last couple of days?"

"I just told you."

"Bullshit."

"No. Mandrell's girlfriend was pretending to be my girlfriend to see what she could find out."

"And you let her?"

"Of course, she's gorgeous, it was easy. I only found out yesterday that she was scamming me. That's why I'm back, but I didn't tell her much and I didn't mind her doing what she was doing. You switched the surveillance cheat on, right?"

"Yeah, I put it on the television circuit when I walked in."

"Switch it to conversational mode, they'd expect us to be talking, if that's what you call what we do."

"Hey, be nice."

"Assuming that they are still listening. Is it working OK?"

He went to check it. The switch was in the linen closet behind a false wall.

"Mick was here yesterday," he called back from down the hall. "So, are you going to whack her? Ms Cabo?"

"Jesus, Jake, you've got some work to do to know when it's appropriate to say that."

"I didn't think it was ever appropriate."

"Smartarse."

"What's on today?" Jake went back to his Gameboy and the packet of Cheezels sitting at the dining table amid the non-homework stuff that was spread everywhere.

"I think I need to pack. Joan got really pissed when I took up with Ms Cabo."

"What, Joan owns this place?"

"Yeah. Didn't I tell you?" I started fiddling around, tidying up some of Jake's mess in the lounge room. "If you're going to live with me, you need to do this for yourself."

"So, where we going?"

"I haven't figured that out yet."

"Chicago, right?" I didn't answer. Jake grabbed my arm with his Cheezel-crumb-ridden hand as I walked past. "Chicago, right?"

"Right." I ruffled his hair, which he hates, and wiped the Cheezels off my shirt. "Got some good intel in Cabo, from the lady next door to Brittany." I went back to tidying.

"Her name was Brittany? Jesus, Jim, how old was she?"

"Twenty-three."

"Mate that's marginal. She's closer to my age than yours."

"Yeah, that's what I said. But the file of info I got from Gwen, the lady next door, has pretty much helped me figure out who's who in the trafficking zoo."

"How old is Gwen?"

I was puzzled by what was taking his attention.

"I don't know, sixty."

"That's more your style."

"How old do you think I am?"

"Sixty."

"Fuck off."

"Did you bang Gwen, too?"

"Jake, Jesus, man…yea sure."

"See, you are James Bond."

"Homeless James, now."

"If you average the 60 and the 23 you get someone your own age."

"What?"

"Why don't you tell Joan you were just collecting intel from Brittany?"

"What did I tell you about being straight with your friends? Besides, she knew I was smitten. Beautiful women make idiots of mortal men. Remember that. Come to think about it, they don't have to be that beautiful."

"Sure."

The doorbell rang. It was Joan. She used the communication device for once.

"We need to talk."

Shit, I hate it when women say that.

"Come up."

"Can you excuse us, Jake." Joan was clearly agitated as she entered the apartment.

"No, let the boy hear it. It will be good for his education to see a grown man cry. Does he know who you are and what I do for a living?"

"Yes."

Jake snatched his bag of Cheezels from the table and bounced onto one of the lounge chairs with a big smile, as if Joan had brought home a copy of his favourite movie.

"Fine. Not happy with our conversation at the gala."

"Agreed."

"Not happy with you traipsing off with Brittany."

"What do you mean traipsing?" Jake asked.

"No questions, Jake, please," I said politely to him, then returned to Joan, "what do you mean *traipsing*?"

"I mean running off somewhere where I can't contact you. She's too young for you, anyway."

"And that would matter to you how?"

"We've got a job to do."

"Ah, the job, what else could it be? Her age is relevant because...?"

No answer.

"What about you and Dave, there was some traipsing going on there too."

"I was collecting intel."

"So was I."

Jake cleared his throat. I shot him the look of a chastised child, the one Tom Hanks does so well.

"So, you weren't fucking Brittany? Sorry, Jake."

"He's used to the swearing."

"Well? Were you?"

"Of course."

"What do you mean, *of course*?" Her voice became anxious.

"I had to get to the bottom of things."

Laughter from Jake and an interesting expression from Joan. I would have said it was hurt if I didn't know better.

"Do you love her?"

"You mean Mandrell's girlfriend?"

"What?"

"Yeah, they sent her to pump me."

Gregarious laughter from Jake.

"And you were just playing along."

"Sure."

"Bullshit," Jake coughed.

"Whose side are you on?" I asked him.

"Batman doesn't lie," Jake suggested.

"OK, I didn't know, at first, that she was a spy," I continued reluctantly. "I went because you went off with Lieutenant America."

"Captain," Jake interrupted.

"Shut up, he's a lieutenant." I did not expect this conversation to have the tone it did. I was now listening very intently, anticipating things that I didn't think were possible, likely, or feasible. "You were dismissive of me, seemingly very interested in him."

"Dave is a sycophantic brown nose with a great bod. I have no interest in pursuing him…again."

"What's sycophantic?"

"Shut up," chorused.

"So, you're not still in love with him?"

"No."

"Oooh," from the crowd.

I removed the space between me and her, now arms-length.

"Because you are in love with me?"

Silence; even Jake stopped crunching.

She waited a while. It took some time for her to compute it herself, clearly unsure of her answer.

"Yes."

Jake jumped up on the lounge, like Tom Cruise, Cheezel bag in one hand, making a fist in the air with the other, screaming a near-silent "Yessss."

"Jake, give us a minute, will you?" I said.

"Jesus, just when it's getting to the good bit," Jake complained as he trundled off to his bedroom. He forgot his Cheezels and his Gameboy so he wouldn't be gone long.

I kissed her, the long overdue kiss of a man who had never been kissed before. My mind evaporated. I lost all sense of where I was and what was happening.

"I can hear you kissing," Jake yelled from his room rupturing the mood. I had no doubt that he could at least feel the radiation.

"Do you have any idea how long I've loved you?"

We were still in each other's arms. She said nothing, just a half smile. I think she actually had no idea.

"My whole life."

"For the first half, I wasn't even born."

"So that's the way it's going to be. My last girlfriend was much younger than you."

"Don't you…"

I kissed her again before she could push me away.

"Is that your compass I can feel on my hip?"

"Sorry. It will snap off in a minute if it gets any more blood, so it won't be a problem."

"Mommy, Daddy, can I come out yet?"

Jake was standing in the hallway looking at us with his best gooey-eyed look.

"You arsehole," I said, "we're not adopting you, forget it. You're too rowdy and messy, and you swear too much, so fuck off." I started to tidy up again. For some reason, domesticity just hit me like a ten-ton bag of Cheezels.

"Don't be mean to him," Joan complained.

"The boy needs to know where he stands, dear. It's not going to happen, not now, too many interruptions. This was my big scene with you and Cheezel kid here trampled all over it."

Jake remembered there were more Cheezels in the bag and went to retrieve them. He sat on the lounge cross-legged as he excavated the remainder of the bag's contents.

"Leave the Cheezels, let's get some brunch," Joan suggested clapping her hands, "and you and I should have dinner tonight when *Leave it to Beaver* here is back home."

"Good idea. I have something I need to give you."

"Is it a surprise?"

"Too hard to say."

CHAPTER FOURTEEN

"What the fuck?" Mick said in a loud whisper as we sat down at an outdoor café, "you look half dead."

The waitress came and we ordered coffee. I certainly needed one as I had a hell of a headache. It had been a long night with Joan and every ounce of fluid was drained from my body. God, I felt good, though. New world, new day. Joan was out of town for forty-eight hours following a lead she had picked up from Dave.

"I think I need some ears inside a warehouse at Naperville."

"Who?"

"The arms-dealing guys Joan's been chasing, haven't you been listening? I got some pretty good intel that this is the HQ of the people we are after."

"I told you that I was not going to get involved face-to-face."

"I need it in two places, actually. A women's dress store on State Street and the warehouse."

"Women's clothing?"

"I thought you liked women's clothing?"

"I told you I was into women, not their clothes. Well, only if they let me."

"In or out? My inclination is to just start shooting people until I get to the right guy but that might not be good for Joan's health or mine."

"And the health of some guy that didn't need to get shot."

"That, too."

"When?"

"Now."

Mick's head exploded with a blast of red blood and brain matter blowing towards me. I was pushed to the floor with the impact of the same bullet on my left shoulder. I scrambled under the table as Mick's body hit the floor in front of me, looking straight at me now with dead eyes. Another shot shattered the table with no sound other than the bullet going through wood and hitting the concrete. I crawled frantically towards the wall nearest to where the shots were coming from above, the roof of the building that housed the restaurant. A waiter took one in the back as he ran past me. A blast of automatic fire pockmarked the pavement in front of me as I stood under the easement with my back to the wall. Then it stopped. I waited, then after a glance back toward the chaos in the restaurant, left quickly staying close to the wall. I had no interest in explaining matters to the authorities or pursuing the assailant. I was unarmed. I paused in the alleyway. I was a mess, with Mick's blood all over me, and I was bleeding but it was hard to tell which blood was mine. Like all things gun-related, I knew someone who could tell me which bit was which.

I was having trouble shaking the image of the blood splash coming toward me from Mick's head. Every time I closed my eyes it was there. It might have been the painkillers the Doc gave me, but I was hallucinating about the shape the splatter took. I was seeing things that weren't there, images of people I had shot in the past. There was a movie, *The Fisher King*, I think, where Robin Williams had it about right when he imagined his shot wife's death as I did Mick's. But this was my pain and it was real. Joan and I had drawn Mick into this and it had cost him his life. Whoever the shooter was he couldn't shoot worth a damn, assuming it was me he was after. Maybe it was a message that they knew who we were and where they could find us. It worried me that they knew we would be at that café and I couldn't figure out how. I wondered if Mick had brought his phone with him. I was fairly certain that they knew he was involved with us; perhaps they were tracking him. That was the best explanation. Brittany had obviously reported back that I had not been converted to their side.

I guessed that a visit to the women's clothing store would be the logical choice of target for some return fire. I should have waited to consult Joan. I knew that, but I didn't. I was angry and I needed them to know I was angry. I was uncertain who this Ames guy was but Eric had been sure he was the linchpin and he looked guilty as hell when I met him. So, Ames would do in exchange for Mick. It would let them know that coming after us had a price.

I was probably less cautious than I should have been but an hour later I was perched high in a church bell tower with a clear view of the rear entrance of the State Street women's clothing store. There was a small, covered platform at the back door and three steps down to the bitumen of the car park, which was an open yard surrounded by a seven-foot brick fence. The distance from where I was to there was under fifteen hundred yards, no problem. Unlike the guy who came after me, I wasn't going to miss.

The gate to the yard was open and I could see Ames's limo parked about twenty feet from the back door, apparently waiting for him with the engine running and the driver inside. That was going to be a very dangerous twenty feet for Ames to traverse and what made it easier for me was that he would be walking pretty much straight toward me. A target moving straight at you is easier to hit than one travelling across your field of view. It would take him five seconds at a normal walking pace to get from the back door to the limo door and I didn't think he was going to make it.

A goon exited the building first and, as expected, gave the nearby rooftops a cursory glance as he went to open the car door. No way he could see me, I was too far away. Then Ames, the man himself, came out next, on the phone, with another goon directly behind him. They were both dead before they got to the bottom of the stairs. The first goon who had moved over to the car was left holding the door of the limo open with one hand and frantically scanning the roofline, gun now in hand, looking for a target. The driver started to back out of the driveway in a panic, leaving the goon to fend for himself. He didn't need to worry for long. I shot the guard standing in the car park and sprayed the driver's side of the car with the rest of the clip. Those .50-calibre rounds would have gone straight through the roof, the guy, and the floor of the car, and still made a mess of the bitumen below. The car went backwards into the wall opposite the driveway and the driver jumped out, dragging his bloodied right leg and returned fire with his handgun. I laughed and stood up so he could see me in the bell tower and waved. The chances of him hitting me with that hand gun were zero. I'm not sure that a bullet from the 9mm handgun he was using could even travel that far, maybe if he aimed it at a forty-five degree angle, it might cover a distance of slightly over a mile. Yet, this idiot was pointing it straight at me. I laugh at these guys in the movies using a handgun at even one hundred yards. If they actually hit anything, they should go buy a lottery ticket. He had the courage of a man stranded in the open, hopelessly outgunned. I reloaded, very deliberately, as he started to run. I blew his brains out, one shot. It pretty much took his head off. He should have picked a safer profession. *And that is how you do that,* I said out loud for the benefit of the sniper they had sent after me as I started to pack up my weapon.

I knew that was really going to piss them off but, fuck 'em. It would probably be the last time any of them were going to be out in public any time soon. My attention now was drawn to Mandrell. He had appearances to keep up, meetings to go to, and weapons to sell, so I wasn't sure that he could spend all his time indoors and he didn't know we were onto him. While Brittany reported back her lack of success with me, she didn't know that we suspected Mandrell and I assumed she didn't know they would come after me. At least, that's what I wanted to think. Would Ames, Mandrell, and Doogie satisfy Joan? I had a bit of a chuckle to myself as I climbed down that steeple. I was like a bad case of the raging zombies, don't go outside or they'll get you.

"You know you started World War Three, right?" Joan said, back in town. She wasn't angry.

"They killed Mick. I needed to respond."

"You were angry."

"That, too."

"How could you be sure...?"

"Sure it was them? He was dropping FEG PA6-3 casings in front of me as I huddled against that wall. Our friends at the women's store were carrying Makarovs."

"I have no idea what that means but you weren't in a state to make clear decisions." She came over and put her hand on my face. "Not that unhappy with the result, though."

"Yeah, I was going to use Mick to verify this guy's position in the organisation, but Eric's file is pretty comprehensive and the fact that they came at me shortly after I paid Ames a visit pretty well sealed it for me. That, and the casings."

"How's the arm?"

"Not as bad as I first thought. Most of the blood was Mick's."

"This guy, Ames, was not the head guy. Logistics maybe."

"How the fuck do you know that?"

"The intel I picked up on my trip. Do you want the details?"

"No. Your source confirmed Ames's involvement?"

"Yes."

"That's good. Not that I could do anything about it now if he wasn't involved. So, Mandrell's the Man."

"Don't think so."

"Whyyyyyy?" I was getting a little frustrated. "Why isn't he the Man? There is no one else."

"Just a feeling. The pieces don't fit."

"You and your fucking pieces, Joan."

"I need this to be right."

"We had better *go to the mattresses* then."

"I actually know what that one means."

"Only because of Meg Ryan in *You've Got Mail,* total chick movie. It's from *The Godfather* not from *You've Got Mail,* not the Jimmy Stewart version."

"I know that."

"No, you don't."

"Who's Jimmy Stewart?"

"Jesus, Joan."

"Where's your gear?"

"I got a bunch of it in the truck. I didn't know what I would need at the clothing store. I didn't go back to the apartment after I whacked Ames in case they came after me. I told Jake to stay at his foster home."

"Good. Pull the battery out of your cell. We'll get a couple of burners."

"What are you going to do?"

"They need me to do this deal. I need to talk to Mandrell."

"So, where to?"

"I got a place. But first, we'll have to unpack that truck and get you some other transport."

As we travelled there was no conversation. I watched people hurry home. It was late in the day and they had homes to go to and they made me wish I had one too. I had the window half down. It was cold and I could smell the rain coming. My interest in the weather had returned, I noted, also what things smelt like and what I was going to do next week if I got the chance. Things I'd had absolutely no interest in when I was in that darker place had started to fill my senses again. *Intermittently, she caught the gist of his sentences and supplied the rest from her subconscious.* Fitzgerald, of course, who but he can walk between words to add the subtle meanings that expose the soul? I was awake and listening to Joan not talking and I supplied the missing pieces of our personal lives from my subconscious. Would malicious forces visit again to crush my beginnings before my new objectives could mature? It mattered little; I knew now that life provided no reassurance and proffered no consequence other than its own atonement.

It was only twenty-four hours before I received a phone call from Joan.

"Mandrell has set up a meeting."

"How did he explain being able to do that?"

"Does it matter? A friend of a friend and so on. And, you're going to love this, it's at that warehouse in Naperville. That place is huge."

"Some good hiding possies for a lawyer with a nasty habit?"

"Sure. If we can get you in there and set up before the meeting, we should be able to tidy this up pretty quick once we find out who the number one guy is."

"Assuming he turns up."

"It's a condition of the deal. So, it wasn't Ames."

"And you think they are being straight with you?"

"They need my electronic sign-off to get the specifications they are after for the T47EP. If he's not there, they don't get it."

"I never did ask you what that shit was."

"It's a targetable electronic destabiliser..."

"Pass. And you get out how?"

"You shoot them all and we walk out the front door and go home."

"With me."

"With you, I hope."

"Joan, do I need to point out the obvious? Mandrell will assume that your insistence on meeting the top guy is not related to exchanging pleasantries."

"Yeah, but he needs verification of the capture of the specifications."

"You mean he won't shoot you because you're involved in the sale of national secrets."

"Something like that but, frankly, it's irrelevant, because you won't let them shoot me."

"So, he's just expecting you to exchange abuse with this guy, the guy who had your father killed, they get the technology and you go home."

"I think he doesn't give a fuck what I try and do because he thinks he'll have it all under control. He'll have enough goons there to control one pissed-off little rich girl, or so he will think."

"Where does he think I am?"

"He thinks you've been shot, he doesn't know how badly. I told him I hadn't heard from you and he knows that's true because you haven't been to my place or on my phone since we started using these burners."

"So how and when do we get me in?"

"I've got a plan."

So, there I was, perched high in the rafters of the warehouse in Naperville. I had followed a maintenance walkway along the roofline to a small platform attached to the gantry crane that ran most of the length of the warehouse on girder rails. The warehouse floor was the size of a football field. If I were James Bond, I would turn the gantry crane on at the appropriate moment and ride on it down the length of the building as I shot at them. But I'm not James Bond and I would rather be still and hidden.

The floor was only sparsely packed. Business must have been good and there were half a dozen vintage muscle cars parked at the southern end. Spoils of war, I assumed. I couldn't see anyone as the sunlight coming through the skylights began to fill the space below. I had been there since three that morning. I was seated with my back against the turret of the crane and chewing on a muesli bar. I had disabled the security camera at the southern end of the ceiling that was looking straight at me. I had put it on a continuous loop, something Mick had shown me how to do. So, I was invisible to the security system and couldn't be seen from the warehouse floor. I had brought enough weaponry to start a war, which was in fact my plan. Joan would be unarmed and her task was to get the hell out of the way once the firing started. Her signal to me identifying Mr Big was to offer to shake his hand. He was my first target.

I kept going over how long it would take me to get out the same way I came in after I had shot the guy and I kept coming up with the same answer; I wasn't going to make it if there was anyone who could shoot worth a damn. Some small comfort was that the AK47s they seemed to favour were hard to control when firing on full automatic. You'd be hard-pressed to hit a barn door with one on that setting if you were over a hundred yards from it. It's better single-shot, but even then, you would struggle to hit a human over 300 yards, especially one that was moving or shooting back. In any case, spraying automatic gunfire 75 feet above their own heads would make me a difficult target unless they were inclined to take their time, something it was important for me to dissuade them from doing. There was, of course, always the lucky shot.

To stay awake, I ran down a list of assault weaponry I would select if I had access to just about anything, which I assumed these guys had. I know the AK47 is reliable and you don't want a jammed gun in a fire-fight, and it does dispense a thirty-calibre-type round that carries a considerable punch, but really? A weapon designed sixty years ago? Who were these guys? Maybe, for mine, a Scar 17 Heavy, the current special ops weapon of choice or, sure, maybe a pimped-out AR15 with an XS50 308 drum mag and a Yankee Hill rail for good looks. At least you're not going to run out of ammo with that gun. Or even an AK74 or an FN P90, but the .57 ammo is harder to come by and it's more of a close-quarter weapon. It's a PDW, personal defence weapon. I understood why they went old school with the AK47, probably still the number one selling assault rifle in the world and they would have plenty in stock. Hopefully, I wasn't about to get shot by one just to prove me wrong about their choice of weaponry.

I love old warehouses, something from a previous life, I guess. They exemplify productivity, progress, and endeavour. I am always in awe of them when I stand inside one. They make me feel small and important all at the same time. That was why I bought that industrial park in Grand Rapids, the one I got diddled out of. The history of these buildings swallows me whole and makes me introspective. They make me feel like I'm about to do something important with my life.

I had drifted off and it was almost ten o'clock before I was woken by Joan and Mandrell entering the building. They were alone, with no escort. Then four goons entered from the Northern doorway and spread out. They walked past Joan and Mandrell and went all the way to the southern end of the building before two of them came back to where Joan was standing. Four other goons entered from the same doorway along with a young guy in a suit who, by the look of him, was unarmed and carrying a laptop that I immediately assumed was to verify the transfer of the secure data. He was escorted by a very familiar figure. Why Brittany was here, I had no idea. All we needed was the Mayor and we could have a charity function, I thought, when in he walked. Mayor Bridgewater, all three hundred pounds of him, camel mohair overcoat, suit and tie, and that crappy old hat he insists on wearing because he thinks it makes him look like Spencer Tracy.

"Mr Mayor," Mandrell said. I could barely hear him.

"Lucas."

"So, Joan, this is the man you have been begging me to introduce you to."

"Detective," the Mayor said, sticking out his hand. Joan took it. Was that the signal?

"You run this show?" Joan asked the Mayor.

Or was that the signal? I brought my weapon to bear. That hat wasn't going to survive. But Mandrell caught my eye with a gesture toward the doorway the mayor had just come through. Another goon entered. He had Jake by the scuff of the neck. My heart stopped.

"Well, I have a little help running it," the Mayor was explaining to Joan as Jake was dragged towards Mandrell, handcuffed and gagged, "though, less now, since you and your friend started shooting up the place. Ames was a real asset."

"I assume your lawyer friend is here somewhere," Mandrell said now full-voiced. "You don't think I'm stupid enough to come to a place like this without taking precautions," he continued, absolutely full of himself. "It's you that is the quarry, my friend, not I. You forget that this is also a good place for you to be shot," he laughed. The goon that had Jake pulled out a handgun and put it to Jake's head. "Come down now or the boy will be killed. Take the gag off and have him call out."

The goon removed the strip of duct tape stuck across Jake's mouth.

"Shoot this fucker," Jake screamed, "shoot them all!" He stamped on the goon's foot and eluded his grasp.

That was the signal. I blew the goon's brains out, the one who'd had a hold of Jake, then I shot Mandrell. I love the fact that the second guy always looks up. The goon who'd had Jake flew backwards, landing in a pool of his own brain matter. Joan grabbed the boy and the handgun from the floor and headed for a pile of crates. The other half a dozen goons opened up on me with their trusty AK47s. The Mayor was waddling for cover but not fast enough. He got one in that fat arse of his, not in the hat in case Joan needed to talk to him. He wasn't going anywhere, instead now lying on the ground groaning, bleeding. The guy with the laptop was lying face down on the floor crying, I think, hands outstretched in front of him to show he wasn't armed but Brittany was still standing. She opened her purse and pulled out a pack of cigarettes and a lighter with a look of resignation like she knew that it would come to this, shaking her head ever so slightly and assuming her fate was sealed. But she wasn't going to demean herself. She had style, that one. The other idiots were standing in the open, spraying fire towards the ceiling. Two more of them got it in the head before the other six figured out they better get some cover. By then, Joan had settled behind the crates with the boy and shot the goon that came running directly towards her and Jake looking for cover and a ticket out.

There was a lull as they all found their hidey holes, so I yelled out as loud as I could, "hold your fire!" To my surprise, they did. I suspected it was only momentary. "We got who we came after. Mandrell and the Mayor can't pay you now. I'm the guy from that other warehouse shootout. It didn't end well for them so why don't the rest of you just FUCK OFF."

It wasn't the most articulate argument I had ever made. There was no response but no return fire either. Then I heard the clang of a gun hitting the floor and one guy walked to the door with his hands on his head, now unarmed. The rest of them were ahead of him by the time he got to the exit. It's hard to get good help these days. I knew that from when I was in business.

Joan did a quick sweep around and gave me the nod. She went over to Brittany, silent. Brittany offered her a cigarette, which she took, and lit it for her. I didn't know Joan smoked. Two of the most beautiful women you could ever wish to see anywhere, standing there trying to kill each other with a stare.

"I'm bleeding," the Mayor whimpered.

"Shut up," Joan responded unsympathetically without losing Brittany's gaze, "if I hear you again, I'll shoot you myself."

Brittany stepped between Joan and her uncle. "He ain't much," Britany said, "but he's family."

Joan removed Jake's handcuffs. Apparently, one key fits all. Jake ran over to the bottom of the gantry ladder to meet me as I climbed down. That was a good hug. Entwined, we made our way over to the girls.

"Who's the crybaby?" I asked, still clinging to Jake with one hand while he held my waist, my gun in the other.

"One of my uncle's flunkies," Brittany answered, blowing smoke in the air to punctuate her answer, "IT, I think."

"You're going to tell the police everything, aren't you, Mr IT?" I said to him, not even bothering to go over and threaten him.

"Yes…of course," he sat up wiping his tears, "I'll help you. I have all the records…please don't shoot me."

"And confirm that Brittany here knew nothing about what was going on, right?"

I got a very cross look from Joan.

"Yeah, that's right, she knew nothing."

"Thanks, big boy," Britany said.

"But she's up to her neck in it," Joan complained.

"You don't mind me killing your only true love?" I asked Brittany, meaning Mandrell.

"He was once, then he just used me, then I got bored. Cabo was an overdue release. I found out this morning what these two arseholes really did for a living. So, no I don't mind that much."

"Shut up, Brittany, the shooting might not be over yet," Joan said, then turned to me and the boy, "all OK?"

"Sure."

"My uncle could use some help."

Another look of derision from Joan.

I went over to one of the half-opened crates and pushed back the lid with the muzzle of my rifle. I'd brought the AWM, which was better at short range and lighter, light enough for me to use as a poking stick with one hand. Jake was still unwilling to let go of my waist.

"That's the stuff, alright. Hey, computer boy, you have all the transaction records, right?"

"Yes," he was standing now, collecting himself as he brushed off his pants, "and bank records."

"You might do OK for yourself, then," Joan said now on the phone to 911, "don't know about your boss, though."

The Mayor had passed out.

"Do you want me to wake him up?" I asked.

Joan was standing over Mandrell's body, looking down at him. Her gun was pointed at his messed-up head, her phone in her other hand. He wasn't going to get any more dead, but I thought she was going to shoot him again, anyway.

"No, I think I'm good."

"Hello, 911, what is your emergency?"

EPILOGUE

I t took six months to tidy up the mess in Chicago. Nobody challenged Joan's statement that she had been drawn to the warehouse because the boy had been kidnapped having been notified by Jake's foster parents who had met Joan through me. One of the warring factions' hitmen had done all the damage apparently in revenge for the previous warehouse attack and had been killed by Joan in the ensuing firefight. It was the guy Joan had shot as he came after her and the boy after he had apparently killed everyone else and wounded the Mayor, he had my gun in his dead hands, the AWM…somehow. I wasn't in attendance by the time the cops got there.

The Mayor did not contradict her statement. I think that was Brittany's doing. To hear the Mayor tell it, he was Mandrell's unwitting pawn. He pleaded out and ratted on his suppliers and Mandrell, not that it mattered much to Mandrell. We already had more than we needed on the guy, anyway, thanks to the audit and Mick's surveillance tapes, as well as the records from the IT Cry Baby. Besides, Mandrell was very much dead and didn't give a shit at that point. The Feds had the Mayor in protective custody and were bleeding him, excuse the pun, for all he knew about the distribution of illegal arms.

In the wake of the scandal, Gwen finished Eric's half-written piece on the goings-on of Mandrell and his criminal associates and it was enthusiastically published in a three-part expose in the *Post*. She had finished it, thankfully, without any mention of beaches in Cabo. Brittany was off somewhere with Lieutenant Dave, lucky guy. It turned out that Joan was right about Dave; he was too busy licking the Mayor's arse to notice who was fucking who. Gwen's book had painted Joan as the hero in shutting down both trafficking syndicates and uncovering the culprits responsible for her father's murder. The public acceptance of Gwen's version led to adulation for Joan and medals for meritorious conduct. It was attention she hated, primarily because of the corruption that the establishment had allowed to fester over many years and that had given rise to her father's death. She resigned from the Force amid media outcries as to how Chicago could lose such quality law enforcement personnel.

Cry Baby did pretty well for himself. He got a three-year suspended sentence after fully cooperating with the police. No one ever found out who shot Ames and his mates at the women's clothing warehouse, or Doogie, for that matter. The authorities lost interest in Doogie even though he was a Homeland Security Agent because of his involvement in the criminal enterprise; no one likes a dirty cop. The police had closed the cases concluding that it was all part of the *Chicago Trafficking Wars,* as that whole sordid matter had become known in the press from the title of Gwen's book. Bridgewater, for reasons best known to his fat arse, couldn't shed any light on the Ames or Doogie murders, in part, at least I am sure, influenced by Brittany's urging to let it lie where it fell and a desire not to let on that he knew much about what Mandrell was doing.

Most important of all, the three of us had set up house in Dallas. Yeah, that's right, me, Jake and the Babe. The adoption was official. Joan had pulled some strings. She said we were a family, even though she had refused to marry me. I was too much of a James Bond type for her, apparently, but more likely it was because she hadn't forgiven me for running away with Brittany. But she'll come around.

What I had found, and for that matter, what I had lost, was unclear to me until the telling of this tale. Life is random, stuff happens. It's not because you are good or bad but because you are here. You can't shoot all the arseholes or let them get you to the point where you want to. It is better to rise above it rather than be crushed beneath it and whether you are rising or squashing is between you and your gods. But you do need to be aware that the gods don't give a shit about you whatever their religious derivation. What you make of the whole thing is partly up to you, but it is just as much up to the tide. The tide had run my way again and I was in full sail, having used the surge generated by those affairs to escape the misery of the shallows that had previously entrapped me. As for tomorrow, we will see.

I was downstairs in my study, finishing this diary with a beer and some peanuts, when in walks Joan. It was late in the day on a fine Sunday afternoon, good weather for a sail.

"What's for dinner?" I asked.

"I might give you a fuck then we'll go get Jake from the gym and go out for a steak."

"Deal," I said. Ain't life grand.

"Jim," she paused and came over to sit on my lap, "you know…I've been thinking about that Council thing."

www.ingramcontent.com/pod-product-compliance
Lightning Source LLC
Chambersburg PA
CBHW040527170726
48295CB00012B/371